HONORED ENEMY

D1557597

Culver A. Modisette

QUANAH PARKER, Chief of the Quahadi Comanches, an honored enemy, and subsequently, an honored friend of the Whites.

HONORED ENEMY

Culver A. Modisette

PublishingWorks, Inc.
2011

PW

PublishingWorks, Inc.,
151 Epping Road
Exeter, NH 03833
603-772-7200
www.PublishingWorks.com

Designed by: Anna Pearlman

LCCN: 2009907335
ISBN-13: 978-1-935557-06-7

ABOUT THE COVER ART: Painted by well-known Western artist Ken Schmidt, the proud warrior astride his war horse was the ruler of the Great Plains. The white ring around the eye of his horse was thought to provide it with keen eyesight, while the lightning bolt on its foreleg assured speed.

Dedicated to the Native Americans of the Southwest, who through the years have been bullied, threatened, and cheated by the government of the United States. The native people suffered the theft of their lands, their freedom, and their natural resources.

Overlooked by many historians and often misinterpreted by the silver screen of Hollywood, they are only recently gaining the recognition they deserve.

AUTHOR'S NOTE

For several hundred years, a little tribe of Native Americans in the Southwest fought off the invading armies of Spain, France, and Mexico to preserve their hunting grounds. That tribe called itself "The People." Other tribes called them "Always Against Us." Texans called them "Comanche" and killed them for their grasslands and buffalo. This is their story. It is also the story of the United States Fourth Cavalry, called upon by Congress to pacify the proud Comanche, Kiowa, and Cheyenne tribes that fought the callous infusion of white buffalo hunters, ranchers, and farmers into their world.

ACKNOWLEDGMENTS

To all those who helped me over the hurdle of first book authorship, I owe a huge debt of gratitude. Among them, the ladies of the Somers, CT. Library: Francine Aloisa, Cecelia Becker and Yvonne Besse, who assisted in my reference work; to my wife for her patience and computer skills; to Chip Kimball of the U.S. Fish and Wildlife Service for her thorough and speedy reference work; to Jeremy Townsend and Kieran Haseler of PublishingWorks for their patience and guidance; and to Gerry Demas, whose idea turned into a book. Thank you all.

—Culver A. Modisette

PART ONE

CYNTHIA

ONE

Parker's Fort, West Texas
May, 1836

The Parker family cabin was one of several grouped together within a perimeter of rough outbuildings, crude barns, and a corral, which contained several milk cows. A handful of chickens hunted noisily in the barnyard. Outside, two men, Silas Parker and brother Ben, were busy splitting firewood. It was a warm spring day, and smoke from the cooking fires drifted lazily on a soft wind.

Lucy Parker, a thin, harried mother of four, was busy in her primitive kitchen, her bare feet stained brown from the dirt floor. She glanced at the empty wood box. "Cynthia. Cynthia Parker!" she repeated, her voice rising. "Where are you, child?" Cynthia appeared in the doorway, nine years old, blonde, barefoot, and dressed in a made-over flour sack, the personification of a frontier waif.

"Oh, there you are, young lady. Go tell your brother that I need more firewood"

Cynthia nodded. "All right, Ma, I'll tell him."

Outside, she found young John, just six years old, more interested in a pet mouse than in his chores.

"Ma needs more firewood. She tole me to tell you," Cynthia said.

John looked stricken. "I jus' did firewood! Criminy, all I do is firewood. Why don't you do some firewood?"

"Cuz," Cynthia replied archly, "ladies don't do no firewood."

"You ain't no lady," John retorted.

Nearby, Silas overheard the conversation. "John, do as you're told!"

"Awright, Pa." John moved slowly towards the wood pile.

Cynthia made a face and stuck out her tongue. "No wood, no vittles, John. That's what Ma said!"

John put his mouse in his pocket and returned the favor of an out-stuck tongue.

"Hush up, you."

Cynthia, having won again in the ongoing brother-sister contest, turned to enter the cabin, when movement across the fields caused her to stop and shade her eyes.

"Ma, something's coming," she called in alarm.

"What?" Lucy replied, preoccupied with preparing supper.

"Somebody's coming, Ma," she called out again. And then, as if a mirage, a huge party of Indian warriors materialized—some on foot, some on ponies. They stopped in a ragged line and silently watched the settlers. Pennants, feathers, and, decorations trembled slightly in the gentle breeze.

Lucy stepped out of the cabin, drying her hands on her apron, and looked up in horror. "Dear God, Indians! Silas! Ben!" She yanked Cynthia back inside the cabin, then dashed out and snatched John from the wood pile. Ben and Silas rushed inside, looking for weapons.

"Lucy, where the hell are the rifles?" Ben shouted.

Silas frantically ransacked the cabin. "They ain't here," he said.

"They're out in the fields with the men," Lucy answered.

"Jesus!" Ben said.

"Cynthia, now you listen real good," Silas ordered. "You run out back of the cabin and tell the men in the fields to come a running. And to bring them rifles. Now scoot!" Overcome with fear, Cynthia fled the cabin.

"John, give me a hand and we'll close the shutters," Lucy said nervously. As they secured the windows, Cynthia returned in a rush, panting with exhaustion.

"The men are comin', Pa," she said.

"Good girl, Cynthia," said Lucy coolly. "Now listen real close, you two. We're gonna take the babies and slip into the woods out back. Cynthia, you carry little Silas and I'll take Orlena. John, you bring as many blankets and quilts as you can carry."

John and Cynthia nodded in understanding. John started gathering quilts as Cynthia held little Silas, who, having awakened from his nap, fretted irritability.

Ben peered out the door. "They've stopped out there, Silas. Kind of lined up."

Silas hefted a hoe, his only weapon. "They're awful quiet."

The Comanches formed a ragged line. There was an eerie silence, broken only by the stamping of hooves and a soft nickering of the ponies. The line parted and two Comanche emerged on horseback carrying a white flag. One was the well-known Comanche war chief, Peta Nokona. They advanced towards the compound, then halted, waiting motionlessly.

"What's the white flag for, Uncle Ben?" Cynthia asked.

"Hope it means they want to talk," Ben answered. "Need all the time we can get."

"Oh, Ben, there's so many," Lucy said softly.

Ben nodded. "I know. But I've only got to talk to two," Ben said calmly, and stepped out of the cabin, carrying a white cloth and an axe.

"Ben, be careful, for God's sake. Be careful!" Lucy pleaded.

Ben showed no signs of hearing her, and walked slowly towards the Indians. He stopped before them and gave the hand signal for peace. The Comanche returned the gesture. In the cabin doorway, the family strained to follow the drama. After much gesticulating and sign language, Ben returned to the cabin. The Comanche watched him intently.

"What do they want?" Silas asked.

"Beef and water," Ben said, laying aside his axe. He dipped into the water bucket.

"Got no beef aside from them old milk cows," Silas said.

"I know! I know!" Ben replied with an edge to his voice. "Must be a hundred of them out there. Coupla milk cows ain't gonna cut it."

"Give them the milk cows, Ben," Lucy pleaded. "We can get along without them."

Ben took a deep breath. "Looks like that's the only card we got to play," Ben said softly. "Need to buy some time."

"God keep you, Ben," Lucy whispered, her eyes filling with tears.

Ben smiled faintly. "Need all the help I can get, Lucy." He squared his shoulders. "Wish me luck!" Ben gathered up several pots and pans as sops for the Comanche and slowly stepped from the cabin, striving to buy time for his family.

As he walked toward the waiting line of Comanche, one of the farm dogs followed him, his tail wagging. The dog smiled up at Ben. "Go back,

Rip! Go home!" The dog placed his forepaws on Ben and whined excitedly. "No, Rip, go back," Ben yelled, as the dog bounded playfully around. As it neared the line of horses, the dog bristled and began a determined barking. Several horses, uneasy at the noise, shied nervously and shifted sideways. Sensing that things were going badly, Ben tried again to calm the dog. "No, Rip! Hush up! Stop that noise! Git! Now git!" Rip, in a state of frenzy, snapped at the legs of the two horses bearing the white flag. The horses danced sideways and the dog, unmindful of Ben's calling, dashed behind the line of warriors, yapping at a high intensity. There was a sudden yelp and then silence.

Ben approached the flag bearers and presented the pots and pans as gifts. They were accepted without expression. As Ben signed his inability to provide beef, there was a murmur of angry voices. The line parted abruptly and a single warrior stepped out and thrust his lance deep into Ben's chest. Convulsively grabbing the lance with both hands, Ben sank slowly to his knees, his blood pouring onto the grass. In unison, the line of warriors surged forward. Ben was lanced several more times and scalped as he lay dying on the green grass of Texas. The Comanche attacked at full cry, sending the people of the fort running for cover and their lives.

"My God, they've killed Ben!" Lucy screamed. In a sudden wave of panic, she gathered her family and they ran, burdened with little ones and blankets, towards a patch of sheltering trees. "Run, Cynthia, run! Hold tight to your little brother! Run, John. Don't look back! Just run!"

"Mama, where's Pa?" Cynthia panted. Stricken, Lucy looked back over her shoulder and screamed for her husband. Silas remained behind to defend his family and was overrun and killed by a Comanche arrow that pierced his chest.

As the settlers ran for their lives, the Comanche intercepted Elder Parker and his wife Sally, grandparents to Cynthia and John. Elder Parker was chopped down and scalped under the horrified gaze of Sally. Immobilized by terror, Sally was scooped up and thrown across his horse by a mounted warrior. Scratching and clawing, Sally fought her captor. Then, in desperation, she rolled off the horse. Infuriated, the warrior wheeled his horse and thrust his lance into Sally's shoulder, effectively pinning her to the ground. Satisfied that she was dying, he whirled his horse, and thundered off into the compound.

Close by, two warriors tore a two-year-old from his mother's grasp, hitting her in the face with the butt of his lance. She fell in a puddle of blood. Lucy, running for safety with her brood, was charged by three warriors. One of the Comanche swept up Cynthia, while the other horsemen dragged John, Lucy, and her two babies back to the burning fort, where several farmers were savagely fighting for their lives.

Gradually, as the combat raged, the guns of the farmers, together with raw courage, turned the tide of the battle. The Comanche pulled back, but not before ransacking the cabins and gathering any books as padding for their war shields. As a last defiance, they torched the cabins and barn.

Meanwhile, Cynthia, in the grasp of a mounted horseman, clung to her captors in terror, having witnessed the fate of her grandmother. As the fort, under a column of smoke, faded into the distance, Cynthia screamed in terror, "Mama! Mama! Help me! Please help me!" Her captor half-turned and slapped her roughly in the face. With a trickle of blood starting from her nose, she hovered near unconsciousness.

They rode all day, stopping that night for water and to rest the horses. At sunrise, the war party halted and donned war paint and feathers for a triumphant entry into their village, exhibiting plunder and captives for tribal approval and adulation. The new bloody scalps were tied to lances.

Two warriors were sent ahead to the village to announce their victorious return. As the war party entered the village, shouting the story of their raid, tribal members clapped and called their welcome. Cynthia, an object of curiosity—a captive with rarely seen blue eyes—was pulled from her horse by tribal women, who derisively stripped her of most of her clothing, poking and pinching her in the process. Cynthia, with her blood-caked face, took refuge under the horse of one of her captors, Peta Nokona, and attempted to defend herself, but the animal's nervous movements knocked her down, and she was attacked noisily by the women.

Peta, nettled by the din, raised his voice. "Enough, old women! Enough! Let her be!" Peta slid from his horse and picked Cynthia up, brushing dust and dirt from her tattered clothing. Searching the crowd, Peta shouted, "Singing Woman. Singing Woman! Come to me!" Answering his call, a petite, dark woman of early middle age stepped from the crowd.

"Yes, Peta, I am here," she said. Peta thrust Cynthia towards her.

"I have a gift for you. You are widowed and childless, and have no help in your lodge. Here, take the Blue Eyes and teach her to be a Comanche."

Singing Woman held Cynthia at arm's length for appraisal. "Yes, yes, I think she will do," she said softly. "I thank Peta for this gift. Yes, I believe she will do. There is much she must learn. And some I must learn. We'll see. We'll see."

Singing Woman turned and led Cynthia through the crowd and towards her lodge, talking loudly to her, while Cynthia, unable to understand the language, stumbled dazedly behind. Upon entering the lodge, Singing Woman stood Cynthia, by now a whimpering, bedraggled, and frightened little girl, by the fire and looked at her critically. Humming softly, Singing Woman appraised her new responsibility. She selected several hides and furs from her sleeping couch and slowly circled the girl, measuring and tucking. Cynthia, although she did not yet realize it, had the good fortune to have been placed in the tutelage of a compassionate soul.

Smoothing Cynthia's blonde hair, Singing Woman smiled. "You do need clothes! And you are so dirty! And you smell like a horse. Well, no matter, no matter. You will do. You will do." She wrapped Cynthia in a blanket. "Come, little Blue Eyes, we will wash you in the creek. Then, at least, you will look better!"

As they left Singing Woman's lodge and walked toward the creek, they attracted a crowd of curious women and girls. Wading into the water, Singing Woman removed Cynthia's blanket, revealing a nude and shockingly white little girl, causing a murmur of wonder from her audience. Embarrassed by her exposure, Cynthia crouched in the water, much to the merriment of the women. "If she bleaches any more in the water, she will look like a ghost," one cackled. "Singing Woman will have a ghost living in her lodge!"

As the shrieks of laughter died down, Singing Woman spoke sharply. "Enough! Enough! Go attend to your chores. I am not concerned about spirits in my lodge. I have been alone long enough. Even a ghost would be welcomed!" The crowd slowly dispersed, and as Singing Woman scrubbed the dirt from Cynthia, at long last, the child gave way to her pent-up emotions and collapsed, sobbing, into the arms of her new mother.

TWO

Indian Territory
1836

Comanche life for Cynthia was very difficult at first. Cynthia, separated from her family, soon learned to do the everyday things that all Comanche girls were expected to do: she carried water and fleshed hides, working them until soft, for clothing and moccasins. She gathered firewood for the cooking fires, watched over the small children, and gradually learned the Comanche language and their customs. As time passed, she lost her white mannerisms and speech. And then, one day, she crossed the threshold into full acceptance by the tribe . . .

Cynthia and an older girl, White Rain, were filling their water skins at a stream. Once finished, Cynthia turned to climb the muddy bank back to her lodge. Above her on the bank, White Rain rudely grabbed Cynthia's filled skins and pushed her back down the bank into the water. "I'll take those, white girl. Here, fill mine," she ordered. She tossed two empty water skins down to Cynthia, who was floundering in the water.

Incensed, Cynthia yelled, "Those are my skins! Give them back!"

White Rain laughed scornfully. "No! You do as I say . . . or you'll be sorry!"

"Give me back my skins!" Cynthia said angrily, wading ashore.

"All right. Here they are," the older girl taunted, as she emptied the water skins over Cynthia.

Enraged, Cynthia scrambled up the bank with two half-filled water skins. "You'll be the one who's sorry," she gritted. Covered with mud, Cynthia swung the skins and knocked the other girl down. Before she could recover, Cynthia was on her like a tigress, pulling her hair, kicking, scratching, and biting. Locked in a muddy embrace, the girls rolled down the bank into the stream. As they fought, a circle of people gathered and silently watched. White Rain, older and heavier, gradually forced Cynthia deeper into the mud. As she thrashed frantically about, Cynthia found a flat stone at the water's edge. With a convulsive effort, she struck the older girl twice in the temple. At the second blow, White Rain slumped over, unconscious, with blood streaming down her face. Struggling out from under her attacker, Cynthia dropped the stone. Impassive, the onlookers looked questioningly at her.

Panting and wiping the mud from her face, she angrily faced the crowd. "Anyone else? Anyone else? I don't . . ." The girl in the mud moaned softly and stirred. Suddenly Cynthia subsided. "I'm sorry. I'm sorry. You shouldn't have pushed me. I'm sorry…can you hear me? Are you all right?" She knelt by the injured girl and wiped the blood from her face. With no offer of assistance from the bystanders, Cynthia struggled to carry White Rain up the bank and back to her lodge, as the crowd watched silently.

As she approached the girl's lodge, her mother, Running Bird, emerged to the sight of her bloody daughter. "What happened?" she screamed. "What have you done to my daughter? White Rain, speak to me! You have blood in your ears!" She turned to Cynthia. "What happened?" she repeated.

"She pushed me into the mud and called me a 'white girl,'" Cynthia explained. She insulted me, so I hit her."

"You what?" Running Bird asked incredulously.

"I hit her," Cynthia answered.

In a fury, Running Bird snatched a burning piece of wood from a nearby fire and launched herself at Cynthia. Off balance, Cynthia fell to the ground and the flaming wood scorched her face. She scrambled to her feet and grappled with Running Bird, whose screams had alerted the entire village. As they fought by the fire, Cynthia suddenly tripped the older woman into the fire, back end first. The mother's screams of rage changed to howls of pain. As the older woman scrambled from the flames, Cynthia retrieved the fallen firebrand and stood over her menacingly. Shaken, Running Bird waved her arms. "No more! No more! I am too old," she said. Cynthia slowly backed away, flinging the firebrand back into the fire. Running Bird hobbled to her lodge, brushing live sparks from her posterior.

Suddenly drained, Cynthia sat down abruptly. "I am not white. I am Comanche," she whispered. Then, more loudly, to the world, "No, not white! I am Comanche, now! Comanche!"

A tribal council convened the next day to investigate the quarrel. Held under a shady tree by the stream, it was headed by Five Wolves, the elder of the tribe. Another member of the council was Peta Nokona, seated cross-legged on a blanket. Standing before them were Cynthia, with a scorched face, White Rain, with a black eye and bruised face, and Running Bird, unmarked to the casual observer, who were summoned to explain their actions.

Clearing his throat, Five Wolves looked solemnly at the women. "We would like an explanation as to why three of our people were fighting with each other like wolves. How did this happen?"

White Rain pointed at Cynthia. "I pushed her into the mud and she hit me."

Five Wolves stared at Cynthia. "Is that true?"

Cynthia nodded. "Yes, it is true. She called me a 'white girl.'"

"And then . . . ?"

"And then I hit her with her own water skins," Cynthia said softly.

"Yes . . . ?"

"Then she fell down and I jumped on her," Cynthia continued.

"Did she fight back?" Five Wolves asked, watching White Rain intently.

"Yes, she was on top of me, so I hit her with a water stone," Cynthia replied.

"And did she stop hitting you then?" the elder inquired.

"Yes, she fell off me without her senses," Cynthia responded.

"Why did you not kill her? She was your enemy," Five Wolves asked pointedly.

Cynthia looked up into the eyes of the old man. "No," she said. "She is not my enemy. She is Comanche."

Five Wolves leaned forward. "You were brave to fight an older, larger girl, and good to a fallen foe. We Comanche do not take pity on a fallen enemy. Our laws and customs are clear. She started the fight, thus you had the right to kill her. But your spirit forbade it."

The old chief turned to Running Bird. "And now, old woman, what have you to say?"

Running Bird pointed angrily at Cynthia. "She brought me my daughter all covered with blood and mud. I was upset!"

"She upset you into your own cooking fire?" the elder asked wryly. Peta Nokona glanced at the old man and stifled a smile.

"And scorched the back of my best tunic," the old lady whined.

Amused, Five Wolves averted his face momentarily. "That fine tunic you always wear working around the village?"

Running Bird nodded vigorously. "Yes that's right. You know the one. It has pretty bead work on the front."

"Of course, of course. I remember it well," the old man said solemnly. He turned to the other council members and they whispered among themselves. After a few uneasy moments, they turned back to the three women. "We direct the blue-eyed one to make Running Bird a new tunic. And, hereafter, White Rain and her mother will treat the Blue Eyes with the respect and dignity due to a Comanche." The women nodded in agreement and touched hands in forgiveness.

As the council dispersed, Peta Nokona, who had been watching Cynthia closely during the proceedings, turned to Five Wolves. "My compliments on a wise judgment. I'm impressed with the Blue Eyes. In several years, she could make a Comanche warrior a good wife."

Five Wolves searched Peta's face. "Ah ha! You noticed, did you? She might be all the wife a man could handle."

"Maybe she'd be the only wife a man might want," Peta said, as he stared thoughtfully at Cynthia.

"One of her might be more than enough," Five Wolves said wryly.

Peta turned back to the elder. "Um, sorry, didn't hear what you said," he mumbled. The old man smiled to himself. "No matter, no matter. We'll see, we'll see," he muttered.

THREE

Indian Territory
1843

Several years passed and Cynthia, now an eligible young woman of fifteen years, had been thoroughly indoctrinated into Comanche life. Her blonde hair, darker now, had been cut short. Her complexion, through exposure to the elements, had darkened. She could pass as a Comanche, except for her eyes. They were bright blue, a dead giveaway that under her dark, outer layer, traces of a white girl remained. She could no longer speak her mother tongue. Her memories of family had almost completely dissipated. She had been given the Comanche name *Naduah*, meaning "Someone Found."

On a warm summer day, she and Singing Woman were busy fleshing hides while tribal life swirled around them. Dogs barked and small, naked children tumbled about. Several babies, secure in cradle boards, were propped against their lodges, while their mothers were busy with chores.

Singing Woman, showing signs of advancing age, hummed to herself as she worked, bent over a hide. She straightened up and looked at Cynthia. "I think it's time for you to think about a husband," she said cautiously. "Your years are right. Have you ever thought about this?"

"Not really," Cynthia said. She scraped the hide furiously. "I like it here with you, Mother."

"Yes, but I am growing old. My time is coming. It is right that you should marry and have strong sons," Singing Woman replied.

Cynthia wrinkled her nose. "Oh, that is so grown up! I don't know if I could be a good mother and a good wife."

The older woman smiled lovingly. "I have no doubt that you can, Naduah. Your sons will become great warriors!"

Cynthia ceased scraping. "Do you think they will have blue eyes?"

Her mother smiled. "Perhaps."

"I hope they don't," Cynthia said wistfully. "Blue eyes make you different. I hate that!"

Singing Woman stopped her fleshing and glanced at Cynthia. "Ah, my little one, in the eyes of a future husband, blue eyes may make you special. Different. Not like the rest of us with brown eyes. All of us want to look special to the one we love."

Cynthia looked closely at her mother. "Do you really think so?" Singing Woman nodded affirmatively. "Peta Nokona. Do you think he might like blue eyes?" Cynthia asked shyly.

"So! You have noticed somebody! Peta Nokona! Don't forget, there are others who might make you a fine husband," the older woman said knowingly.

"I know," Cynthia said forlornly. "But there is something about Peta. I . . . I just like to look at him. He probably doesn't even know who I am."

"Of course he does, silly," Singing Woman said soothingly. "He brought you to me, remember?"

"That was a long time ago, when I was just a child."

"Yes, that is true. Peta is a fine man and a great warrior. But he has never taken a wife."

Cynthia brightened. "That's right, isn't it? Why do you think he has never taken a wife?"

Singing Woman patted Cynthia softly on the head. "Maybe he has not found the one he wants," she said slyly. "Maybe he's looking for someone special."

Cynthia hesitated. "Do you really think so? Do you think that he . . . uh . . . that he might like blue eyes?"

Singing Woman laughed. "So now you think that blue eyes might make you special? I thought you hated blue eyes?" Cynthia giggled and resumed fleshing at a quickened pace.

A week passed of soft summer days and starlit nights. Tribal life proceeded at a leisurely pace. While the women did most of the drudge work, the men rested, smoking, telling stories, and gambling. Naked children tumbled about, while babies, in their cradle-boards, watched with large, dark eyes. The Old Ones braided rawhide ropes and made bow strings and arrows while gossiping with friends. Close by, older children laughed and shouted as the played in the clear waters of a small stream.

Sitting cross-legged on a blanket outside his lodge, Peta Nokona painstakingly carved a piece of cedar. He held his work at arm's length and examined it critically. "Needs more off the sides," he mumbled to himself.

Five Wolves approached. "So, Peta, you are making chips to start your cooking fire?" he asked innocently.

Peta looked up and smiled. "Not quite, my friend. This is to be my first courtship flute. I have decided upon a wife." He put the flute to his lips and blew several experimental notes.

"About time," said Five Wolves. "Does the lucky girl know?"

Peta shook his head and held out the flute. "No. Here, you try it. You've had more experience with these things than I have." Five Wolves took the flute and shook it, dislodging several wood chips.

"Works better with the chips out," he said, playing a few notes.

"Not bad!" said Peta approvingly. "Considering that you haven't played one of these for many winters!"

"Never mind," Five Wolves answered. "It worked for me. Now, listen, I want you to hear the most important part." Putting the flute to his lips, he played a plaintive melody, closing with a special trill. "Hear that?" he asked. "Right at the end? That's the important part! It works. Trust me. That special trill! It persuaded my wife!" He handed the flute back to Peta. "Probably should take a little more wood off the sides."

Peta accepted the flute. "Don't you want to know who I've decided upon to be my wife?" he said in a slightly injured tone.

"I already know," Five Wolves said patronizingly.

Peta was startled. "No, you don't. I just decided yesterday."

Five Wolves smiled and shook his head." No you didn't. You've known for a long time!"

Flustered, Peta stared at his flute. "Um . . . well . . . maybe I have."

As he walked away, Five Wolves said, "Remember what I said. Keep practicing."

Peta nodded and, somewhat perplexed, inspected his flute carefully. Putting it to his lips, he attempted the trill. After several attempts, he succeeded in mastering the notes. Wrapping the flute in a soft skin, Peta smiled to himself and entered his lodge.

Later that evening, Peta stationed himself by the stream bank. The sounds of the village were muffled in the distance, and the evening birds were stilled. A whip-poor-will sang close by, and the horse herd, guarded by several teenage boys, grazed contentedly.

As part of her daily chores, Cynthia provided water for her lodge. In the waning evening, she approached the stream to fill her water skins. As she bent to fill the containers, she heard, for the first time, the soft notes of a courtship flute. Glancing over her shoulder, she noticed Peta, and hastily averted her eyes. Strangely uneasy, she retreated towards the village, her water skins only half filled. As she entered her lodge, she placed the half-filled water skins on the ground.

Singing Woman looked up from her sewing. "Why are the skins not full?" she asked.

"He was there! I saw him!" Cynthia said excitedly. "It was him!"

"Who is 'him'?"

"Peta Nokona!" Cynthia said weakly.

"Yes?" said the older woman knowingly.

"He was blowing a whistle."

"No. A flute. He was playing a courtship flute."

"He was? A courtship flute? What comes of that?" Cynthia wondered.

"Was anybody else there?"

"No, nobody else. Just me. I was filling my water skins."

"Good. Did he speak to you?"

"No."

"Did you speak to him?"

"No. Should I have?" Cynthia worried.

"No, you did the right thing," Singing Woman reassured her.

"What does all this mean?" Cynthia wondered.

Singing Woman wrapped her arms around her daughter. "It is a Comanche custom, Naduah, that a man wishing to marry shows his love to his chosen one by singing to her with a courtship flute." She stroked Cynthia's head tenderly. "And you, my little Blue Eyes, have been chosen by Peta Nokona to be his wife. If, of course, you wish it and I approve it!"

"Are you sure? Maybe he was just practicing. Maybe he was waiting for another girl. Me? Do you really think so?"

Singing Woman smiled and nodded. "Yes, I really think so. I can remember when it happened to me, many winters past."

Tears started in Cynthia's eyes. "Maybe his family won't like me because I am not true Comanche, not one of The People. Maybe they will not approve of me."

Singing Woman shook her head disapprovingly. "You are getting too far ahead of this thing. But I will tell you this: If Peta truly wants you for his wife, his family will welcome you. And, as one of The People."

Heartened, Cynthia wiped her tears away. "What should I do?"

"He will be out there again tomorrow night. This time you must show him that you have heard his song, and that you like it."

"How do I do that?" Cynthia asked.

"You stand up, after filling your skins, and look at him shyly. You smile just a little at him and come back here to the lodge," she directed.

"What if it rains?"

"Don't worry. I won't let it." Singing Woman laughed.

The next evening was clear and gentle, and Peta returned to his place in the shadows, ever more confident in the magic of his flute. Its haunting notes drifted on the evening breeze. Moonrise was heralded by its strong white light. Cynthia, carrying her water skins, neared the stream, and knelt, filling them slowly, emptying them repeatedly as a cleansing measure. As she worked, the wistful notes of the flute floated softly across the quiet water. Once finished, she stood up.

As Peta played his most practiced trill, the music took on an added dimension. Cynthia smiled shyly at him, then lowered her head modestly, and hurried back to her lodge. Peta's song resumed with an exuberant overtone.

Entering the lodge, Cynthia was breathless. "He was there. Just as you said!"

Singing Woman looked up from her sewing. "Did he play his flute?" she asked.

"Yes, and then he stopped and looked at me and the moon came out," Cynthia said dreamily.

"And what did you do?"

"Just what you said. I smiled at him and hurried back here."

"Good." Singing Woman paused. "The water skins. Where are they?"

"I don't know," Cynthia said blankly. "I must have left them by the stream."

Singing Woman smiled. "That's all right. You had much on your mind. Now, about tomorrow night. You must wear your finest things—your softest moccasins, your beaded tunic. I will paint you in Comanche custom. Then you will go out and meet Peta by the stream. Then we will know. Do you understand?"

Cynthia nodded. "Yes, and I . . ."

There was a scratching on the outside of the lodge. Singing Woman looked up from her sewing. "What's that?" she asked.

Cynthia opened the lodge flap and peered outside. "There's nobody here," she replied. "But look, my water skins are here, and all filled!"

Singing Woman looked at her gravely. "I wonder what could have done this? Maybe the spirits are among us tonight in the bright moonlight. Yes, it must be the spirits," she said with a knowing smile.

Fulfilling Cynthia's weather worries, a steady rain dampened village life for the next two days. The third day, however, dawned bright and clear with the promise of a half-moon evening.

In their lodge, Singing Woman and her daughter prepared for the next step in tribal tradition. In the high fashion of Comanche custom, the part in Cynthia's hair was painted red along its entire length. Her eyes were accented by red lines above the lids and yellow lines below, crossing at the corners. Her cheeks were painted with a solid circle of red. She wore a deer skin blouse and skirt, heavily beaded, as were her moccasins.

Singing Woman held her daughter at arm's length. "Yes, that's about right," she said. "We have to save a few tricks for your wedding day." She dug into a leather pouch and produced a scrap of mirror. "Here, Blue Eyes," she said. "See for yourself."

Cynthia looked into the mirror and marveled at her appearance. "Do I really look like that?" She hesitated. "Do you think there's too much red? Maybe some green around the eyes?"

"No, no, you're just right. Leave well enough alone." Singing Woman waved her hand, wand-like. "See? I have made a duckling into a swan!"

"Well, if you say so," Cynthia said uncertainly. She paused. "Do I really look like a swan?"

Singing Woman laughed. "Of course you do," she said reassuringly. "Now listen to me. As the moon rises, you must go out to the stream and meet Peta. You will know what to say. But let him speak first. Now, go my Blue Eyes, with my blessing."

Timidly, Cynthia opened the lodge flap and walked towards the stream, casting sideways glances to see if anybody was watching. As she neared the water's edge, she heard Peta's courtship song lilting in the pale moonlight. Peta then rose from the shadows and came towards her. "I wondered if you heard my song?" he asked.

"Yes, it is a very nice song," Cynthia replied, her eyes averted.

"Would you like to hear it again?" Peta asked.

"Yes, that would be very nice." Putting the flute to his lips, Peta played his love song, concluding with the special trill.

"I really like the ending," Cynthia said.

Peta looked startled. "You do?" He repeated the trill. "That part?" Cynthia nodded in assent. "I call that part the 'Five Wolves Trill.'"

"I think Five Wolves is a very wise man," Cynthia said.

"He is wise in more ways than you can imagine," Peta answered.

"Yes, I am sure he is."

"If it pleases you, I would like to have Five Wolves call on Singing Woman tomorrow, when the sun is high," Peta said.

"Yes, that would please me. I will tell my mother."

Peta hesitantly reached out and touched Cynthia's hand. "Before you go, I want you to know how pretty you are in the shine of the moon," he whispered.

Cynthia lowered her head. "Um . . . thank you," she murmured. Raising her eyes, she asked archly, "Do you say that to all the swans?"

"Swans?" Peta repeated blankly.

"Oh, never mind. It's just a little riddle," Cynthia responded as she retreated towards her lodge.

"Swans?" Peta wondered aloud as Cynthia turned away. "Swans?"

It was a warm autumn day in the village, and Five Wolves, resplendent in his finery, stalked through the village, leading two horses. Each horse was decorated—tails tied with ribbons, bodies painted with various designs. As he walked past the Old Ones making bows and arrows, they looked up from their work and nudged each other. By now, Five Wolves had attracted a curious crowd of all ages, who trailed along behind him. Unruffled, he stalked on. Arriving at Singing Woman's lodge, he tied the horses. Hearing the commotion, she stepped out from her lodge, noting that there were two horses, rather than the customary one.

"Five Wolves! I am pleased to see you. Please come in," she said, smiling.

Five Wolves nodded. "Thank you. We should talk"

Inside the lodge, Five Wolves was seated on a buffalo skin beside his hostess, who dipped a cup of broth from a pot and handed it to her guest. "Now, honored guest, what is it that you would say to me?" she asked pleasantly.

Five Wolves sipped his broth. "As you see, I bring gifts from Peta Nokona," he said pompously.

"Yes, they are fine-looking horses," she said innocently. "But why would Peta Nokona send me gifts? I am just a poor old woman."

Five Wolves, ever the diplomat, finished his broth and set the cup down. "No, no. You are not old. Mature, perhaps, but not old. Anyway, Peta wishes your permission to marry Naduah, the Blue Eyes. And, of course, if you agree, then you will no longer be poor."

"I see," Singing Woman said. "But before I can give you an answer, I must talk with Naduah. Her happiness is very important to me."

"I understand. We will await your answer." Five Wolves rose, sipping the last of his broth.

Upon his departure, Cynthia scrambled through the lodge flap and ran to her mother ecstatically. "I heard every word," Cynthia said excitedly. "I can't believe it!"

The two women, holding each other in a loving embrace, whirled giddily around the lodge. "Peta Nokona! Who would have believed it? Me? Naduah! I can't believe it!" Cynthia repeated.

Regaining her composure, Singing Woman smoothed her skirt. "Enough of this," she said. "Comanche law says that if I release those two horses outside, we have rejected the marriage offer. However, if I lead the horses to the herd, then we have accepted the offer. Naduah, what do you think I should do?"

"Keep the horses! Keep the horses! Hold their halter ropes tightly!" Cynthia sqealed deliriously. "Don't let them get away!"

"Don't worry, they don't have a chance," replied Singing Woman, who then walked from her lodge and led the horses to the herd, taking pains that her actions were observed by the village. Five Wolves's audience had remained silent, but at Singing Woman's actions, there was a knowing murmur. Several hundred yards away, Five Wolves and Peta watch intently as Singing Woman approached the herd. They nodded solemnly at each other.

"Well, it is done," Five Wolves said.

Peta gripped his friend's arm. "Yes, it is done. My thanks to you."

"You are welcome. Hopefully you'll feel the same ten winters from now. And now that you have no further use for that flute, I have a son who thinks he's in love."

Peta handed him the flute. "Here," he said. "It worked for me. Be sure to show him the trill."

Later that day, Five Wolves let it be known that Peta and Naduah were to marry and that a celebratory feast would be held the next afternoon. While Comanche custom did not require ritualized nuptials other than agreement to marry by both parties, a feast was always welcomed.

Resting on buffalo robes in the center of the village, Peta and Naduah accepted the good wishes of their friends. Peta, handsome in ornately beaded, soft buckskin, and hair plated in two braids each tied with strips of red cloth, joked and laughed with his fellow warriors. Cynthia, painted lovingly by Singing Woman, sat next to him, relishing her new status. She had become the darling of the tribe.

As the celebration grew in levity and noise, Cynthia turned to Peta. "Do you notice anything different about me?" she asked shyly.

"You look beautiful," Peta responded.

"Yes, thank you. But what's different about me?"

"Ah . . . um . . . you're my wife now. That's different," Peta said lamely.

"No, silly. It's my ears. Do you like them?" Her ears had been painted bright red on the inside by Singing Woman, who saved this as her crowning touch.

"Oh, the ears. I thought you were blushing," Peta teased.

Before Cynthia could attempt one-upmanship again, a handful of mounted warriors whirled into the center of the village. Astride their best ponies, painted and beribboned for the occasion, the young men gave a breathtaking display of horsemanship: they swung over and under their mounts, picking up small objects off the ground, sat backwards, and stood on their saddles. The exhibition concluded when the riders, at full gallop, swung under the necks of their ponies and shot arrows into a small target. The crowd shouted its appreciation, and the warriors raised their bows in salute to Peta and his new bride.

As night approached and the feasting diminished, the flickering fires illuminated the celebrants, as well as several tribal dogs, who sensed prosperous scavenging.

Peta stood up. "We thank our people for this feast. It was a good thing," he said. "But now I—we—must leave you to refresh ourselves in the cool waters of the stream."

On the stream bank, lit only by a thin sliver of moon, the bride and groom eagerly sought each other, undressing and slipping into the water. Other than the sounds of a distant whip-poor-will and the gurgle of water, there was absolute silence. Except for a subdued moaning.

After several years, Naduah gave birth to her first child, a son. He was given the name Quanah, the Comanche word for *fragrance*, and he had grey eyes.

FOUR

Indian Territory
Autumn, 1860

On a grassy meadow adjoining their village, Peta held school for his young son. The curriculum included the rudiments of Comanche life, with a heavy emphasis on ponies, their training, and care. Quanah repeated riding maneuvers time and time again. Although taught to ride almost from infancy, Quanah took his share of spills and falls. The Old Ones of the tribe, the weapons-makers, taught the boy the intricacies of the bow, arrow, and lance. He learned to keep his bowstring dry, as moisture would stretch it, making it unusable. And after long hours of practice, he was able to hit any target, moving or still, within thirty yards. At a gallop, swung from the neck of his pony, he could drive an arrow into a ten-inch target.

Peta watched intently as his son thundered past him, slid to the side of his pony, and drilled an arrow into a target. Quanah reined up in front of Peta with a big smile on his face. Unobtrusive, at the edge of the meadow, Weckeah, a handsome child, watched in awe as her idol practiced being a man.

Quanah leaned over and patted his pony affectionately "How was that?"

"It was all right," Peta said condescendingly. "How many arrows did you shoot?"

"One. That's all I could," Quanah said, perplexed. "Why?"

"Get off your pony and come here," Peta said gently. From a bundle of skins, he unwrapped a rusted, damaged rifle.

"What's that for?" Quanah asked mystified.

"It's to teach you a lesson," his father responded. "Now, when this rifle is fired, what must you do to make it fire again?"

"Reload?"

Peta nodded. "That's right. Now watch me. I'm going to pretend I have just fired this rifle at you and missed. Now, I have to reload. I want you to count as I reload. Ready?" Quanah nodded, as Peta began to simulate pouring powder down the rifle barrel.

"One, two, three, four, five, six, seven, eight, nine, ten, eleven, twelve . . ." Quanah counted. Next Peta seated an imaginary wad over the powder charge with his ram-rod. ". . . Thirteen, fourteen, fifteen, sixteen . . ." Peta dropped a simulated bullet down the barrel, stamped it firmly, and then seated a patch over the bullet. Peta withdrew the ramrod

"Stop counting," he said. "What's your count?"

"Fifty-eight," Quanah answered. "I counted to fifty-eight."

"Good. Now I'm going to ride by that target and fire six arrows into it. I want you to count again. Count how long it takes me to shoot these six arrows." Peta carefully selected five shafts from his quiver, and gripped them between his teeth. He nocked the sixth arrow to his bow string, then removed the other arrows from his mouth. "Now, Quanah, start counting when I shoot my first arrow, and keep counting until I have shot my sixth. Understand?" Quanah nodded. Peta again gripped the arrows between his teeth, and thundered across the meadow. As he approached the target, he slid off his seat, clung to the far side of his pony, and released his first arrow. The pony abruptly wheeled, and Peta fired his second.

"One, two, three, four, five, six, seven, eight, nine . . ." Quanah counted. As one, Peta and his pony, galloped and wheeled in stunning displays of horsemanship. ". . . Ten, eleven, twelve, thirteen, fourteen, fifteen . . ."

As his last arrow hit its target, Peta charged up to Quanah, raised his bow in salute, and slid from his pony. Brushing dust from his clothing, Peta looked inquiringly at the boy. "So what was your count?"

Quanah looked stunned. "Thirty-nine, I think."

"That sounds about right," Peta said. "Now, do you know what I'm trying to show you?"

"Um . . . I . . . ah . . . I think so," Quanah stammered uncertainly.

"Tell me," Peta said.

"That it takes a long time to reload a rifle."

"Truly. What else?"

"That you can shoot six arrows quickly?"

"Yes, that is so. Anything else?"

Quanah fumbled. "Um . . ."

Peta placed his hand on his son's shoulder. "Quanah, some day you will be a war chief of the Comanche, and you must know how and when to strike your enemies. For instance, pretend you are attacking some Tejanos who are killing our buffalo. They have rifles. You have lances, bows, and arrows. What should you do?"

Quanah paused. "Yes, their rifles take long to reload. We can shoot faster with our bows. I would wait until the Tejanos have fired at us, and then attack, shoot six arrows, and ride out of range before they can fire their guns," Quanah said excitedly.

"Good. That is right. But one caution," Peta said.

"Caution?"

"Yes. There are stories that some Tejanos have guns that shoot many times without reloading. Watch out for that," Peta warned. "Such weapons could change many things."

FIVE

Fort Belknap, Texas
1860

Fort Belknap was one of seven so-called "forts" utilized by the Texas Rangers and the U.S. cavalry. Despite its name, it had no defensive walls or pickets, but was rather a cluster of rough-hewn buildings open to the plains that served as meeting rooms, living quarters, and offices to military personnel. It was originally established to protect the frontier against hostile raids, however, the military demands of the Civil War limited its use.

In one of the crude offices, three men met quietly. Charlie McKnight, local rancher and renowned tracker, sat next to Jim Loving, another rancher. The third man, Sam Ross, was a newly commissioned officer in a recently formed local militia known as the "Texas Rangers." The slamming of a door announced the arrival of a fourth man, John Baylor, the tainted ex-agent of the Texas Comanche Reservation. "Sorry I'm late. Have I missed anything?" he asked.

Ross placed a bottle and four glasses on the table. "Nope. Here. Wet your whistle."

Baylor filled his glass and raised it in salute. "Luck." The other three nodded in acknowledgment.

Ross wiped his mouth on his sleeve. "Need some help." The bottle passed around again.

"What kind of help?" McKnight asked.

Ross tipped back in his chair. "You all know about the Comanche Reservation that the Texas legislature set up in 1855?"

"Something like twenty-three thousand acres, wasn't it?" Loving asked.

Ross nodded. "Yup, and the problem is that them Comanches are being shoved off their land by cowmen and such."

Baylor interrupted angrily. "Them savages don't need all that country. All they wanta do is steal people's horses and massacre their families! I oughta know! I was their agent, them bastards!"

Ross waved off the comment. "C'mon, John. Calm down. Anyhow, as I was sayin', them Comanche ain't so damned pleased. And now the hide-hunters are wipin' out their buffalo, which ain't helpin' much neither."

"Serves 'em right," Baylor growled. "Sonsabitches!"

Loving stared at Baylor. "Guess we know where you stand, John," he said sardonically.

"Damn straight!" Baylor looked pleased.

"Let's get back on the subject," Ross said. "Folks hereabouts are some spooked by a couple of Comanche raids. Nothin' big, but a warning. Until two days ago."

McKnight glanced at him. "You mean the Sherman killings?"

Ross nodded. "That's right. I figure that prolly was revenge for the Paint Creek massacre you pulled off, John."

Baylor brightened. "Yeah, we killed thirteen bucks and took their hair, by God!"

"And the Sherman family paid for it. Miss Sherman and her unborn babe," McKnight said, his voice rising.

Ross slammed his hand on the table in irritation. "All right! All right! Enough! The question is, what do we do next? Smooth it over, or hunt down the killers?"

McKnight fiddled with his glass. "The Shermans are neighbors to me. So you know how I feel about them. But we don't know much about them Comanche. How many? Where they come from and where they are now? And if we find 'em, will the chiefs turn over them that killed the Shermans, or we hafta fight everybody? Touchy situation!"

"Good points, Charlie," Ross said. "John, you've made it pretty clear how you feel. How about you, Jim?"

Loving lit a cigar and studied it closely. He looked up. "Well, Cap'n," he drawled, "I'm just a plain old cowhand tryin' to make a livin'. And I do believe in live and let live. But this Sherman thing does make me wonder some. If we let 'em get away with this, there'll be hell to pay. And I wouldn't count on the chiefs helpin' none. It'll be a fight for sure."

"You're damned right!" Baylor said loudly.

Piqued, Ross turned to Baylor. "You've said your piece, John. Thank you." Ross looked at McKnight. "Think you could find 'em?"

McKnight scratched his nose. "Maybe. Need another scout."

"Anything else?"

"Bunch of riders from around here who know the lay of the land and how to fight it. Some soldier boys. Cavalry might help some."

"When can you start?" Ross asked.

McKnight stood up. "When can you get me the men?"

Ross smiled. "Fair enough. Be ready to pull out in two days. I'll take care of the details." He turned to Baylor. "No, John, you can't come. You've done enough damage already."

"You don't say? Well, Mr. Ross, Texas Ranger, you ain't seen the half of it!" Baylor said belligerently.

"Spare me," Ross retorted, as the group headed towards the door.

McKnight tapped Ross on the shoulder. "I know the man I want as scout. I'll get him. We'll leave at first light tomorrow. Join up with you later."

Baylor sidled up to McKnight. "I got thirteen of them bastards. You're gonna hafta go some to beat that!" he said unpleasantly.

McKnight stared at Baylor and shook his head incredulously.

"What?" said Baylor, bewildered. "What? What?"

SIX

Comanche Village, West Texas
November 1860

For his fall camp, Peta had selected a meadow fronting on a modest stream. Early frost had turned the meadow grass to a soft beige. The tribal horse herd, tended by teenaged boys, stood ankle-deep in the stream and drank noisily. Cooking fires burned brightly in the growing twilight, as the women of the tribe prepared food for their lodges. An early chill in the air gave warning of the coming winter.

Two scouts, astride their ponies, trotted into the center of the camp, halting at Peta's lodge. Peta stepped from his lodge and the men exchanged greetings. "You have the look of scouts with something to say," Peta said.

"The buffalo come, Peta," the older of the two scouts said. "Many, many buffalo."

"How far?" Peta asked.

The younger scout held up one finger. "Maybe one sleep."

Peta nodded. "Did you see any other people? Tejanos? Apaches? White hunters?"

Both scouts shook their heads. "No. No people. We saw only fat cows and bulls."

"Good!" Peta said. "We will leave when the sun rises and make a hunting camp. Women with children and the Old Ones will stay here with the camp guards." The scouts nodded and left to alert the village.

Inside Peta's lodge, Pecos and Topsannah joined the excited chatter of their mother and older brother. Peta held up his hands and silenced the noise. "Quanah, you and Pecos will ride with me tomorrow. You are old enough to help in the running. Naduah, you and Topsannah will stay here."

Cynthia looked at her husband, measuring his words. "Are you sure?" she said. "They are so young!"

Peta nodded. "Yes, I am sure. They will do well. They have been waiting for this!"

Cynthia bowed her head. "I am sure they have. But I haven't. They're so young! Please watch them carefully." She placed a hand on each boy. "Your father honors you with your first running. Be careful. Stay close to him. Understand?"

"Yes! Yes," Quanah said jubilantly. He turned to Pecos. "How many arrows do you have? I have nine."

"I have seven," Pecos replied.

Peta stifled a smile. "Real buffalo hunters need twenty arrows—each. Maybe you should stay with the women."

"No, no, we'll get more," Quanah argued. "Come on, Pecos, old Red Elk will have some extras." The brothers scrambled from the lodge in search of the arrow-maker.

Peta turned to Cynthia. "Don't fret, Naduah," he said tenderly. "Pecos will hold our horses. The next hunt will be his first real running. And Quanah will ride next to me."

Cynthia nodded in understanding, but felt a lingering sense of doubt.

As the sun set, the village bustled about, packing for the hunt. The riders carefully selected their best runners, elite ponies trained for the hunt, while a number of skilled women butchers, who were included in the hunting party, sharpened knives. Those not selected packed food and necessities for the party. Around the camp fires, warriors sharpened lance points and arrow heads. Others decorated their ponies' tails, manes, and bodies as a protective measure ordained by the buffalo gods.

The Hunting Dance had begun in the center of the camp. As the drums throbbed and the dancers assembled, Peta and his two sons stood at the edge of the crowd.

Peta looked at his sons proudly. "Tomorrow you will do a man's work," he said. "Do it well. Trust your pony. Ride close to the buffalo. Shoot strong and straight." He drew a buffalo in the dust. "Shoot between his shoulder and his rib on a downwards slant so that your arrow will strike his heart. If you wound him, keep away. Your pony will see to that. And be sure to keep your long halter rope in your hand as you ride. If you fall off and let go of the rope, your pony will run free with the buffalo herd and you will be all alone. Do you understand?" Both boys nodded vigorously, stamping to the beat of the drums. "Good. Now go watch the dancers. But you can't dance until after your first running. Watch! Don't dance!" Yelping with excitement, the boys plunged into the crowd.

Led by Sam Ross, the cavalry unit plodded across the open plains. Two scouts roamed in wide sweeps ahead of the columns, studying the ground for any telltale signs of Indian presence. Two days of searching had produced nothing.

As he rode slowly in advance, Charlie McKnight's attention was caught by a flutter of movement in the prairie grass. He dismounted and picked up a battered Bible. Inscribed on the fly leaf was the name *Sherman*. He cantered back to the column, and waved in the other scout.

Ross rode up. "What you find?"

McKnight handed the Bible to Ross. "Look at the first page," he said.

Ross turned the page. "Sherman! Looks like we're on the right trail!"

McKnight nodded. "Seems so."

"Any tracks?" Ross asked.

"Nope. Not yet." He turned to Dave, the second scout. "You seen anything?"

Dave shook his head. "Nothin' yet."

Ross beckoned to his sergeant. "Sergeant, rest the horses. Dismount the men and stand to."

As the sergeant trotted back to the column, McKnight pointed ahead. "Sam, seems I remember a sweet water creek up ahead. Good camp site. Comanche could be there. Worth a look."

"How much time you need?" Ross asked.

"Coupla days should do it."

"You got it."

"Need help?" Dave asked.

"Nope. One man job," McKnight replied.

Dave squinted at him. "Luck," he said. "Keep yer head down and yer hair on!"

McKnight grinned. "I'll try."

The following day McKnight rode cautiously through tall buffalo grass and tangles of green scrub. Every few minutes he dismounted and searched the ground. Topping a low rise, he could make out the glitter of water—the sweet water creek he was seeking. A slight breeze ruffled his shirt. He stopped, stood in his stirrups, and sniffed the wind. "Wood smoke. Betcha two bits!" he muttered to himself. McKnight dismounted. In a crouch, he tied his horse to a bush and drew his rifle from its scabbard. After removing his hat, he slipped silently through the brush. After several minutes, he topped a bluff fronting on the creek.

On the far side of the creek was a Comanche encampment with its horse herd grazing close by. Evening was approaching and the village showed signs of increased activity. Lying on his belly, McKnight watched as a hunting party gathered in the center of the village. The sound of drums heralded the Hunting Dance, as the Comanche gathered to celebrate. After counting the lodges and estimating the number of horses, McKnight quietly backed off the bluff and remounted. He walked the horse until out of earshot of the village, then broke into a gallop towards the waiting columns.

A day later, McKnight neared Ross's bivouac. Slowing his pace on uneven ground, McKnight was challenged by a sentry. "Don't shoot ol' Charlie!" McKnight shouted as he trotted into the midst of the camp.

Sam Ross approached him. "You all right?" he asked.

McKnight slid from his horse. "Yeah, I'm in one piece. Little worried about that horse, though. Needs a little corn and some rest."

"Find anything?" Ross asked, handing the scout a tin cup of coffee.

McKnight drank gratefully. "Jackpot!" he answered. There was a murmur of excitement in the camp.

"Where? How many?" Ross asked.

"Best guess about a day's hard ride. Best guess about a hundred Comanche. Big pony herd. Maybe fifty, sixty lodges, right on the creek."

"Think they did the Sherman killin'?"

McKnight shrugged. "Maybe. No way of tellin'."

"Maybe? That the best you can do?" Ross asked impatiently.

"Gonna hafta be," the scout answered. "Looked like there was a huntin' party gettin' ready to pull out. Just a guess."

Ross rubbed his eyes. "Charlie, how good are yer guesses?"

"Fair to middlin', I s'pose," the scout answered amiably. "Two outta three usually on the money."

Ross brightened. "I'll settle for that!"

McKnight smiled. "Why don't we go find out?"

"Damn straight!" Ross said, his voice rising. "That's what we come for! Let's move out!"

SEVEN

Comanche Village, West Texas
November 1860

The next morning, the Comanche camp boiled with activity. Lodges were struck by the women and loaded on their travois. Older children, allowed to be part of the hunt for the first time, ran excitedly through the camp, mimicking the hunters, while others played the part of dead and wounded buffalo. Village dogs barked and happily chased the children.

The hunting party gradually formed in the center of the village. Quanah and Pecos, astride their favorite ponies, feigned nonchalance under the gaze of envious friends who had yet to join a running.

"Aren't you excited?" asked a boy.

"No, not really," Quanah said condescendingly.

"Are you scared," asked another.

"Us? Scared? It's the buffalo that should be scared!" Pecos said with false bravado.

"Maybe so. Just don't fall off your pony during the running!"

Quanah smiled and patted his pony affectionately. "My pony friend won't let me fall off. He knows all about the running."

Standing quietly away from the noisy crowd, Weckeah, now a pretty young lady, hesitantly stepped forward and offered Quanah a sprig of sage. "This is for good luck," she said. "It will protect you during the running."

Quanah smiled. "Thank you, Weckeah. I will kill a buffalo just for you. Your very own buffalo!"

Weckeah looked at Quanah adoringly. "That would be very nice! I've never had a buffalo all my own!"

"It will be my gift to you," Quanah said, relishing his newfound status.

"Please be careful, Quanah," she said softly.

Quanah nodded. "Don't worry, Weckeah," he said. "I'll be all right."

Red Elk stepped from the crowd and approached the two boys. He held up a bundle of arrows for all to see. "For our two new runners, I give these arrows as a sign of good medicine," he said. "The shafts are of young dogwood, for strength, and the feathers of the wild turkey will cause the arrows to fly straight and true. Take them with my blessing."

As Pecos and Quanah accepted the gift, Peta rode alongside. "As a young man, Red Elk was a mighty hunter," he said to the crowd. "He brings honor to our lodge with this gift. We thank him."

Pecos admired the arrows. "We will bring Red Elk a fat cow killed by one of these arrows," he said as the crowd applauded.

Gradually the crowd dispersed as the hunting party slowly wended its way out of the village. Cynthia, holding Topsannah by the hand, approached Peta and her two sons. "My heart rides with you, my love," she said to her husband.

Peta reached down and gripped her outstretched hand. "Watch over my little Topsannah for me," he said.

Turning to her sons, she placed a hand on the leg of each boy, and looked lovingly up into their faces. "Be brave and be careful, my sons. Bring honor to your father and to our lodge." The boys touched her hands in farewell, and rode slowly from the camp.

Cynthia and her daughter, standing alone, watched the hunters gradually fade into the distance. Cynthia, overcome with concern, failed to notice Topsannah as she gathered several sprigs of sage. She smelled them solemnly and then placed them in her mother's open hand. Absorbed in her thoughts, they slipped, unnoticed, to the ground.

After a six-hour ride, the Comanche made a hunting camp in close proximity to the buffalo herd. Makeshift one-night shelters made from grass and branches were quickly set up. Everyday ponies were segregated from the "runners," who were pampered and painted with feathers and tribal designs, expected to bring good fortune to their riders and safe passage for themselves.

With the coming of dawn, the hunters abandoned their camp, mounted their runners, and rode slowly towards the ridge overlooking the herd.

Older warriors and experienced hunters rode ahead, discouraging younger hunters from breaking ranks and spooking the animals. Several scouts joined the party, having studied the buffalo earlier. The novice hunters, Pecos among them, were designated to hold the horses, while the older tribesmen crawled silently to the top of the ridge.

There below, massed across the prairie, was a sea of feeding buffalo, gazing peacefully in the early light of morning. Awkward calves gamboled by their mothers, while bulls and young cows fed placidly. Young bulls pawed the earth and butted heads, while the older males dug into the soil with their stubby horns, twisting and turning their ponderous heads, their thin, short tails erect. It was a sight to behold, and the Comanche watched in quiet reverence. They withdrew carefully from the ridge and returned to their runners, murmuring prayers and words of encouragement to the excited ponies, who sensing the proximity of the herd, pranced excitedly. For both rider and runner, it was a climactic moment.

Upon mounting their horses, the riders spread out and quietly led their ponies over the ridge, relying on the buffalo's poor eyesight for the element of surprise. As the band approached the herd, several bulls raised their heads and pawed the ground, bellowing belligerently. The Comanche edged closer to the herd, their bows readied, with additional arrows clutched in their hand or between their teeth. Suddenly, a bowstring twanged and a fat cow stumbled, walked several steps, and collapsed, with the feathers of an arrow protruding from her side. Several animals, dimly suspicious, approached the fallen cow curiously then returned to grazing. On a pre-determined signal, the Comanche, as one man, attacked. Panic-stricken, the animals scattered haphazardly.

Quanah, riding hard, overtook a cow with her calf, which was having difficulty in keeping pace with its mother. Drawing close to the cow's right side, Quanah's pony brought him within an arm's length of the animal's flank. Quanah pulled his bow to the arrow's head and aimed at the cow's vulnerable shoulder. The frightened calf crowded close to his mother for protection. Quanah hesitated, then switched his aim to a large bull on his opposite side. His drove his arrow deep into the bull, which suddenly swerved towards the pony and its rider. Trained for just such an occasion, the runner veered sharply away from the wounded bull, which suddenly stumbled and pitched headfirst into the grass.

By now, the herd had rumbled out of range, and Quanah's runner had lost its jump. He reined to a stop and looked warily about him. The herd was in full flight, filling the air with dust and a thunderous rumble. In its wake were black, huddled figures on the prairie—the wounded, dead, and dying buffalo.

A small group of animals, separated from the main herd, curled back towards Quanah. Coming hard in pursuit, Peta expertly dropped a cow. As he nocked another arrow at full gallop, his pony stumbled and sent Peta hurtling through the air. Clinging to his halter rope, Peta hit the ground, rolled over, and ran back to his runner, which had struggled to its feet. Wiping blood and dirt from his face and spitting prairie grass, Peta, bruised both in body and ego, remounted and rode slowly up to his son, who had witnessed his father's fall.

"Are you all right?" Quanah asked.

Peta felt his arms gingerly. "I think so."

"What happened?" Quanah asked, suddenly relieved.

"My runner stepped in a hole, I guess."

"Is he hurt?"

"Only his pride."

"How about you?"

"Same as my runner," Peta said wanly. "Don't tell your mother."

Quanah nodded. "I won't."

"There is a lesson in all this," Peta said.

Quanah smiled. "I think I know."

"What is it?"

"Never let go of your halter rope," Quanah said confidently.

Peta nodded. "There's one more thing."

"What?"

"Ask your runner not to step in a hole!" Peta said with a straight face. He reached out and patted his pony affectionately. In response, the pony lifted its tail and defecated nonchalantly. Peta burst into laughter and tapped his runner gently on the head with his bow.

The hunt was over. Skinners swarmed onto the field with their butchering knives. Each hunter searched the fallen animals, seeking to identify his kill by the markings on his arrows embedded in the carcass. Chattering and laughing, the skinners gutted the buffalo and cut choice pieces for the horse-holders and non-hunters. Pack horses were loaded with dripping meat and bloody hides. It had been a successful hunt. No injuries, and the buffalo killed were fat with fine hides. In early evening, the hunting party started slowly back to its main camp.

EIGHT

Texas Frontier
December 18–19, 1860

As midnight approached, the Ranger camp assembled into columns. The usual confusion accompanying a military maneuver in the black of night was rampant. Horses saddled in the dark and equipment lashed to unhappy mules caused blue language to become commonplace. A cantankerous horse objected to an overly tight cinch and bucked its rider into the darkness, much to the muffled delight of his friends. A sergeant, moving through the columns to check their readiness, stumbled into the thrown rider.

"Soldier," he said, "if you ain't man enough to ride that animal, I'm gonna leave you here with the pack mules!"

"No such thing, Sarge. Old Molly here was just a tad touchy about leavin' all this nice grass hereabouts. She's fine now," a voice from the darkness replied.

"She better be. You get bucked off in that Comanche camp an' it's gonna be your ass and your hair, too," the sergeant growled. "An' you can't afford to lose neither," he added. A burst of subdued laughter came from the ranks. At a soft-spoken command, the columns moved out, with all metal objects muffled.

Several hours later, as they neared the Comanche camp, Ross halted the columns. As the men dismounted, the two scouts joined him. "Sam, we'll be comin' to the crick shortly. Comanche are on the far side. This side has a high bluff, facing the camp. Seems like if we were to cross the crick above the camp and attack from behind 'em, we could push them people right up against that bluff," McKnight said.

"Sounds reasonable. What do you think, Dave?" Ross asked.

The scout nodded. "Yeah, sounds good to me. We'll hit 'em with the sleep still in their eyes!"

"All right, it should work," Ross said. "Let's move. Real quiet."

The columns remounted and soon arrived at the creek, where the horses were watered and the men filled their canteens. The first streaks of daylight appeared to the east. "First light, Sam. Better get a move on," McKnight warned.

"Sergeant, let's move," Ross ordered.

The sergeant saluted. "Yes sir," he said and turned to the ranks. "Let's go, boys. An' be terrible quiet." The columns broke into a trot. The only sounds were those of creaking leather, the horses, and the tentative notes of awakening birds. Sunrise was fast approaching.

A low ridge appeared in the early light. Ross signaled a halt. "Sergeant, all officers here on the double," Ross ordered. Within moments, a small knot of officers joined Ross and the scouts. "Boys, the Comanche camp is just over that rise ahead, on the banks of the crick. Pony herd should be close by. We're gonna attack over that ridge, stampede them ponies, an' drive right through the village. Comanche will prolly make a run for it across the crick, but there's a bluff there. Makes runnin' difficult. Any questions?" Ross paused. "No? Then good luck and good hunting!"

The officers rejoined their men. Weapons were readied, chin straps tightened, and saddles and cinches double-checked. At the cry, "Let's go, boys! Remember the Shermans!" the columns charged, their sabers drawn and pistols cocked.

The sleeping village was jolted awake by the thunder of hooves and the shouts of the attackers. Struggling from their lodges in their sleeping robes, the tribes people were thrust into a bloody hell. Screaming children were run over by charging horses. Women, trying to protect their little ones, were shot in cold blood, others fell from saber cuts. Confused by the noise and chaos, the Old Ones fell under a hail of bullets, as their lodges were toppled by the troops. Singing their death songs, the handful of warriors left to guard the village were quickly overwhelmed and scalped. The soldiers, unlike the Rangers, showed no mercy to the women. The village was quickly set ablaze. Burning lodges filled the air with sparks and smoke.

Clutching Topsannah, Cynthia scrambled from her lodge and ran awkwardly out of the village towards the terrified pony herd. As the animals milled about in confusion, she caught a bay and mounted, holding tenaciously to her daughter. Panic-stricken, she galloped from the village, sobbing in terror.

A Ranger, attempting to quiet the herd, saw her gallop past, drew his pistol, and chased her. As he rode alongside her pony, he saw that she was carrying a small child. Holstering his weapon, he reached out in an attempt to grab her reins, but Cynthia, screaming, fought him off. After several tries, the Ranger forced her pony to a stop, as its rider clawed and scratched. "Hold on, woman! I ain't gonna hurt you and your papoose," he said. "But if you don't stop that infernal hollerin', I might change my mind." He led his captives back to the village and Sam Ross. "Here's another one, Cap'n," he said. "A real scrapper!"

Ross glanced at Cynthia. "With a baby to boot," he said. Cynthia's screams turned into wailing. "Calm down, woman, we ain't gonna harm your kid." Cynthia turned to Ross and raised her head. As she cried out in Comanche, she made eye contact with the Ranger. "My God!" Ross blurted. "She has blue eyes!"

McKnight joined them. "Who has blue eyes?" he asked.

"This squaw right here. Her eyes are honest-to-God blue!" Ross said in astonishment.

McKnight turned to Cynthia and squinted. "Well I'll be damned if they ain't! You speak any English? Can you understand me?"

Cynthia, now hysterical, spoke in Comanche. "My two sons! My husband! Where are they? Did you kill them, too? You Tejanos butchers! My poor babies!"

Ross shrugged. "Can you understand her, Charlie?"

McKnight shook his head. "Nope. Only know a few words of Comanche. But I'll give it a try." He spoke several words to Cynthia, embellished with sign language. "You are safe with us. We will not harm your child. Do you understand?" Cynthia did not seem to understand and continued to cry hysterically.

"Anybody here speak Comanche?" Ross called out.

"Fella over yonder is part Mex. He might speak some. I'll go get him," a Ranger volunteered.

Ross led Cynthia into a clump of trees, out of the sun. As she crouched on the ground, a crowd of curious soldiers and Rangers gathered to stare.

CULVER MODISETTE

"Ain't that a sight? A squaw with blue eyes!"

"She's gotta be white somewhere under there. An' look, don't she seem to have some blondish kinda hair?"

"Yessir, by God, she sure does. Wonder who she is?"

"Lucky she dint get kilt, what with her babe an' all!"

As the interpreter approached, the crowd parted to let him through. "I am called Carlos, Capitan," he said. "I can speak to her."

Ross nodded. "Carlos, ask her name."

"What is your name? How are you called?" Carlos asked in Comanche.

Startled, Cynthia replied, "I am called Naduah."

Carlos turned to Ross. "Her name is Naduah."

"What's that mean in English?"

"*Naduah* means 'someone found,'" Carlos answered. Cynthia broke into sobs.

"She thinks her two sons have been kilt, or left to starve on the prairie," he added.

"Ask her if she can speak any English, or if she can remember her real white name." Carlos proceeded, but all questions were met with blank stares by Cynthia.

"Don't seem she knows, Sam," McKnight offered.

Ross nodded. "Seems I recall folks some time back talkin' about a family named Parker who had a girl taken by the Comanche."

McKnight took off his hat and scratched his head. "Yeah, that's right. Heard the same thing. What was her first name? Started with a *C*, I think. Carol, Clara . . . no. Celeste . . . no, that don't sound right."

"You're close. It was . . . it was Cynthia! Yup, that's what it was!" Ross added. As Ross spoke her name, Cynthia stiffened and rubbed her eyes with two dirty fists. She stared down at her feet in confusion.

"Cyn . . . Cyn . . . Cyncee . . . Cin me . . . Cincee Ann," she whispered.

There was a stir among the crowd. "Well I'll be go-to-Hell! It's her!" said McKnight in disbelief."

"Damned if it ain't!" Ross exclaimed. "Carlos, tell her she's safe with us. Tell her we'll take care of her child. Tell her we'll take her back to her real family!" Carlos relayed the message, which caused Cynthia to resume her wailing. "What's the matter with her now? Think she'd want to get back to her white family!" Ross said in annoyance.

40

"Ah Capitan," Carlos said wryly. "Wrong family. She cries to go back to her Comanche family—her husband, and her two sons. She no want to go back to white family. She say give her back her pony and she will go look for her real family."

"Can't do that," Ross said flatly. She's gotta go back to her folks. Them Parkers. They can worry about her. She ain't got a choice. Tell her that." As Carlos translated, Cynthia's grief became overwhelming. Feeling the first twinges of guilt and remorse, the crowd slowly dispersed, and the detachment readied for its return to Fort Belknap.

As the columns picked their way through the bloody remains of the village, Carlos rode up to Ross. "Capitan, may I speak?" he asked.

"Yup, what's on your mind, Carlos?"

"Capitan, Naduah. We talk. She say this camp was on buffalo hunt. Dint kill no Shermans. Dint kill nobody. Just buffalo!"

Stunned, Ross pulled his horse up short. "What? What did you say?"

"Capitan . . . I think maybe we kilt wrong people!"

Ross's voice rose. "Don't tell me that! I don't want to hear it! You hear me? We done what we had to do! It's over! Done!"

"But, Capitan . . ." Carlos said softly.

"It's over, damn it! That's enough! Carlos, get back to your unit!" Ross ordered angrily. Chastened, Carlos rejoined the ranks. Thunderstruck, Ross sagged in his saddle. "Jesus, Mary, and Joseph!" he whispered.

It was a victorious ride back to Fort Belknap, with several men flaunting trophies of the slaughter: war shields, lances, bows and arrows, and even a few drying scalps. Riding behind Ross and McKnight was the disconsolate figure of Cynthia, slumped on her pony, clutching little Topsannah, who fretted from hunger pains.

As the successful hunting party approached its main camp, columns of black smoke ominously marked its location. Gripped with foreboding, Peta and the hunters urged their ponies to a gallop. Quanah and Pecos, riding by their father's side, became uneasy at their elders' concern.

Topping a rise overlooking the camp, the hunters looked with horror upon a scene of carnage and slaughter. Bodies were strewn everywhere—some scalped, others mutilated from saber cuts. Dying mothers clung to dead children. Old people were crumpled grotesquely among the smoldering lodges; some displayed bullet wounds and saber cuts, others looked like they had been trampled by charging horses.

The hunters leapt from their ponies and searched frantically for family members. A bloody figure crawled from the surrounding brush. It was old Red Elk. He had been shot in the back. Blood bubbled from his mouth. "Have they gone?" he quavered.

Peta steadied the old man. "Who did this? Who did this?" he demanded.

Red Elk sank to the ground. "Bluecoats and Tejanos," he answered weakly, coughing blood.

"Naduah! Topsannah!" Peta called hoarsely. "Topsannah! Naduah!" He lifted Red Elk. "Have you seen my family!"

Red Elk clung desperately to Peta. "I don't know. So much noise . . . so suddenly . . . so many dead. I don't know. There were too many." His voice broke, as he slumped to the ground.

"Quanah, Pecos, find your mother and sister." Peta's rage increased. "Tejanos, I spit upon you, you mad dogs! Your blood will spill, I promise you! I promise you!" He knelt beside Red Elk. "When did this happen?"

"One sleep past," whispered the old man. "Before sunrise. Too many guns! Too much noise! Too many dead!"

Peta gently wiped the blood from the old man's mouth, then with his sons frantically searched the camp for signs of his family, all to no avail. Their bodies were nowhere to be found.

As the day drew to its end, amid the grief of the tribesmen, Peta gathered his sons. "We have looked everywhere," Quanah said. "Where could they be?"

"Maybe they escaped," Pecos offered. "Maybe they rode away. Or maybe they're hiding in the brush."

"Maybe," Peta said. "Keep looking."

The boys redoubled their search efforts, but found nothing. As the sun set blood red on the horizon, its dying light only increased their despair. The Nokona family, missing two of its members, gathered about a small fire and mourned its loss.

NINE

Camp Cooper, Texas
January, 1861

A cold snow drifted across the barren road leading to Camp Cooper. A wagon, driven by a thin, elderly man clad in his Sunday best—black clothes topped by a shaggy buffalo coat—jounced towards the fort. Sitting erect on the wagon seat, he was absorbed in thought. His nose dripped from the cold.

Upon his arrival, the man found the Post Commandant's office, climbed down from his wagon, and clumped up its wooden stairs. He opened the door and looked about inquiringly. A clerk looked up from his paper work. "Yes, sir. Somethin' I can do for you?" he asked. The man wiped his nose on a bandanna.

"Lookin' for the sutler."

"That'll be the third house on the left," the clerk replied.

The man rubbed his hands together. "Colder'n tarnation out there," he said. "Cap'n Ross around?"

"Prolly at the sutler's."

The man put his fur hat and mittens back on. "All right if I leave my horse here?" he asked.

The clerk nodded. "Sure thing. We'll take care of him."

"Much obliged."

The man walked to the sutler's weather-beaten house, climbed the porch stairs, and knocked on the door. A stout, florid woman of middle age, whose appearance belied the rigors of frontier life, answered the door. "Come in! Come in!" she beamed. "Wipe your feet, if you please. I'm Mrs. Stage, wife to the sutler. We been expectin' you, Mister, uh . . ."

The man took off his hat. "Parker, ma'am. Isaac Parker."

Mrs. Stage took his hat and heavy coat. "Can I get you some hot coffee, Mr. Parker?" she asked.

"Be mighty nice, ma'am. Thank you." Mrs. Stage bustled about and returned with a steaming cup of coffee. Isaac Parker wrapped his cold hands around the mug gratefully.

"You must be about froze," she said. "My land, what a day to travel!"

Mrs. Stage led Parker into a modest sitting room, its rough-hewn planked floor partially covered by a battered rug and heated by a pot-bellied stove. Crowded into the room were Ross, McKnight, Carlos, the sutler, John Stage, post physician Dr. James Rogers, post commander Col. Kenneth McCarthy, and Cynthia with her child.

Clutching Topsannah, Cynthia was almost unrecognizable. She was scrubbed clean and wore a simple dress. Topsannah, similarly washed, wore a crude nightgown and knit booties. She was bright, alert, and fascinated by her surroundings. Col. McCarthy rose from his chair. "Mr. Parker, welcome, sir. You made good time getting here. I'm Col. McCarthy, post commandant."

The men shook hands. "My pleasure, Colonel," Parker said.

"Ross. Cap'n Ross, Texas Rangers." Sam said rising from his seat.

After introducing Isaac to the rest of the men in the room, Ross gestured towards Cynthia, who was crouched in a chair, eyes riveted to the floor. "Well, sir, there she is," he said briskly. "We think maybe her name was—is—Cynthia Ann. She look familiar?"

Parker approached Cynthia and stared at her intently. "As God is my witness, it could be her. Cynthia? Cynthia Ann? Look at me girl!" He forced her head up. "Are we kin, girl? Answer me!" Cynthia was motionless and unresponsive. "Can you understand me, little lady? I'm Isaac Parker. We may be flesh and blood, you and me. You hear me? Cynthia?" Parker placed his hand on Cynthia's shoulder. She shuddered, recoiled, and slapped his hand away without looking up. Parker was stricken.

Doctor Rogers stepped up to Parker. "She's been through a lot, Mr. Parker," he said soothingly. "You have to give her some time!"

"My God, man, she may be our own! My own flesh and blood! As God is my witness, I'm here to help her back to a Christian life. It's my Christian duty!"

Mrs. Stage reached out to him. "She don't know that, Mr. Parker. You have to give her some time, as Dr. Rogers says. She's a pretty scared young lady about now."

Parker became increasingly irritated. "Scared? What she so all-fired scared about? I'm here to bring her back to her real, gen-u-wine God-fearin' family, if she's really Cynthia Ann Parker! She know that?"

Mrs. Stage shook her head. "Right about now, Mr. Parker, she don't know what to think. She's seen her Indian kin and friends shot down in front of her eyes. She don't know where her husband and two boys are, if they're dead or alive. She an' her babe have been hauled up here and pestered by total strangers who speak a different language, and now you're here to take her away to a different world. So I'd say that's enough to scare anybody, wouldn't you say, Mr. Parker?"

There was a long silence. Parker twisted his fingers in agitation. "You're right, I expect. You're right," he said in a low voice. "Yes, it's just that it's a shock to see one of your own, you know, so different, we never expected to see, that is . . ." His voice trailed off.

McKnight shifted uncomfortably in his chair. "Sam, why don't you and me step into the kitchen for a minute?" he said.

"Yeah, good idea. Excuse us, folks. Be right back," Ross responded gratefully, then retired to the kitchen with McKnight and John Stage.

Stage pointed to a wood box. "Bottle's over there, gents."

"Well, John, now that you mention it," McKnight said appreciatively. He lifted the cover of the wood box, retrieved a bottle, pulled the cork, and took a substantial swig. Wiping his mouth on his sleeve, he pointed towards the living room. "I'll tell you boys, this ain't no fun," he said.

Ross took the bottle. "For sure. Figger we'd been better off if we hadn't caught that squaw at all."

"You're right," McKnight agreed. "Gimme another whack at that bottle."

Having emptied the bottle, the men rejoined the others in the next room, where a chastened Isaac Parker had taken a low-key approach to Cynthia, realizing that she could not understand him. Carlos, unable to establish a meaningful rapport with Cynthia, lapsed into a prolonged silence. Parker pulled a chair up, facing Cynthia. As he did so, she burst into sobs, rocking in her chair. Wailing in Comanche, she held tightly to Topsannah, who, bewildered by her mother's distress, started to cry.

Unnerved, Parker glanced around the room. "What'd I do? What's the matter with her? She afraid of me? What have them heathen done to her?"

Carlos shifted uneasily in his seat. "She say same as before. Same as when we caught her. Wants to go back to husband and sons. Thinks maybe we kilt them. Wants to go find them," he said hesitantly.

Col. McCarthy spoke up. "Well, Mr. Parker, you can see our problem. I cannot release her to go back to her Indians, so I guess it's up to you to take her back to her real family. And the sooner the better, sir," he added. The old man nodded in agreement.

"I understand, Colonel. You're right, of course." He handed Cynthia a soiled bandanna. "Here, young lady. Take this and dry your face. You and me and your papoose are goin' back to Fort Worth. Then you can live like white folks with your brother Silas and your sister Orlena." He paused. "You remember Silas and Orlena?"

Cynthia stopped wailing. She raised her head for the first time and stared at Parker. She blinked several times, as if to clear her mind, then silently mouthed the words *Silas* and *Orlena*. A hush fell across the room. Cynthia, straining, silently mouthed the names again—at first inaudibly, and then more definitively. "Si . . . Sil . . . Sila . . . Silas . . . O . . . O . . . Or . . . Orlena . . ." she mumbled, then broke into a torrent of tears, collapsing into the protective arms of Mrs. Stage.

Parker leaped up and raised his arms. "It's her all right," he shouted. "At last! She's come back to us! Praise be to God! She's come home!"

Mrs. Stage tearfully embraced Cynthia. "Yes, Lord! Oh, thank you, God! She's goin' home at last. Your long-lost lamb, she's goin' home!"

The next day was a cold, gray winter morning with patches of snow on the ground. A biting north wind scoured the parade ground. A wagon driven by Isaac Parker rattled out from the camp carrying two passengers huddled under buffalo robes. The figures soon blended into the landscape as they headed toward white civilization. The only sounds were those of the wind and of a baby crying, and that soon faded into silence.

PART TWO

MEDICINE LODGE

TEN

Comanche Village, West Texas
1863

Two years had passed since the attack on the village, and Quanah and Pecos had become novice warriors in the Quahadi band—one of the five tribes that formed the Comanche nation. Their father, Peta Nokona, while still a leading warrior among the Comanches, could not erase the sadness brought about by the abrupt disappearance of his wife and daughter. As an added aggravation, an old wound from a brush with the Tonkawas had flared up, limiting his daily life and participation in raiding parties. But when a war party was planned against the Apache, who had violated Comanche hunting grounds, the warrior in Peta rose once more and he eagerly led painted riders from camp. Several days later, the war party that had departed so confidently returned in disarray. Two warriors had been killed and three wounded, among them Peta. As the defeated riders rode slowly into camp, dragging several travois burdened with the wounded, the village wailed as one; a long, lingering cry of grief and anguish .Families of the dead slashed their legs, arms, and breasts in grief, and women cut their hair off.

As the wounded were reverently carried from the travois, Peta struggled to sit up. Quanah and Pecos rushed to their father's side. Near tears, Pecos's voice broke. "Father, are you badly hurt?" he asked.

Peta coughed blood. "No, I'm all right," he said wanly. "No tears, no tears from a Comanche. Never."

"But does it hurt?" Pecos asked.

"Some, but I'm home now. I'll feel better." His latest wound, in his lower back, oozed dark blood through crude bandages.

"I'll repay those Apache!" Quanah said angrily. "I'll carry your war shield against them! They'll pay in blood! Just you, you . . ." his voice trailed off emotionally.

"There will be time for that," Peta said. "Help me into our lodge."

Peta was lifted from the travois by his sons, who placed him gently on a bed of skins. Despite intense pain, Peta maintained a silent stoicism, while his wound was packed with cobwebs to coagulate the seeping blood. He was then washed by village women, who plied him with warm broth, while Singing Woman fussed over him, arranging his sleeping robes.

"There now, you need to sleep," she said softly. "The cobwebs will close that wound. I'll be right here if you need anything."

Peta watched her. "You are a good friend. Remember when I found you, the Mexican ranch, you were so little, like the Blue Eyes?"

"Yes, I remember a little. It was so long ago," she said brokenly, tears streaking her cheeks. "I am Comanche now. For many years, you have been good to me."

"Like one of my family. You . . . you cared for Naduah," Peta mumbled, semi-conscious.

Surprised, Quanah looked in askance at Singing Woman. "You were taken by my father? My mother? She was taken, too? By my father?"

Singing Woman smiled and patted Quanah's arm. "Yes, that is so. Your father found Naduah many years ago and asked me to be her mother. Haven't you ever wondered about her name? *Naduah*—Someone Found."

"I asked her once, but she said I was too young to understand," Quanah said.

"I'm sure you were."

"What tribe was she?" Quanah asked.

Singing Woman, adjusting Peta's sleeping robes, looked up at the boy. "No tribe. She was white." Quanah and Pecos gasped in astonishment

"White? White? I am part white?" Quanah asked, thunderstruck.

"Probably," Singing Woman said, humming softly.

"Then I'm part white, too?" Pecos questioned.

"I'm afraid so," she answered.

Quanah rubbed his arm abrasively. "I don't see any white there!"

Pecos followed suit. "Look at my arm," he said. "There's no white anywhere! No, I am not white."

"What color are you then?" Singing Woman asked solemnly.

"Comanche color. Same as my brother. Same as my little sister. Comanche color, not white!" Quanah answered.

Singing Woman turned and faced the boys. "That is so," she replied. "Your sister, wherever she is, like you is Comanche. And you should be proud of that! Many great men have been Comanche, Peta Nokona among them. But Comanche color? What is that? I have brown skin, yet I am Comanche. Your mother had white skin, yet she is Comanche. Old Red Elk, his skin was another color and he was Comanche! So if you are Comanche, does the color of your skin really matter? Does it make you brave in battle? No. Does it bring you many horses? No. Does it make our enemies fear you? No. But being one of The People, ah, that is different! Do you understand what I am telling you? Now be quiet and let your father sleep."

Pecos and Quanah nodded their heads somberly, and quietly left the lodge, examining their bodies for any telltale trace of white blood.

"Maybe she's wrong," Pecos said in desperation. "Maybe she's so old she can't remember things as they were. Do you believe her?"

"I don't know," Quanah offered. "But what I know is that you and me are Comanche. And that's good enough for me. Anyway, I don't believe that kind of old woman talk"

As the days passed, Peta became weaker, breathing with difficulty, and lapsing into unconsciousness. His sons, Singing Woman, and several villagers kept a close watch over him. A tribal medicine man passed sacred amulets over his body and burned sprigs of sage and cedar, fanning the smoke over the dying man. His low chanting to the Grandfathers filled the lodge.

When the lodge was quiet once again, Peta opened his eyes and beckoned to Quanah and Pecos. "My sons," he whispered. "Come closer." Pecos and Quanah obediently moved closer to their father. Peta closed his eyes. "I have been blessed with two fine sons," he said weakly.

"We have tried to bring honor to our lodge," Quanah said.

Peta opened his eyes. "And so you have, and I am proud of you for it."

"When you are better, we will have many good times together," Pecos's voice quavered.

Peta reached out and touched each boy. "I will be joining the Grandfathers soon and will become part of the Great Mystery," he said. "But before I leave, you should know that I found your mother many years ago and brought her here. She has been a good mother and wife and a true Comanche. Hear me. Some of our people may look upon you as part white, as weak, as having no honor. Be unmindful of such people, my sons. Lead our people! Take my place and turn their eyes ahead! Look into the sunrise, not the sunset! Do you hear me?

"Now, Pecos, our brothers of the Kotoseka tribe band have asked for you to join them—an honor that pleases me. But, Quanah, I want you to remain here with the Quahadis."

The two boys grasped their father's hands. "Yes father, we hear. We will do as you say. Your spirit will guide us," Quanah whispered.

Peta closed his eyes. "I am sorry I will miss seeing you become Comanche warriors, leaders of our people. But, maybe, from the land of the Grandfathers, I can watch over you."

Singing Woman hushed him. "Peta, you must rest now."

"I am very tired, but I can . . ." his voice trailed off, and Peta Nokona, a giant among the Comanche tribes, died in the presence of his family.

ELEVEN

Comanche Village, West Texas
May, 1865

Two years had passed since his father's death, and Quanah, now a strapping young man, had become a noted warrior. However, as a young man without a family, he had no visible wealth, ordinarily measured in the ownership of horses. Thus his interest in Weckeah, the comely daughter of the band's chief, Yellow Bear, was brushed aside by her father. Weckeah, he maintained, was worth many horses in the marriage market. When Quanah learned that Weckeah was to be given to another suitor, he was heartbroken.

Several days after the announcement, Quanah and Weckeah met furtively in the shadows of the village. Quanah gathered the girl in a loving embrace. "I won't allow it!" he said.

"Won't allow what?" Weckeah asked.

"I won't allow your father to give you to that fat, rich nothing!"

"I know! I know!" Weckeah said despondently. "But my father is our chief. There is nothing we can do about it."

"There must be something we can do," Quanah said despairingly. "I won't lose you! I won't! Old Yellow Bear has got to change his mind!"

"I don't think he will," Weckeah replied mournfully. "You've tried reasoning with him."

"That old man! He won't listen to reason," Quanah said bitterly.

"It's the horses, Quanah. He thinks you're too poor. No horses," Weckeah said softly.

Quanah angrily held her at arm's length. "Is that what you think, too?"

"Oh no, my love. But it doesn't matter what I think. Or what you think!"

Quanah folded his arms. "It's those damned horses. If only he'd wait a little. I can get horses—a few raids—but it takes time!"

Weckeah brushed tears from her eyes. "Quanah, I've waited so long for you. Since we were very little. Remember? But my father won't wait. I know him! He's made up his mind. He just won't wait!"

Quanah sighed. "You're right. But I'm not going to let you go. I'll think of something. I'll even steal you, if I have to!"

Weckeah caught her breath. "But that's against tribal law," she said aghast. "You could be killed for that!"

"Old Yellow Bear will have to catch me first," Quanah said stubbornly.

"But where would we go? Where would we live? No Comanche band would take us in!"

Quanah brooded. "I'll think of a way. I'll think of something!"

Weckeah glanced over her shoulder warily. "I have to get back. Father will miss me." As she turned to go, Quanah reached for her hand.

"Meet me here at the same time tomorrow night," he whispered as he took her into his arms.

"Oh, Quanah, I do love you so. Please be careful!"

"Don't worry. It will work out. You'll see."

The next day was cold and wet. A steady drizzle drove the villagers into their warm, dry lodges. In early evening, Weckeah flitted through the darkness and joined Quanah, embracing him as the rain streamed down their young faces.

"I can't stay long. My father wonders why I go out in the rain," she said.

Quanah stroked her face lovingly. "It's all arranged," he said.

"What's arranged?"

"Two sleeps from now, we will run away from your father and that stupid person who wants to buy you," he said exultantly.

Weckeah pulled back from Quanah in alarm. "Are you serious? Where will we go? Where will we live?"

"It's all arranged, just as I said," he replied soothingly. "We'll start our own band at a new place. Eleven of my warrior friends will join us."

"What if my father comes after us? You know he will try to kill you!"

"He won't catch us," Quanah said confidently. "Trust me. My friends and I know of places he has never seen. We'll be safe."

Weckeah wavered. "Truly? You and my father fighting is a great sadness."

Quanah played his trump card. "And later, when we have taken many horses, I will give old Yellow Bear more horses than he can imagine for you! Then we will be at peace with him."

"Do you truly think so?" she asked.

"Yes, I know so!"

"I pray you are right," she said, as the rain pattered down more heavily. "Yes, I will go with you. I'll be ready."

"Be careful that your father doesn't become suspicious," Quanah cautioned. "This will be a great thing! You'll see! And best of all, we'll be together!"

Weckeah hugged Quanah emotionally. "Truly, you are my love," she said, and, turning to go, splashed through widening puddles to her father's lodge.

Two nights later, Quanah paced nervously in a grove of trees outside the village as he awaited Weckeah. She slipped from her father's lodge, carrying a small bundle of possessions. After a hurried embrace, the lovers ran hand in hand from the grove to where eleven young warriors waited astride their ponies. The young lovers were silently welcomed. After quietly pledging allegiance to Quanah by touching the couple with their bows, the party rode away at a walk. When they were far from the village, they sped up to a canter, and finally to an exuberant gallop.

Within a few years, Quanah's band became a thriving Comanche village of some sixty people. Many women joined its ranks, some widowed, some "found" by Comanche raiders, bringing with them domestic tranquility and children. Food was plentiful, buffalo were abundant, and the young men had time to pursue their great adventures—horse-stealing and raiding. Under Quanah's leadership, both ventures were successful, and slowly the little band accumulated a substantial pony herd, the basis of tribal wealth.

While life was good, Quanah kept his band far from the reach of Yellow Bear, knowing full well the consequences should they meet. Several times Quanah moved his village hastily under cover of darkness, in an effort to elude Yellow Bear, who became more and more frustrated at his inability to reclaim his daughter. And then, one glorious summer day, it all came to a head. . . .

A small, canvas-topped wagon train of renegade Mexican traders, despised as *Comancheros* by the Whites, approached Quanah's camp. As a source of guns, powder, cloth, metal cooking pots, and virulent whiskey, they were always a welcomed sight. Under the leadership of Jose Tayofa, this particular group of *Comancheros* was fine-tuned to its market's needs, and as a result, was very successful.

The Comanche conducted a brisk trade with the Comancheros, exchanging stolen horses and cattle for needed goods. At the head of an excited, chattering group of villagers, Quanah and Toyofa met in front of the wagons. Each held up his hand in the sign of peace. "It is good to see you again, Quanah," Toyofa said. "Your village has grown since the last time we met."

"We have been lucky," Quanah answered. "Much food and no spotted sickness."

As they spoke, a distant camp guard signaled the approach of unknown horsemen. "Quanah, be aware! Many ponies coming towards us!" he said excitedly, pointing to the east.

Quanah whirled his horse and galloped towards his villagers. "Everybody go back to the village," he ordered. "Our warriors gather here with me!" There was a wild scramble as women and children ran back to their lodges. The Comancheros, veterans of many such alarms, prudently retired to their wagons, nervously fingering rifles and pistols.

As the column neared, it was apparent that it was Chief Yellow Bear's band, led by the warrior himself. The old chief, given to increasing weight, wore his graying hair parted in the middle, with two braids falling loosely down his back. He had snapping black eyes and a jagged scar on his left cheek, a reminder of a near-fatal encounter with the animal whose name he bore.

Recognizing each other, the two bands hastily prepared for combat—shields uncovered, arrows nocked, and lances readied. In two lines, headed by Yellow Bear and Quanah, the bands faced each other across the wagons. The tribesmen fell silent as Comanche faced Comanche. The stamping of hooves and the snorting of their horses seemed unnaturally loud.

Yellow Bear was the first to break ranks, riding up and down his line, posturing and shouting. "Quanah, you woman-stealer, sing your death song!" he bellowed. "Your time has come!"

"Spare me your words, old man," Quanah replied defiantly. "The

Grandfathers are waiting for you right now!"

Yellow Bear shook his lance angrily at Quanah. "Old man? Old man? Come see how this old man fights! Young, insolent pups!"

Quanah laughed. "Pups maybe, but pups with sharp teeth!" The warriors on both sides were becoming restless. A blood bath was imminent.

As the tension mounted, a diminutive figure detached itself from the wagon train and walked towards the hostiles. It was Singing Woman, now an elder, who had come to trade buffalo robes for cooking pots. Yellow Bear waved her away. "Leave, woman, before you get hurt," he said impatiently. "This is not a woman's place!"

"No, I will not leave," Singing Woman said stubbornly. "Now is the time for a true Comanche to speak. And if it must be a woman, then so be it!"

Recognizing his opportunity, Quanah rode closer to the old woman. "My warriors would never hurt you, Singing Woman," he said gently. "Now, what would you say to us?"

Flustered, Yellow Bear walked his pony in a circle. "Go ahead, but make it quick, old woman. I have a score to settle!"

Singing Woman climbed unsteadily onto a wagon. "Hear me, my friends," she shouted. "I have seen many winters, and speak only the truth. We Comanche were once as many as the rain drops. We had many ponies and our young men rode far and wide. Then came the sickness called the "spotted death" and many of our people died. Next came the Whites and Tejanos, and more of us died. Is it not enough that we lose our men, women, and children to the Tejanos, that we lose even more to the Apaches, and to sickness? Has it come to the day when we Comanche kill our own? Do we have so many young men that we can kill them carelessly? Already we must steal women and children to maintain our numbers. And now we want to eat our own like crazed dogs? Hear me! Put away your weapons! Make peace among yourselves! Think of tomorrow, and the next day, and the years after that! Be true Comanches today, or there will be no Comanches tomorrow! I have spoken." She concluded her impassioned speech to an embarrassed silence.

As Singing Woman stepped down from the wagon, the ranks of Quanah's warriors parted and Weckeah, leading a small child by the hand, walked slowly towards her father. "Hello, father," she said gently.

Overwhelmed, Yellow Bear sat his pony in stunned silence. Then, as if awakening from a dream, he returned to reality. "Weckeah, I am so glad to see you! You are well?"

"Yes, I am very well," his daughter replied. "And you?"

"Yes, yes, I am well. Who is that with you?" he asked, pointing to the child.

Weckeah beamed. "Father, I want you to meet your grandson."

"My grandson! How old?"

Weckeah slicked the baby's hair. "Almost two winters. He is growing quickly and needs a grandfather to teach him Comanche ways."

Yellow Bear extended his arms toward the child. "Here, let me look at him," he said, and lifted the little boy onto his saddle, where grandson and grandfather regarded each other with interest. Smiling, Yellow Bear held the little boy aloft and showed him proudly to his riders. "I have a grandson!" he shouted. "A grandson!" he repeated. "He will make a fine warrior! See how bright his eyes are! And such sturdy legs!" As Yellow Bear's young men crowded around him, admiring the boy, there was a palpable lessening of tension as weapons were sheathed.

Quanah rode slowly towards Weckeah and her father. Yellow Bear watched him closely. Quanah made the peace sign as he approached. The old chief hesitantly did the same.

"Hello, Chief Yellow Bear," Quanah said formally.

Yellow Bear cleared his throat. "Hello," he replied. "You have a fine son, I think."

"And you a fine grandson."

"How is he called?" the old man asked.

Weckeah spoke up. "We call him Little Moon, but that is only a child's name. We were waiting for his grandfather to give him his true Comanche name."

Yellow Bear nodded. "Just right. You were wise to wait."

"You are well?" Quanah asked.

"Yes, and I am pleased to see my daughter."

"She is a good wife and mother," Quanah added.

"I am pleased to hear that. Now about all this . . ." The old chief waved his arms about.

"Before you say more," Quanah interrupted. "I have something I have wanted to tell you, something to give you."

"What is that?" Yellow Bear asked cautiously.

"It is something I have owed you for two winters."

The chief's eyes narrowed. "Two winters?"

Quanah twisted in his saddle. "The last time I saw you, I forgot to pay for Weckeah. I believe her price was three horses"

"That is the truth," said Yellow Bear.

Having waited years to make good on his promise to Weckeah, Quanah savored the moment. "Chief Yellow Bear, your daughter is worth much more to me than three horses. I am giving you ten horses for her, as I promised when I was poor!"

"Ten horses! Are you serious?" Yellow Bear asked in stunned disbelief.

"Ten horses! Yes, she is worth even more. I am a lucky man. See what a fine son she has given me . . . um . . . us," Quanah added.

Yellow Bear reached across his horse and gripped Quanah's arm. "Singing Woman was right!" he exclaimed. "No more fighting between brothers! We are as one!"

Quanah nodded. "Yes, she was right. Our people will celebrate her wisdom around their campfires. And I will welcome Weckeah's father to my lodge." The two warriors touched hands and the riders from each band greeted each other as brothers.

The Comancheros' wagons were quickly engulfed with crowds of Comanches, men, women, and children shouting and laughing as they bargained with the traders for colored beads, blankets, pots and pans, colored cloth, needles, firearms, powder, lead, and rot-gut whiskey. The buffalo robes, hides, and stolen horses and cattle offered in return made the Comancheros wealthy. As Quanah rode slowly through the happy throng, an old Comanchero nudged his leader.

"Hey Tayofa," he asked. "Ain't that the young buck called Quanah?"

Jose Tayofa nodded. "Si, he has that look, like a leader," he said thoughtfully. "I think I would not crowd him too much."

Later that night, Yellow Bear and his new son-in-law sat cross-legged on a buffalo robe as a fire burned in the center of his lodge. His wives were busy sewing skins and beading moccasins. Yellow Bear lit his pipe. "Join me?" he asked, extending the pipe. Quanah nodded and accepted the pipe. He smoked it silently then passed it back. "Quanah, there are things we must talk about," he said quietly.

"Truly."

"I fear for our people," Yellow Bear said. "I fear for the mountains and the rivers. I fear for the meadows and the plains. I fear for our brothers, the buffalo."

"The Whites?" Quanah asked.

"The Whites, yes. Especially the Tejanos and the filthy hide-hunters. Wagons full of new Whites cross our hunting lands each day. The land promised us forever by the treaty with the Tejanos. The Whites want that land for themselves. They do not honor their word. Their promises mean nothing. Can we ever trust them?"

"I share your concerns," Quanah said. "I, too, fear for the future of our people. The Whites kill the buffalo for their hides and tongues, even their bones, and leave the meat to rot in the sun. The crows and coyotes have become fat. Now the buffalo are almost gone, when before they were like leaves in the woods. Our people cannot live without our brothers, the buffalo."

Yellow Bear stared into the fire. "What do you think we should do?"

"What choice do we have?" Quanah asked.

Yellow Bear shifted his gaze to the younger man. "We have two choices," he said. "We can pack up our lodges and go and live on a reservation, as the Whites call it, and accept the White man's ways, or—"

"Or we can fight!" Quanah exploded. "I will not live like a donkey in a corral. I am Comanche and I will fight! Like my father would have fought! Like my grandfather would have fought!"

Yellow Bear shook his head. "No, Quanah," he said, pointing a finger at him. "We! We will fight! All five bands of our people will fight! Not one! Not two or three! But all five!"

Maybe then the Whites will listen to us!"

Quanah bowed his head. "You are right," he said. "But first, the hide-hunters must go."

The old chief stood up. "It is well," he said. "Let us talk more of this tomorrow."

The two men gripped each others arm. "Tomorrow we will ride out and see these things for ourselves," Quanah answered.

TWELVE

Indian Territory
May, 1867

The morning's song sparrows, having welcomed the dawn with bursts of song, were silent by the time Quanah and Yellow Bird departed from the village. Quanah rode a magnificent black horse of which he was obviously proud. "A fine-looking horse, Quanah," Yellow Bear said. "Does he run the buffalo?"

"Truly. He is my best runner," Quanah replied. "He has never failed me."

Yellow Bear nodded. "You are lucky. Watch over him carefully. Somebody might steal him."

"I know. We are like brothers, that horse and me. Like family."

"Does he sleep in your lodge, yet?" the old chief teased.

"Not yet," Quanah laughed. "But I think he'd like to."

Yellow Bear grew serious. "Quanah, riding this land with you may help our hearts decide what we should do."

Quanah nodded. "Not only the Comanche, but all the Indian People."

The two men cantered across the rolling plains, flushing prairie chickens and bob-o-links as they rode. Late in the day, as they rested their horses, a smudge of smoke curled from a clump of trees, alerting the riders. Gripping their weapons, they secured their ponies and crawled carefully to the crest of an overlooking ridge. Below them was an emigrant wagon train, pulled by oxen, making evening camp. The wagons were gathered in a loose circle. As the oxen stolidly pulled their loads, their drivers whistled, shouted, and cracked their long whips. Cooking fires had been lighted and a scattering of women and children were unpacking for the night. A little blonde girl, dragging a well-worn doll, played about the edge of the circle, while her mother was preoccupied with dinner preparations. Lying flat on their bellies, Quanah and Yellow Bear watched with interest. Yellow Bear nudged Quanah. "Look at them," he whispered. "On our land without even asking."

"They don't care," Quanah answered. "Probably most of them don't even know. Like that Little Yellow Hair there."

"If we tell them to leave, they refuse. Then if our riders scare them, they call for the Bluecoats to protect them. And on our land!"

"Truly," Quanah replied. "That's how people get killed. And we get blamed."

Having satisfied their curiosity, the men backed off the ridge and returned to their horses. As they prepared to mount, a movement in the brush caused their horses to prick up their ears. The men instinctively reached for their weapons. The brush parted, revealing the Little Yellow Hair. She gazed at them and smiled. "Hello," she said, radiating innocence. Quanah and Yellow Bear looked at each other in astonishment. "My name is Charity," she announced. "What's yours?" The two men retreated several steps. Charity held up her doll. "This is Emily. She's only three years old." Quanah glanced at his companion, who shrugged .Charity thrust the doll towards Quanah. "Here," she said. "Would you like to hold her?" Quanah gingerly accepted the doll, and nodded his appreciation. He handed the doll back to the child. "Emily says she likes you," the little girl said solemnly.

Quanah turned to Yellow Bear. "The Little Yellow Hair has no fear."

"Truly! She would make a good Comanche," Yellow Bear marveled.

Quanah glanced sharply at the old man. "Probably. But not today," he said.

Yellow Bear smiled faintly. "Just a thought."

"I can't understand you. You talk funny. You should speak more normal," the little Yellow Hair scolded.

Quanah reached over to his horse and removed several eagle feathers from its mane and handed them to Charity. "Here," he said. "A gift for the Little Yellow Hair and her doll."

Charity giggled. "What pretty feathers! Emily thanks you, don't you, Emily?" She took the feathers and tickled Emily with them.

Yellow Bear looked about nervously. "Quanah, we must go. Some one will come looking for her." Quanah nodded and the two men swung up into their saddles.

Charity looked up at them. "Aren't you going to tell me your names?" she asked.

The riders waved at the child and galloped off into the early evening.

As they receded into the distance, Charity's mother topped the ridge, distraught. "Charity! Charity! Where are you?" she called anxiously. Seeing her daughter, her anxiety turned to annoyance. "Charity, what are you doing way out here? You know it's dangerous to leave camp alone!"

Crestfallen, Charity held up the eagle feathers. "Yes, Momma," she said. "But look what the men gave me! Aren't they pretty? Emily likes them, too."

Stunned, the mother pulled her child close. "What men?" she asked.

Charity pulled from her mother's grasp and pointed. "They just rode away," she said. "See them? Way off there!" Her mother quickly identified the riders for what they were and pressed her hands to her face in disbelief. She pulled her daughter closer. "They didn't talk right, Momma. I couldn't understand them very well. They talked funny, but one of them gave me these pretty feathers for keeps."

Huddled on the ridge top together, the mother sorted through her fears as Charity tickled Emily with her feathers.

The next day, the two Comanche somberly rode out yet again to another confrontation with Manifest Destiny.

"Yesterday, Quanah, so many wagons, where do you think they come from?" Yellow Bear asked.

"I don't know. But they keep coming," Quanah replied.

"I do not understand these things. All at once. Many, many Whites. Are we being punished by the Creator? Have we done something that displeases Him?" the old man questioned.

Quanah waved his hand dismissively. "No!" he said emphatically. "We live as the Comanche have always lived! As our fathers and grandfathers lived. They were not punished!"

"Truly," Yellow Bear agreed. "They never saw their brothers, the buffalo, slaughtered just for their skins!"

Quanah nodded. "The wasteful killing of our buffalo is something they did not see."

"Today our hunters must ride far to find animals for food and clothing. Our buffalo brothers are scattered by too many white hunters, too much shooting, too much killing," the old chief said.

They rode steadily for several hours, stopping occasionally to rest their horses. As the sun rose to in the sky, they halted at a small stream. While their horses drank, the men shared a piece of jerky. They ate silently, squatting on their heels and sipping water from the stream.

As they rose to leave, a puff of wind shook the leaves of a nearby cottonwood. Quanah stiffened and sniffed the breeze. "Phew, that's a bad smell," he said.

Yellow Bear wrinkled his nose. "Bad, really bad! Coming from upwind."

They remounted and slowly followed their noses. Emerging from a shallow canyon, an unforgettable sight confronted them: Hundreds of buffalo carcasses were rotting in the sun. Only the hides had been taken, leaving thousands of pounds of meat to fester in the heat. As they rode closer, appalled at the sight, there was a constant buzzing flies swarming the dark bodies. The riders covered their noses with their hands in a futile effort to block the stench. A cloud of jays, crows, and buzzards reluctantly took flight as the men approached.

"There's enough meat here for every Comanche band through the snow months," Yellow Bear said in disbelief.

"Now it's only fit for the wolves and buzzards," Quanah said bitterly. As the riders picked their way through the decaying bodies, they crossed a small stream. Several lonely cottonwoods showed axe marks. A fire ring was smothered in trash, rancid clothing, rusty tin cans, rotting hides and paper. Shattered whiskey and beer bottles littered the ground. Wagon tracks led away from the camp.

"Watch your pony's feet," Yellow Bear warned.

Quanah pointed to an empty whiskey bottle. "Look," he said in disgust. "They drink foolish water!"

Yellow Bear waved his arms in anger. "Pig people! They are pig people! See how they live! They have no respect for the land. No respect for the buffalo! No respect for the Comanche." He drew a finger across his throat. "They offend me much!"

Enraged, Quanah nocked an arrow to his bow, and drove it into the ashes of the fire ring. "No more! No more! Now, Yellow Bear, it is the hide-hunter who will be hunted. We will take their scalps, but leave the meat!"

THIRTEEN

Fort Harker, Kansas
1867

Alarmed at the waves of white settlers encroaching upon the land promised to them by treaties with the U.S. Government, and angered by the wanton slaughter of their basic food supply by white buffalo hunters, the Comanche, Kiowa, and Cheyenne swept across the plains in retaliatory raids. No rancher, farmer, trading post, wagon train, or hunting camp was safe. Striking at dawn, when least expected, the painted warriors terrorized the frontier, killing at random, and stealing women and children. Ranchers were left without livestock, as whooping riders stampeded their herds.

The U.S. Cavalry, decimated by four years of conflict in the east, was stretched too thinly across the frontier to be effective. A local militia company, known as the Texas Rangers, was dispatched, but was constantly harried and led on fruitless forays by an enemy who appeared and then disappeared, blending into the countryside. Cries for help from Texas and southwestern newspapers soon reached Washington, which had been too caught up in the War Between the States to pay much heed. But when the outpouring became overwhelming, an "Indian Peace Commission" was formed and yet another meeting with the tribes and political and military officials was called. Despite previous abuses of their treaties with the United States Government, the Indians once again cautiously agreed to the meeting.

The gathering was to be known as "The Medicine Lodge Council," and was to be held on the banks of the Medicine River in Kansas, where, once a year, the Kiowa bathed in its sacred healing waters. In addition to the Kiowa, representatives of the Comanche, Cheyenne, Arapaho, and Kiowa-Apache would be in attendance.

But from the outset, the Peace Commission had already committed a major blunder by inviting only three of the five bands of Comanche which comprised the Comanche nation. This oversight would only further strain relations between Washington and the Comanche people.

Serving as a supply station for the Council, Fort Harker, Kansas, was a scene of tumult and confusion as some two hundred freight wagons were loaded with military supplies and gifts for the Indians. Unhappy mules, in teams of six, were hitched to the white-topped wagons, as teamsters cursed, whistled, and shouted, trying to be heard over the uproar. Two wagons, hitched to relatively untrained mules, were overturned by the bucking of the animals. A handful of spectators, delighted by the entertainment, offered free advice to the frantic teamsters. Once quieted, the wagons were loaded with barrels of flour, sugar, molasses, medallions, coffee, military clothing, bolts of brightly colored cloth, and trinkets. Three other wagons, hitched to teams of well-trained mules, stood off to the edge of the bedlam, where soldiers laboriously loaded them with heavy boxes of ammunition. Each box was marked *Gatling*.

One wagon was driven by young Billy Dixon, who had run away from home in Missouri at the age of fourteen and headed for the Golden West, seeking adventure on the frontier. As a youngster, he had signed on to drive bull trains which supplied Army outposts in Kansas. Now, at the ripe old age of seventeen, he was a seasoned driver of mules, oxen, and horses. Loading supplies for the Medicine Lodge Council, Dixon eagerly anticipated his first encounter with the Southwestern tribes.

As the last box was stored in his wagon, a sweating freight handler spat tobacco juice. "All lashed and loaded, Sonny," he drawled. "Think you kin handle them shave-tails, boy?"

Dixon smiled. "Expect so, corporal. No complaints yet."

The soldier chuckled cynically. "Better keep yer head down out there, Buster. See if you kin keep yer hair on!"

"Do my best."

The handler shifted his chaw from his right to left cheek. "Well good luck to ya, kid. And remember me to all them redskins out there!"

Dixon fiddled with his reins. "I'll be happy to say howdy for ya."

The soldier hitched up his pants. He squinted quizzically at Dixon, and wiped his mouth on his sleeve. "Guess you might at that," he said grudgingly.

Gradually the train took shape. Wagon master Jared Simpson, astride a bay horse, pleaded, cajoled, and cursed the train into a semblance of order. At his command, it moved slowly from the fort, headed for Medicine Lodge, Kansas.

When the last wagon in the procession cleared Fort Harker, the lead wagon was out of sight several miles ahead. A Seventh Cavalry escort jingled on its flank as a huge cloud of dust rose in its wake. From time to time, the march was interrupted by individual wagons pulled by headstrong mules, which broke from line. Until the mules calmed down, blue language rolled across the plains.

Three days passed as Dixon's mules plodded along at a steady pace, resigned to good behavior. As the wagon jolted ahead, the wagon master rode up alongside. Grizzled and wearing sweat-stained buckskins, Jared Simpson sat erect in his saddle, overseeing his formidable responsibility from beneath a battered Stetson.

Dixon glanced at the trail boss. "Mr. Simpson, sir, how much longer till we get there?"

Simpson maintained his vigil. "Be there tomorra, God, weather, and Injuns permitting," he replied without looking up.

"Yessir, that's good news! Um, what kind of Indians?"

Simpson glanced briefly at Dixon. "What kind?" he repeated. "How does Kiowa, Comanche, Cheyenne, Apache, and Arapaho sound? They'll all be there."

Dixon was awed. "Hoooo boy!" he exulted. "I've been waiting a long time to see somethin' like this!"

Simpson suppressed a smile. "Yup, you're gonna see some of the best and some of the worst. Sometimes hard to tell them apart."

Dixon's eyes widened. "How do you do that?" he asked innocently.

"Not sure," Simpson replied solemnly. "Last time I tried, made a mistake."

"What happened?"

"Guessed wrong and got kilt," Simpson replied gravely.

Dixon looked at the older man sheepishly. "Aw shoot!" he said, returning to earth.

Later that day, as the column plodded ahead, several lines of mounted Indians in family groupings appeared in the distance, all heading towards a common destination. As the lines moved across the plains, a scattering of Indians flanked each side of the wagon train. A small band of buffalo, confused by the turmoil, milled about near the supply column.

Two armed soldiers, Privates Cass and Gaudet, left the line and walked toward the bewildered animals. Cass fired wildly at a buffalo. "I got one! I got one!" he yelled boisterously, pointing at a wounded bull.

Private Gaudet fired rapidly at several cows. "I got two!" he exulted.

Private Cass fired a final shot. "Aw shoot," he lamented. "They're outta range."

At the sound of gunfire, the supply column halted. Leaving the dead and wounded buffalo on the prairie, the two hunters turned to rejoin the column. Their Sergeant, Lem Pinney, approached them in a fit of anger.

"Cease fire, you idiots!" he bellowed. "Who gave you permission to leave this here column and to fire at them animals? Get your asses back to the column, on the double!"

"Awright, Sarge, awright!" Gaudet said soothingly. "Don't get excited!"

The sergeant's voice rose an octave. "Excited? Me? Excited? I ought to beat the crap outta you two! You know what you could have done? Do you? Do you?"

"We jus' plugged a few of them buffs, Sarge. That's all," Cass explained. He turned to Gaudet. "Ain't that right, Lou?"

Gaudet nodded vigorously. "That's right, Sarge. We dint mean no harm."

Sergeant Pinney scowled. "We dint mean no harm. We dint mean no harm," he repeated sarcastically. "You meatheads look over there." Pinney pointed to the Indian columns in the distance that paced the supply wagons. "See them Indians? Goin' to a peace council. Want us to stop killin' their buffalo. And you knot heads shoot a bunch of them animals right smack under their noses! You tryn' to start your own little war, or are you just plain stupid?"

"No, no, it's not like that. We were jus' having some fun, Sarge. Honest. We dint mean no harm!" Cass explained lamely.

Sergeant Pinney moved menacingly towards the soldiers. "You done the harm all right, whether you meant to or not! Now git! On the double! Report to Lieutenant Gallup. Now! Move! Move!"

As the chastised privates scuttled back to the train, Sergeant Pinney watched the Indian columns carefully. Suddenly, a lone rider left the column and galloped toward the wagons. Increasingly apprehensive, Sergeant Pinney turned and shouted to the train. "Send Lieutenant Gallup out here on the double!" Lieutenant Gallup arrived in a rush.

"Report, Sergeant."

Pinney fixed his eyes on the rider. "Sir, two dumb-assed privates just kilt some buffalo right smack in front of them," he said, pointing towards the Indians. "And we're about to have a visitor who's prolly mad as hell!"

"Very well, Sergeant," Gallup answered, gauging the oncoming rider.

As the two men watched, the rider thundered up to them and reined his pony to a stop. Sitting erect in a primitive saddle, he wore a buckskin shirt, fringed leggings, a porcupine quill chest plate, and a single feather in his hair. A decorated strap was worn over one shoulder. He carried a rifle, its stock studded with copper nails, in the crook of his arm. Lieutenant Gallup made the peace sign.

"Sergeant," he asked. "What tribe is he?"

"He's a Kiowa, sir. Looks like an important one. That strap across his shoulder means he's a member of the Ten Bravest Society. Yes, sir, this is a special fella!"

Gallup nodded. "You speak their language?"

"No. sir. But one of our teamsters is part Kiowa."

"Very well, Sergeant. Get him out here on the double!" Pinney turned and ran back to the train. Awaiting the interpreter, the two men sized each other up. Attempting to fill the void, Gallup cleared his throat. "We're sorry about this," he offered. "It was a mistake, um . . ." His voice trailed off as he realized his words were not understood.

There was a brief, awkward silence before Sergeant Pinney arrived with an older man of obvious Indian features. He was unarmed, and when he removed his hat, in deference to the meeting, his head had been shaved on one side, with thick hair on the other. He put his hat back on, then snatched it off when he recognized the Indian rider.

Sergeant Pinney wiped the sweat from his face. "His name is Lopez, sir."

Lopez nervously fingered the brim of his hat. "Por Dios!" he exclaimed. "It's him!"

"It's who?" the officer asked.

"Si, Lieutenant," he said excitedly. "It's Satanta! White Bear! Great Chief of the Kiowa!"

"Can you understand his talk, Lopez?"

Lopez hesitated. "I think so." The Kiowa Chief stared curiously at Lopez and, pointing to his head, spoke to him in their tongue.

"What'd he say?" Pinney asked.

"He sees I am Kiowa and knows he can trust me."

"How'd he know you're Kiowa?" Gallup questioned

"My hair."

"Your hair?" Pinney asked.

"Si, Sergant. It is like my father's hair. He was Kiowa. Black Leg Society."

Gallup was puzzled. "Black Leg Society?"

"Greatest warriors of Kiowa People. Black Leg because on war trail so much, legs always black from dirt and mud," Lopez explained.

"I see," Gallup said, eyeing the rider with a new respect.

As the Indian and Gallup spoke, the men of the wagon train strained to determine what was happening. A cavalry lieutenant and his sergeant broke off from the train to help, but Gallup waved them back, fearing their presence might provoke the Kiowa unnecessarily. "Stay with the wagons. Don't need any more people," he shouted. The cavalrymen waved in acknowledgement, but remained mounted, watching the Kiowa closely.

Undaunted by the presence of cavalry, White Bear rode his pony back and forth in front of the three men, gesticulating and speaking angrily. "He's very angry about those buffalo," Lopez translated.

"Yes, I'm sure he is," Gallup replied. "Tell him we will not permit this to happen again. Tell him that the men who did this will be punished." As Lopez translated, the Kiowa glowered at the whites. Lopez finished his translation and turned to Gallup.

"Si, Lieutenant, I tol' him. But he say those buffalo are still dead. Wants to know if you can bring them back to life?"

Gallup shook his head. "Tell him I would if I could," the officer said apologetically. White Bear watched Gallup's expression closely. It was apparent he needed no further answers to his questions, for he suddenly burst into an impassioned speech while whirling his pony in circles. Lieutenant Gallup was impressed.

"What'd he say?"

"He say . . . he say . . . has the white man become a child that needlessly kills and does not eat? When the Kiowa kills buffalo, he does it so his people will not starve. He has spoken!" As Lopez finished his translation, the incensed Kiowa rode his pony in a circle around the three men, and then galloped off to rejoin his tribesmen.

Sergeant Pinney wiped sweat from his eyes. "Whew," he offered. "That coulda been nasty!"

"Pass the word, Sergeant," Gallup ordered. "Any more buffalo shooting and the shooter will be wearing irons." Sergeant Pinney acknowledged the order and the men headed back to the train "Lopez," Lieutenant Gallup said, "you did a good job out there. I appreciate your help." He reached into his pocket and produced a cigar, which he offered to his interpreter. "Here, have a smoke after supper."

Lopez smiled. "Gracias. Lieutenant. Now I can tell my children and grandchildren that I have met the famous Kiowa Chief, White Bear, and that he is a friend of mine!"

FOURTEEN

Medicine Lodge Creek, Kansas
October 19, 1867

Upon its arrival at the treaty site, the wagon train disgorged quantities of supplies and a large number of white canvas tents, which were to house officials, visitors, and dignitaries of both renown and notoriety. They were erected in neat, orderly rows on the grassy, park-like opening on the bank of the river.

The mood of the encampment was festive, as bands of Indians, with their families, flooded into the area. A number of teamsters, expert with their long black whips, exhibited their skills in informal competitions. The cracks and pops, some as loud as pistol shots, caused a few nervous glances of concern among the whites as well as the Indians. The military, with much fanfare, installed two Gatling guns in positions overlooking the camp, a presence not lost among the tribesmen.

Having successfully completed his job as a teamster, Billy Dixon was free to roam the encampment, where the cream and the dregs of the West had gathered—traders, soldiers, mountain men, generals, scouts for the military, politicians, the elite light cavalry of the plains, and the tribes people of the Comanche, Kiowa, Cheyenne, Apache, and Arapaho all gathered in one place. For a young man who had dreamt of such things, the reality was overwhelming. He listened to the varied dialects and saw famous Indian warriors at arms length.

While roaming near the Cheyenne camp, he noticed Jared Simpson chatting with a man he did not recognize. Of medium height, with a dark complexion, he could have passed as an Indian. He wore a black broad-brimmed hat, turned up at the front.

"Billy! C'mon over here. Someone I want you to meet," Simpson called out.

"Yes, sir, Mr. Simpson," Dixon replied.

Simpson smothered a smile. "Billy, this here is Amos Chapman. Lives off and on with the Cheyenne. Speaks their tongue. Amos, say hello to Billy Dixon who come all the way out here from Missouri to see some Indians."

"Howdy, Amos Chapman. You really live with the Cheyenne?" Dixon marveled.

"Some," Chapman replied.

Dixon was impressed. "Mr. Chapman, I sure would like to talk to you, and maybe trade for some Indian stuff," Dixon said seriously.

"Tell you what," Chapman said. "I'll come by your tent around sundown. See what we can stir up."

"Much obliged," Billy said. "I don't know much about Indians and stuff, but I'm a quick learner."

Simpson winked at Chapman. "Sure hope so, son. Otherwise all you'll have left is the hair on your head and the lint in your belly button!"

Simpson walked away as the crowd parted, giving way to a striking warrior riding a coal black horse. He was dressed in buckskins and his brass hoop earrings glittered in the sun. Two long braids, garnished with strips of red flannel and otter fur, hung far down his back. A chest plate of porcupine quills contrasted with his fringed shirt and leggings. Brass bells hung from his horse's bridle and jingled as it walked.

Dixon stared in awe. "Amos, who is that?"

"That, Billy Dixon, is Quanah, Chief of the Quahadi band of the Comanche," Chapman answered.

"He sure looks like a Chief!"

"I tell you something, Billy Dixon," Chapman said. "Remember this. There are five bands of Comanche that make up their nation. Each band separate from the other. Each band has its own chief. Each band speaks for itself. Quanah is Chief of the Quahadi band. White people call them the 'Antelope' band. They were not invited to the Council. The Kotseka band, called the 'Buffalo Eaters,' they were not invited, either. Only three of the five Comanche bands were invited."

"Why?" Billy asked. "Somebody mad at them?'"

Chapman shrugged. "Don't know. Pretty dumb. Not a wise thing."

"How come Quanah is here if his band ain't invited ?"

"People say he is here to watch and listen," Chapman replied. "Hey, enough talk. See you at sundown."

FIFTEEN

Medicine Lodge Creek, Kansas
October 20, 1867

As Treaty Day neared, a cross section of western tribes flooded into the Council area. Each tribe camped by itself, in some cases not trusting its neighbors. They erected their lodges some distance from any military presence, drawing upon bitter experience.

The treaty-makers from Washington, conspicuous in their black city clothing, contrasted vividly with brightly garbed scouts, warriors, and military personnel. Housed in large, roomy tents, the politicos were pampered by servants and military stewards.

In two large canvas tents at the edge of the military encampment, nine newspaper correspondents and their artists assigned to report the Council relaxed amid cigar smoke and a shared bottle of whiskey.

Roland Phillips, correspondent for the *Chicago Sun,* stood in the doorway of the tent watching the turmoil. "This is really something to see!" he said to his tent mates. Peter Forbes, a cub reporter for the *St. Louis Day,* and Chris Ford of the *Boston Times* joined him in the doorway.

"Sure is," Forbes said. "Supposed to be the biggest thing of its kind ever. Great story for my readers."

Seated on his cot, Chris Ford poured himself a drink and held it aloft in a salute. "My story for the *Boston Times* is about those poor devils out there looking for justice," he said.

Phillips looked at him critically. "Justice? From those scalawags back East? I don't think so!"

"Why do you say that?" Forbes asked. "There's two sides to every question you know."

Phillips lit a cigar. "That's right," he agreed. "But I betcha a good cigar that I can predict right now how this so-called 'Council' is gonna play out."

Forbes shook his head. "Aw, c'mon now," he said. "How do you figure that?"

Phillips waved his cigar expansively. "Well, first we're gonna tell our red brothers how much we love 'em. Then we're gonna give them some pots and pans and hats and medallions to prove our love, so to speak. Next we're gonna promise them more stuff, like food and clothing. But there's a catch . . ."

"What's that?" Forbes asked.

Phillips smiled sardonically. "The catch, my friend, is that to get all this stuff, our red brothers will have to move onto a reservation."

"That's not so bad," Forbes answered. "They'll get taken care of by Uncle Sam."

Chris Ford spoke up. "Make that 'taken' by Uncle Sam."

Forbes raised his eyebrows. "Meanin'?"

"Meaning that they're at the mercy of an Indian Agent, who runs the reservation," Ford said. "If he's a crook, which most of them are, he'll fill his pockets at the expense of the Indians, the very people he's supposed to be helping!"

Phillips raised his hand. "And that's not all. Part of the deal is that our red brothers have to become farmers! Farmers!" he repeated, his voice rising. "Sod busters! A Cheyenne, Kiowa, or Comanche behind a plow? Are we serious? These people are the best horsemen in the world! Their life centers around the running of the buffalo. Farmers? I don't think so!"

Forbes persisted. "But the buffalo are disappearing."

"You're right. That's the bald truth." Phillips replied. "But do you know why the buffalo are disappearing? Because the white hide-hunters are wiping out the herds. Shooting thousands of animals for their skins, leaving the meat to rot! That's why! It's a damned disgrace! And another thing, you know what the hides are used for? Well, I'll tell you what they're used for. Industrial belting!"

"I thought they were used for coats and robes. Things like that," Forbes replied.

"Some are," Phillips conceded. "But the big mills back east have found that buffalo hide makes the best belting to drive their machines. Isn't that a twist? Our Industrial Revolution runs on leather belting provided by the Stone Age!"

Ford poured himself a drink. "But listen to this!" He said. "Here's the hook! We're gonna tell them to sign a treaty which will call for peace between us forever. And then, and here's the kicker, as the price for peace and protection, we'll tell them they have to give up all the land outside the reservation where they've lived and hunted for hundreds of years! 'Justice' you say? What justice?" Ford shook his head in doubt. "You can't be serious! Nobody in his right mind would agree to those terms!"

From the back of the tent, a correspondent dressed in typical city fashion spoke for the first time, his voice tinged with a British accent. "Henry Morgan Stanley here, *New York Herald*," he stated." I'm afraid they have no choice, old boy. You see, this is a case of Stone Age man opposing our so-called 'progress.' The die is cast, and, unfortunately, the Indian doesn't realize it. His day has come and gone!"

"Stone Age? Isn't that a bit of a stretch?" Forbes inquired.

"Not at all," Stanley replied. "Consider, my good fellow, what we have here. One side employs stone axes, clubs, spears, bows and arrows, lives in skin tents, and follows the buffalo for food, clothing, and necessities. The other side has access to firearms, railroads, steam engines, cities, huge populations, and newspapers, for which we are all grateful I'm sure, and an insatiable hunger for land."

Forbes looked dubious. "Well, when you put it that way. I've never really thought of it like that."

"Perfectly all right, young man," Stanley said graciously. "Not many people have. You know, a few months ago I spent some time in the field with General Hancock chasing some poor devil Kiowa and Comanche. Just a few days out there opened my eyes. The odds are not with those wild people. They are brave, incredible horsemen, excellent warriors, and are fighting for their homeland. But they can't win! And probably by the end of this treaty charade, they will come to that realization."

Forbes looked uncomfortable. "You make it sound so cut and dried," he responded.

Stanley smiled thinly. "Exactly! The hard, cold facts are that we sympathize with them, that they move us with their dignity, but gentlemen, half a continent will not be left open as buffalo pasture and hunting grounds!"

"Stone Age. Interesting perspective," Phillips commented, as he reached for a bottle and four glasses. When all glasses were filled, he proposed a toast. "Gentlemen, here's something that's strictly from our age," he announced. "Join me in a drink to justice!"

Stanley fondled his glass and held it to the light. "I say, gentlemen," he said. "Do you know what the Comanche call this? They call it 'foolish water,' and, by Jove, I think they have a point!"

SIXTEEN

Medicine Lodge Council Encampment
October 26, 1867

The next morning brought an air of anticipation to the encampment, as the tribal spokesmen drifted into the Council site with their entourages.

Seated on empty flour barrels, Billy Dixon, wearing a necklace that he had traded for a cloth coat, and Amos Chapman, wearing his new cloth coat, were interested observers. Chapman pointed out notable Indians to Billy, who watched exitedly. "See that warrior with the strap over his shoulder? That's Satanta. The whites call him 'White Bear.' Very great Kiowa warrior! The strap means he's a member of the Ten Bravest Society. When he goes into battle, he stakes himself to the ground with a lance through that strap. Then he fights there until he is killed or is released by a brother warrior. See the one with the silk hat? That's Kicking Bird, another Kiowa. Very important man! Look in front of him, kinda smallish, that's Lone Wolf. Kiowa, too."

Dixon was wide-eyed. "You sure know everyone!"

"Not yet, but I'm workin' on it," Amos said. "Now, over there by the big tree, that's Wolf Sleeve. He's Apache. Next to him is Yellow Horse, sub-chief of the Arapaho. See him? No, over there," he said, pointing to a crowd of Indians.

"Yeah, yeah, I see him now," Dixon replied.

Chapman continued. "Over to the left, there, just walking in, that's Toshaway. The one with the tall hat with the big star on it, he's Comanche. The whites call him 'Silver Brooch.' Next to him is Ten Bears. See his spectacles? He says all important Whites wear spectacles, so he got a pair for himself. Comanche, too. Just in front of Ten Bears is another Comanche, Long Hat."

"I saw a bunch of Cheyenne around," Dixon said. "Their leaders here?"

Chapman searched the crowd. "Yup, there they are, up front. See the two with the Peace Medals around their necks? That's Black Kettle on the left and Little Robe on the right. And that one talking with White Bear, that's Black Eagle, another Kiowa. And see that white man talkin' to the Bluecoat under the canopy?"

"The one with the big mustache?" Dixon asked.

"Yeah, that's Phillip McCusker," Chapman said. "Lives with the Comanche. Has a Comanche wife."

"What's he here for?"

"Interpreter," Amos replied. "Speaks good Comanche."

"I see. Who interprets for the other tribes? Them Kiowa, Cheyenne, and Apache?"

Chapman shrugged. "Dunno, but they better hope it ain't one of them fellas in a black suit."

By mid-morning, the Council had gathered in a grove of trees bordering a river. A large, open-air structure of poles and an open roof laced with leafy branches provided welcomed shade. The white dignitaries were seated on crude benches. The Indians sat cross-legged on the ground.

Sergeant Lem Pinney, resplendent in full-dress uniform and elegant helmet, ignored the stir of admiration his uniform created throughout the audience and commenced the day's agenda. "This Council will come to order. The Honorable N.G. Taylor, Commissions of Indian Affairs for the United States of America, presiding. Mr. Phillip McCusker and Mr. John Smith will serve as interpreters."

The eight members of the press corps crowded onto two crude benchs. The ninth member, a brash cub reporter on his first assignment, sat on the ground. Chris Ford nudged a companion. "We'll see how 'honorable' he is," he whispered.

Commissioner Taylor rose to his feet and cleared his throat. "I bring our Indian brothers greetings from the Great White Chief in Washington. He wishes you to know that he wants only peace and plenty for you. He wishes no more war between our people.

But he fears for the future of the Indian people, as the white people and the Bluecoats are as blades of grass, they are so many, while our red brothers become fewer each year, like snow flakes melting in the spring sun." There was a pause for translation. The Indians were impassive. Taylor continued. "The Great Chief wishes you to come and live on a reservation, where you will be protected, and he will give you food, clothing, and shelter. The reservation land will be yours forever, forbidden to all outsiders."

There was another pause for translation. The references to *reservation* caused a stir among the audience. Taylor spoke on. "And there is more. Each member of your tribe will be given three hundred and twenty acres of land to keep as his own, providing that he cultivates and farms it. Plows and farming tools will be given to you by the Great Chief." The Indians exchanged stunned looks. There was a noticeable restlessness among them. Taylor warmed to his task. "And in return for all these good things, our red brothers will be asked to give up any rights to land outside the reservation." There was a profound silence during the translation. The interpreters glanced nervously at the Commission. Hurriedly, Taylor finished his message. "However, knowing that our brothers cherish their buffalo hunts, you will be allowed to hunt buffalo off the reservation as long as there are enough animals to justify the hunt. The Great Chief will also forbid any hunting or trespassing on your land south of the Arkansas River. That land will be yours forever." Taylor turned to Senator Henderson. "Now Senator Henderson will say a few words to you."

Senator Henderson rose. "Thank you, Commissioner Taylor. I bring greetings to our brothers from Congress, the Big Council in Washington. We extend our hand in friendship to our red brothers and hope they will take that hand. You have heard many things today which you must consider for the well-being of your people. I urge you to counsel with your wise men tonight around the fire in your lodge. Think upon what has been said. It is your best path. It is in the best interests of your children, and their children! We ask that you return to this Council tomorrow, prepared to make your mark upon the paper which will give you peace and plenty. After you make your mark, the

Great White Chief has asked me to give you the gifts he has sent you as a sign of his good faith. And now, General William Tecumseh Sherman, a great warrior and Chief of the Bluecoats, wishes to speak to you."

Sherman stood up. "Many of you know me. You know I speak the truth. Sometimes the truth is like a stone, hard to chew, hard to swallow. But hear me now! You can no more stop us than you can stop the sun or the moon. You must submit and do the best you can!"

Upon the translation, the commissioners rose, signifying the conclusion of the day's agenda. The tribesmen, in stunned silence, remain seated, as if frozen to the ground. The correspondents scribbled furiously. "So that's it!" Forbes exclaimed. "The mailed fist! Take it or leave it! Our stone-age friends are in a real fix!"

"I wouldn't miss tomorrow for anything!" Chris Ford said. "What do you think the chiefs will do?"

"Maybe they'll massacre the whole bunch of us!" Forbes said semi-seriously.

"The thought has crossed my mind," his companion admitted.

"Naw, that won't happen. But they don't have much choice, do they? All that military, soldier boys, and generals with Gatling guns, they're not here for fun. And that's not lost on our friends. Their time is running out. I just hope they realize it. It could get pretty bloody, pretty ugly if they don't!" Phillips added.

Chris Ford looked up from his notes. "There's going to be some soul-searching in the lodges tonight! By the way, General Sherman, know what his middle name is?"

Phillips paused. "Tecumseh?"

"Yup. Good Indian name," Ford said. "If he's got any Indian blood in his veins, it sure as hell doesn't show!"

"Pretty ironic, isn't it?" Phillips commented. "Guess we can be glad about something, though."

"What's that?"

"Decisions," Phillips said. "Only decision we have to make tonight is whose bourbon are we gonna drink!"

Later that evening, a meeting convened in the lodge of Ten Bears, a Comanche highly respected by his tribesmen. The chiefs of the three

Comanche bands invited to the Council were seated cross-legged by the fire. Although his band was not invited to the Council, Quanah was present as a spectator. A pipe was passed around the circle of participants. After several minutes of silence, Ten Bears set the pipe down and donned his spectacles. "You have all heard with your own ears the words of the White Chiefs," he said softly.

"After hearing the words of the Bluecoat Chief, my heart is like a stone," Silver Brooch said. "Truly, his words were like a rock."

Black Eagle nodded. "Do you think he speaks the truth?"

Long Hat brought his fists together. "He is known as a hard man. My mind does not want to believe him, but my heart tells me he is to be feared."

Ten Bears spoke again. "Two winters ago, I traveled the long trail to Washington to see for myself how these Whites live. And I saw things my mind would not accept! The Whites are like leaves in the woods, they are so many! They travel in iron wagons that spit fire and smoke! They live in lodges made of wood that are crowded together in places called 'cities.' I have seen these things with my own eyes. We are an island in a lake of Whites!"

"They ask us to make this treaty with them. Yet they have broken every treaty they have ever made with us," Silver Brooch said bitterly. "How do we know that they will not break this treaty, as they did the others? They are liars! They have no honor!"

"What you say is the truth," Ten Bears said soothingly. "But we must do what is best for our children and grandchildren. We must look over the horizon into the next world."

Black Eagle interrupted angrily. "We will become tillers of the soil on a reservation ruled by Whites! They will control our food, our clothing, even our lives! Farmers! Ugh!" He spat disgustedly into his palm.

Long Hat spoke slowly. "I am troubled by having to give up the land that we have hunted and roamed for so many years. We are being squeezed into a little space. My heart is on the ground!"

Ten Bears removed his glasses. "I understand," he said thoughtfully, "and feel much as you do. But what choice do we have? If we do not make our mark on the treaty paper, then we must fight the Bluecoats. And, yes, we would fight them well. And win some battles. But for how long? Two moons? Two winters? Eventually we would lose our villages, our ponies, our food—everything. Then, when all the killing is over, we would go to the reservation. But how many of us would be left? My heart tells me not many. The Comanche, once a proud and feared people, would be a handful of starving children, Old Ones, and grieving widows. All our young men would be dead. I have spoken."

There was a momentary silence that was eventually broken by Black Eagle. "Our brothers, the buffalo, are leaving us. Where before the land was black with them, now it is white with their bones. Will they ever return to us? Some say yes, but I do not think so."

Long Hat nodded in agreement. "The white hunters are a stone in my moccasin. They have no respect for our brothers, only for the money they get for their hides and bones. The wolves grow fat on the piles of meat left to rot. The coyotes and buzzards have full bellies."

"Truly," Silver Brooch agreed. "We must think about these things in our lodges tonight, so we will all walk the same path tomorrow."

"We must ask the grandfathers for their wisdom tonight," Black Eagle said in a subdued voice. It was clear that the meeting had concluded.

Quanah, who had been listening carefully, stood up. "I have heard your words," he said grimly. "You speak for only three bands of our people. I cannot speak for any but the Quahadi. But hear me! Tell the White Chiefs that the Quahadis are warriors and will surrender only when the Bluecoats come and whip us!"

There was a strained silence, broken only by the crackling of the fire, as Quanah stalked from the lodge.

The following morning, a soft breeze dissipated the lodge smoke that wreathed the encampment, allowing a bright sun to warm the late October day. The Council ground was bustling with activity, as preparations were completed for the day's deliberations.

As Billy Dixon aired his bed roll, he detected movement far out from the camp.

At the crest of a rise, where the light blue of early morning met the autumn brown of the prairie, there flowed a glittering, feather-fluttering wave, half a mile in length. Fifteen hundred of the finest warriors of the Cheyenne Nation, adorned in full battle regalia and well armed, made their way to the Council ground at a trot. When about a quarter of a mile from the encampment, the warriors charged at full gallop, singing, chanting, and whirling their weapons over their heads. When only some two hundred yards from the camp, they reined to an abrupt halt.

General Harney, respected by the tribesman as an honorable man, walked out alone and met the line, complimenting the chiefs on their spectacular demonstration, which pleased them greatly. At the general's suggestion, the Cheyenne dismounted and the Chiefs took their places at the Council.

Phillip McCusker was chatting with friends when he noticed Quanah in a crowd of Comanche tribes people and hailed him. "Are you Quanah of the Quahadis?" he asked in Comanche tongue.

Quanah regarded him cautiously. "I am."

"I am called 'McCusker.' Interpreter."

"You speak our tongue well, for a white man," Quanah said suspiciously.

"My wife is Comanche. I live with her people," McCusker explained. "The Comanche have become my people, too."

"You're the wrong color."

"My skin, maybe, My heart, no."

"What would you say to me?" Quanah asked.

"I have heard of your mother," McCusker said. Quanah remained passive. "I know that your mother and sister were lost when the Bluecoats attacked their village long ago."

"That is the truth," Quanah acknowledged.

"Well, they weren't killed. They were taken by the Bluecoats and sent back to your mother's white family in Texas."

Quanah stared at McCusker. "Taken? Are you sure?"

"Yes, I am sure. I have talked to those who have seen them. But . . ."

"They are well?" Quanah asked, hesitantly.

McCusker coughed. "No, Quanah. Your sister died of fever and your mother soon after. About seven years ago." There was a pause.

"Her white family. How are they called?" Quanah asked softly.

"Her white family is called 'Parker.' She was called 'Cynthia' by the Whites. Cynthia Ann Parker."

"So I am part Comanche, the Quanah part, and part white, the Parker part?"

"You can look at it that way."

"Quanah Parker to the Whites maybe. To the Comanche, I am Quanah, son of Peta Nokona!"

McCusker extended his hand. "I am sorry to tell you these things, Quanah, but I thought you would want to know."

Quanah shook his hand. "Yes, I am relieved to know. No longer will I wonder. My heart is heavy, but at the same time, lighter. My thanks." McCusker walked away, leaving Quanah—now Quanah Parker—standing with his thoughts as the crowd swirled around him.

SEVENTEEN

Medicine Lodge Creek, Kansas
October 27, 1867

The Peace Council was once again called to order on a brisk autumn morning by Sergeant Pinney in his splendid dress uniform. Commissioner Taylor was the first speaker. "Today, the Great White Chief in Washington has asked that his red brothers tell him of their concerns so that he can make their path smoother. He awaits your words."

Silver Brooch rose to speak first as his interpreter cleared his throat. "My young men are a scoff among the other nations. I shall wait until next spring to see if these things you promise will be given to us. If they are not, I and my young men will return, with our wild brothers, to live on the prairie. I have spoken." The Peace Council officials, seated at a long table, seemed unmoved as they whispered to one another.

When Ten Bears stood up and prepared to speak next, there was a palpable air of anticipation among the Council. He waited patiently for the crowd to quiet down, then removed his spectacles. "My heart is filled with joy when I see you here, as the brook fills with water when the snows melt in the spring, and I feel glad, as the ponies do, when the fresh grass starts in the beginning of the year. I heard of your coming when I was many sleeps away, and I made but few camps before I met you. I knew that you had come to do good to me and to my people. I looked for benefits which would last forever, and so my face shines with joy as I look upon you. My people have never first drawn a bow or fired a gun against the Whites. There has been trouble on the line between us, and my young men have danced the War Dance. But it was not begun by us. It was you who sent the first soldier, and we who sent the second.

"Two years ago, I came upon this road, following the buffalo, that my wives and children might have their cheeks plump and their bodies warm. But the soldiers fired on us, and since that time, there has been a noise like that of a thunderstorm, and we have not known which way to go. Nor have we been made to cry alone. The blue-dressed soldiers came from out of the night, when it was dark and still, and for campfires they lit our lodges. Instead of hunting game, they killed my braves, and the warriors of the tribe cut short their hair for the dead. So it was in Texas. They made sorrow come in our camps, and we went out like buffalo bulls when their cows are attacked. When we found them, we killed them, and their scalps hang in our lodges. The Comanches are not weak and blind, like the pups of a dog when seven sleeps old. They are strong and far-sighted like grown horses. We took their road and we went on it. The white women cried and our women laughed. But there are things which you have said to me I do not like. They were not sweet, like sugar, but bitter, like gourds. You said that you wanted to put us upon a reservation, to build us houses and make us medicine lodges. I do not want them. I was born on the prairie, where the wind blew free and there was nothing to break the light of the sun. I was born where there were no enclosures and everything drew a free breath. I want to die there and not within walls. I know every stream and every wood between the Rio Grande and the Arkansas Rivers. I have hunted and lived over that country. I lived like my fathers before me, and like them, I lived happily. When I was in Washington, the Great White Father told me that the Comanche land was ours, and that no one should hinder us in living on it. So, why do you ask us to leave the rivers and the sun and the wind and live in houses?

"Do not ask us to give up the buffalo for the sheep. The young men have heard talk of this and it has made them sad and angry. Do not speak of it more. I love to carry out the talk I get from the Great Father. When I get goods and presents, I and my people feel glad, since it shows that he holds us in his eye. If the Texans had kept out of my country, there might have been peace. But that which you now say we must live in is too small. The Texans have taken away the places where the grass grew thickest and the timber was best. Had we kept that, we might have done the things you ask. But it is too late. The Whites have the country which we loved, and we wish only to wander on the prairie until we die. Any good thing you say to me shall not be forgotten. I shall carry it as near to my heart as my children, and it shall be as often on my tongue as the name of the Great Spirit. I want no blood upon my land to stain the grass. I want it all pure and clear, and I wish it so that all who go through among my people may find peace when they come, and leave it when they go out. I have spoken." Ten Bears remained standing for several moments, as his words hung in the air. He then sat down, breaking the spell. The treaty officials exchanged uneasy glances.

Beneath the canopy, Roland Phillips scribbled frantically as he wrote his dispatch.

"I've heard a lot of speeches, gentlemen," he said to his fellows. "But never one like that! My God! It was magnificent!"

Henry Stanley paused in his writing. "And from a wild Indian, eh? The politicians in Washington, and London, for that matter, could take some lessons from Mr. Ten Bears! Put him in front of Congress and make that speech, without notes, mind you, and he could change the entire Indian Policy of this country. Guaranteed!"

Striving to fill the void of silence, Commissioner Taylor attempted to push the agenda. "Yes, well, moving on, we thank our red brothers for sharing their thoughts with us. Now we ask all the chiefs to come to the table and make their mark on the treaty paper. Then the Great White Father will give you gifts and presents."

The chiefs dutifully made their marks on the treaty agreement, except Lone Wolf of the Cheyenne who refused. But it was too little and too late to deny the Treaty.

As the last chief signed, Taylor continued. "I hereby adjourn this Council and pronounce that the reservations, from this day forward, are preserved for the absolute and undisturbed use and occupation of the Indian tribes described herein. The Government of the United States hereby solemnly pledges that no persons, except those herein authorized, shall be permitted to pass over, settle upon, or reside in the territory herein described."

The splendidly adorned Sergeant Pinney rose. "The supply wagons will unload in that open meadow," he said, indicating to a nearby open area. He pounded his gavel. "This council is hereby concluded."

At that, soldiers began emptying the supply wagons of their gifts and presents for the tribesmen: barrels of sugar, molasses, flour, dried fruit, and coffee; boxes of Army pants, hats, shirts, socks, great coats, pots and pans, mirrors, blankets and hatchets; bolts of calico and flannel, in a rainbow of colors; and boxes of multi-colored beads. The goods were gathered in three huge piles, amid a general uproar, as the Indians gazed upon the mind-boggling treasures.

General Harney, in charge of the distribution, waved to his bugler who sounded several notes to quiet the crowd. He beckoned to the interpreters " My friends, let the Cheyenne take the middle pile of presents, the Apache and Arapaho, the pile to the left, and the Comanche and Kiowa, the pile to the right. Your chiefs will oversee the distribution."

Amid the ensuing uproar, Indians walked off wearing two hats, several great coats, some even with umbrellas. Pack horses were overburdened. Travois were loaded to the point of immobility.

As the crowd slowly dispersed, there were still some unclaimed gifts. The Indians streamed back to their lodges, leaving the area littered with unwanted clothing, both used and new. As Billy Dixon gazed at the remnants of the gift-giving, he noticed Amos Chapman, on horseback, picking his way through the litter. Dixon waved at the scout. "Hey, Amos! What're you doing?"

Amos grinned. "Tryin' to find some new pants. Need a pair?"

"Might at that," Dixon said. "How come there's so many pants laying around?"

"Indians don't like pants," Amos explained. "Just don't feel right."

"Amos, you hear that speech by Ten Bears?"

"Yeah, I did," Amos replied. "Ain't he somethin'?"

"You think he's right?" Dixon asked.

"Course he's right!" Chapman answered.

"Maybe we're on the wrong side," Dixon said hesitantly.

"Could be," Amos conceded. "But you an' me ain't gonna change anything. Best we can do is play square with everyone and keep our nose clean."

"Seems my mother told me them rules when I was little tyke. Guess she was right," Dixon concluded.

"Your ma was a smart woman, Billy," Amos said. "Too bad them stuffed shirts and scalawags in Washington didn't have that kind of upbringin'."

EIGHTEEN

Indian Territory
1868

Despite all the lofty speeches at the Medicine Lodge Treaty Council, the treaty was broken through misunderstanding, government hypocrisy, and outright greed, within a year. The U.S. Government failed to understand that the Comanche nation had not agreed to the treaty, only three of the five bands had done so. Furthermore, the tribes subscribing to the agreement did not understand that Texas, a long-time enemy, was part of the United States. Raids for horses, cattle, women, and children, therefore, continued in the Lone Star State. Ranchers drove their herds across treaty land on their way to the nearest railhead. Hide-hunters, oblivious of treaty boundaries, pursued the Texas buffalo herd and slaughtered the animals by the hundreds of thousands. Outraged by what they considered a flagrant disregard for truth, honesty, and respect by the Whites, the Kiowa, Cheyenne, and Comanche rose in a bloody fury to protect their homeland and the future of their people.

A trail herd of longhorns moved steadily across the prairie, raising a cloud of arid dust. Drovers, obviously nervous, kept watch over the herd and the surrounding countryside. The trail boss, a laconic black man, pulled his horse up next to Charlie McKnight, distinguished by his prematurely grey beard. "Washita River up ahead, Mr. McKnight."

McKnight stood in his stirrups. "Yup, see it, Bose," he answered. "Far side is Indian Territory. Let's get the herd across while it's still light."

"Yes, sir. Right now," Bose said, with a half salute.

As evening approached, the last of the herd struggled out of the river and moved inland. Bose reported back to his boss. "Beddin' 'em down for the night, Mr. McKnight. Plenty of grass."

McKnight beckoned to his trail boss. "Tell the boys to keep their eyes open and their heads down tonight. Tell the nighthawks to be careful!"

Bose nodded. "No sign of Feathers so far," he offered.

McKnight grimaced. "We both know that don't mean a thing!"

Bose smiled. "Yeah, this country's still got the bark on." He wheeled his horse and galloped off to warn his riders.

McKnight's concerns were realized when in the darkest part of the night the herd was stampeded by a screeching, blanket-waving band of warriors. Helpless before the charging cattle, the drovers were lucky to survive. It took several days to gather the scattered herd, and even then a number of cattle were missing. Some lost. Others, a substitute for buffalo meat.

As the herd regrouped, McKnight gathered his drovers at the chuck wagon. Coffee mug in hand, he surveyed his weary riders. "Well, boys, it's not as if we ain't been warned. Best thing to come of this stampede is that nobody got hurt."

"We gonna move the herd through the Territory, Mr McKnight?" Bose asked.

McKnight pushed his hat back on his head. "Don't think so. Bad start here on the Washita. Prolly best if we go around. Get out of the Territory."

Bose poured coffee grounds from his cup. "Awright, boys, you heard the man. Got work to do." The riders mounted up and the trail herd veered west, out of harm's way.

In an isolated hunting camp south of the Arkansas River in Indian Territory, two tents had been pitched near a pile of hides, a number of which were pegged out on the ground to dry. A chuck wagon and its two mules comprised the rest of the camp. A hunter, with his two skinners, readied for the day's hunt, while the cook, a slight, balding older man, bustled about cleaning up after breakfast.

"Be back afore sundown, Cookie," the hunter said. "May need the wagon."

The cook looked up. "Just let me know. Good huntin'."

The hunter and his skinners rode out for the day's work. Nearing a small group of animals, the hunter quietly set up for his shoot. He spread his cartridges on his bandana, tested the wind, and arranged his shooting sticks. Satisfied, he adjusted the windage on his Sharps, and dry-fired to check the trigger pull. He slipped a cartridge into the chamber, aimed carefully, and squeezed off his first round. With the boom of the rifle, a bull dropped abruptly. Others in the group paid little attention to him, and continued grazing contentedly. The hunter continued firing, until the ground in front of him was littered with dead and dying animals.

Back at the camp, the cook was unloading flour from the wagon, blissfully unaware of three Comanche riders who silently sat on their ponies watching him. As he hefted a sack of flour, an arrow hissed into his back. With a look of surprise, the cook turned to face the intruders. "Get outta' here! Leave me alone!" he choked, staggering against the wagon. "Biscuits for supper, can't you . . . see . . . I!" He pitched forward on his face, and the sack of flour in his arms split open as it hit the ground, leaving a white, snowy patch beneath him, which slowly turned red with blood. The warriors looted the wagon and the tents. Piling the hides and camp gear together, they set them on fire. They took the mules with them, leaving the camp a blazing pyre.

Meanwhile, the hunter, hard at work, had killed a dozen buffalo. The skinners were busy stripping hides from the carcasses when a distant column of black smoke caught their attention. The three men hastily mounted and galloped back to camp. When they arrived, the fire was reduced to smoldering ashes. Appalled at the sight, they hurriedly dug a shallow grave and buried the cook.

The first skinner, looked nervously about, and took off his hat. "Somebody should say some words over Cookie," he said.

"Let's get the hell outta here while we can!" the other skinner urged.

"Them ain't the right words," the hunter said. "Here, I'll do it." The men took off their hats and stood at the grave's edge. The hunter picked up the fatal arrow.

"Poor old Cookie," he said. "Never did nobody no harm, 'cept maybe with his biscuits. It was a Comanche arrow, Cookie. Thought you'd like to know. Anyhow, they dint scalp you, bein' bald an' all." He paused. "Awright, boys, let's get outta' here!"

The somber hunting party, minus one of its members, left hurriedly, having paid the penalty for trespassing on lands forbidden them by treaty.

A crude home dug into a bank of earth sheltered an emigrant family of farmers, comprised of two children, their mother, father, and grandfather. Dirt poor, the children were barefoot, clad in flour sacks and hand-me-downs. The farm consisted of a handful of chickens, which clucked and scratched both inside and outside of the dugout, two dairy cows, a large pig, one horse, a plow, and a wagon. The family had unknowingly settled on Indian land.

As the family ate its sparse noon meal, several Comanche riders boldly circled the dugout. Two other warriors opened the corral, releasing the cows. At the insistent barking of their dog, the farmer peered outside. Shouting a warning to his family, he pulled up his suspenders and dashed out of the doorway. Shotgun in hand, he led their horse into the dugout and hauled the wagon tight to the door. By this time, the Comanche had leisurely riddled the pig with arrows. A rider slid from his pony and attempted to catch one of the squawking chickens, which ran in every direction, much to the amusement of his fellow warriors. Risking his life, the farmer tied a white cloth to the barrel of his shotgun, waved it out the door, and stepped out into the open. Impressed by his bravery, the Comanche stopped. Two riders cautiously approached him.

"You go!" one of the riders said emphatically, pointing to the East. "You go now!" The second rider nodded in agreement, and then, in one quick movement, slid from his pony and caught a chicken by its neck. He vaulted back into the saddle, with the squawking, flapping chicken firmly in his grasp.

The farmer watched, wide-eyed. "Yes, yes, we go. Right now we go!" Then, in an effort to buy time, and perhaps their lives, he pointed at the chickens. "Them chickens, it's all right! You kin have 'em!" The warriors regarded him curiously. The farmer flapped his arms imitating a chicken. "It's all right, them chickens, we're just leavin'," he said fervently.

The two riders looked at each other and smiled faintly. "He makes a pretty good chicken," observed one warrior.

"He hasn't said anything about the pig," his companion said.

The farmer touched his brow in an ingratiating salute and hurried back into the dugout. By this time the family had hastily gathered its few possessions and hitched the horse to the wagon. As they left, with the mother fearfully sheltering her brood, one of the children noticed the pig. "Mama," he said through tears, "Why'd they shoot Lucille? She wasn't doing nothin'."

The mother glanced fearfully at the Comanche. "Hush up, child," she said. "They're probably hungry. Anyways, we couldn't take Lucille with us, no how."

"Hush up, everybody," the grandfather whispered. "Just hush up!"

As the farmer drove the wagon, with its terrified passengers, past the corral, a warrior wrested the shotgun from the his grasp. The farmer held up his hand in the peace sign. "Peace be with us!" he quavered.

As the wagon headed east, in the direction of the nearest ranch, the warriors, yipping excitedly, ransacked and torched the dugout.

The farm wagon rattled across the prairie for several hours. The neighboring ranch they so desperately anticipated as a safe haven came into view. Except it was no longer a ranch. It was a smoldering ruin, with livestock strewn about, riddled with arrows. Near the well, the owner lay on his back, lanced and scalped. Ranch hands and family were scattered among the ruins, united in death. One living thing remained: a little girl, who had crawled from beneath her mother's body. She sat bolt up-right in the smoke and carnage, playing with her Indian doll.

The mother covered her face in horror. "Oh, my God! My God! Those poor people!"

"It coulda' been us," the farmer said grimly. "By the Grace of God, it coulda been us! Sarah, fetch that little tyke. Dad and me will bury her folks." The two men located several shovels in the ruins and dug a mass grave, all the while nervously scanning the horizon.

The mother plucked absently at her shawl. "This awful country," she wailed. "This God-forsaken, terrible country. Lord God have mercy . . ."

"Stop it, Mother," the farmer ordered. "Stop it! Now go fetch that little tyke!" He took his wife by the shoulders and shook her. "You hear me? Help the Lord take care of that little thing! Mother! You hear me?"

As if awakening from a dream, the woman gathered herself. She climbed down from the wagon and ran towards the child. "Oh dear, yes, of course, good Lord, that poor little thing! I'm coming, dear. I'm here, you poor baby!" She scooped the child from the carnage and cuddled her, as her tears wet the little girl's grimy face.

As the raids grew in intensity and frequency, ranchers, farmers, and everyday citizens demanded protection from the states of Kansas and Texas, as well as the Federal government. But help was slow in coming, until Civil War hero General William Tecumseh Sherman was nearly killed while on an inspection tour of the frontier. A Kiowa war party allowed his party to pass unharmed, but wiped out a wagon train close behind. Sherman responded quickly. He ordered Colonel Ranald Slidell Mackenzie, a decorated Civil War commander, to subjugate the hostile tribes who were terrorizing the southwestern frontier in rapidly spreading guerrilla warfare. Although nobody realized it at the time, this was the turning point of the Indian wars in the Southwest.

PART THREE

BAD HAND

NINETEEN

Fort Concho, Texas
February 1871

Private Wiley Wirth, company clerk of the Fourth Cavalry, was absorbed in a game of solitaire. Hunched over his desk, he pondered his next move. Behind him his office door opened. Wirth remained fixated on the cards. "Close the damn door. You're lettin' the heat out," he growled.

Colonel Ranald S. Mackenzie, the newly arrived post commander, glanced over the clerk's shoulder. "Play the red jack on the black queen," he said.

"Yeah, right," the clerk replied. He turned around and came face to face with his worst nightmare. "Yes, sir! Yes, sir!" he mumbled, dropping the cards and snapping to attention.

The newcomer smiled faintly. "I'm Colonel Mackenzie, your new commanding officer."

In a panic, the clerk saluted several times. "Yes, sir. But we dint expect you for a coupla days, sir."

"So it seems, Private . . . uh . . ."

"Wirth, sir. Private Wiley Wirth, Fourth Cavalry, United States Army, sir!"

Mackenzie glanced around the office. "Tell me, Private Wirth, where is the officer of the day?"

The clerk remained at attention. "Sir, the officer of the day is hunting."

Mackenzie ran his finger across a dusty desk top. "Oh? And what is the officer of the day hunting, Private? I hope you'll tell me he is hunting Indians?"

Private Wirth squirmed unhappily. "Um, no, sir. The officer of the day is believed to be hunting prairie chickens. You know, sir, for supper. Like that, sir."

Mackenzie examined the dust on his fingers. "I see. And tell me, Private Wirth, where are the rest of the Fourth Cavalry's officers?"

The clerk swallowed hard. "Um . . . I . . . they," he stammered.

"Go on, Private. They what?" Mackenzie asked calmly.

A drop of perspiration appeared on the clerk's forehead. "They're with the officer of the day, sir."

"Thank you, Private Wirth," his commandant replied. "Now if you will be good enough to show me to my quarters."

"Yes, sir. Right this way, sir," said the relieved clerk. Private Wirth picked up the Colonel's trunk and led him to the post commanders living quarters. "Anything else I can do, sir?" he asked, as he set the trunk down.

Mackenzie surveyed his quarters critically. "No, I think not, Private. But please convey to the officers of the post that I am looking forward to meeting them this evening at eight o'clock in the commandant's office. Oh, one last thing, Private Wirth. Please see that my grey pacer is well taken care of. A little extra grain or corn, perhaps?"

Private Wirth saluted. "Yes sir, Colonel. Right away ,sir," he said and left hurriedly.

The officers of the Fourth Cavalry gathered to meet their new commandant. There was an apprehensive murmur in the room. As the office door opened, a silence fell over the room. An officer barked attention, and the men rose as one. Mackenzie strode into the room. "Be seated, gentlemen," he said. "I believe you know who I am, but I don't know who you are. However, I am sure we will be known to each other in the very near future." The officers individually and collectively nodded their heads in affirmation. Mackenzie continued briskly. "Thank you, gentlemen. I am pleased to learn that many of you are devoted hunters. However, from this point on, we will limit our hunting to Indians." He looked slowly around the room. "Do I make myself clear?"

"Yes, sir," the officers said in unison.

"Very well, gentlemen," he continued. This post is an eyesore. I want it cleaned up. And I want it to stay that way. Understood?"

"Yes, sir," the officers responded.

"Tomorrow we will begin a new training program for the men. I want each of them to spend more time on the firing range. I want to be informed of their progress." Mackenzie paused.

"Yes, sir," the officers responded.

"And, gentlemen, I will hold an inspection tomorrow morning at roll call. Are there any further questions? As I see no hands raised, you are dismissed."

The next morning dawned clear and cold. Morning roll call was held on the parade ground at the center of the fort. Mackenzie stood on the porch of his office, watching the proceedings. As the roll call concluded, he walked slowly down the porch steps, drawing on his gloves. All eyes were on him as he stepped in front of the ranks.

The officer of the day saluted. "All present and accounted for, sir. Ready for your inspection, Colonel."

Mackenzie returned the salute. "Very well, Lieutenant Carter," he replied. Lieutenant Carter appeared startled that Mackenzie knew his name.

Mackenzie walked slowly through the ranks, looking carefully at each trooper. Here and there he adjusted a button and straightened a hat. Standing stiffly at attention, staring straight ahead, the men were without expression. When he reached the last man, the trooper broke into a broad smile. Mackenzie stopped and looked at the man curiously.

"Do we know each other, trooper?" he asked.

"Yes, sir. We sure do," replied the trooper, still at attention.

"How so, Corporal?"

"Second Connecticut Volunteers, Colonel. I was with you at Petersburg, and the fights at Winchester and Cedar Creek, and Opaquan and Fisher's Hill. And Middletown, Virginny, too."

Mackenzie brightened. "Guess both of us remember those names pretty well. What's your name, trooper?"

"Davis, sir. Corporal Whit Davis. From Somers, Connecticut."

"I am pleased to see you again, Corporal!" the officer said loudly, for the benefit of the ranks. Then he lowered his voice dramatically. "Just between you and me, Corporal, there's at least two of us in this outfit who've had our ass shot at pretty regularly!"

Trooper Davis grinned. "We sure have, sir. Um, how's your hand, Colonel? Battle of Petersburg, wasn't it?"

Mackenzie extended his disfigured right hand. "Still got the hand, Corporal. Seems to work fine with just three fingers."

Corporal Davis bobbed his head. "I figgered."

The Colonel continued. "Have to rely on experienced troopers like you, Corporal Davis. We've got a big job to do."

"You kin count on me, sir," Davis said, his ego rising.

"Appreciate that, Corporal Whit Davis from Somers, Connecticut," the Colonel answered.

He rejoined the officer of the day, fronting the troopers, and cleared his throat. "Stand at ease, men. I am Colonel Ranald Mackenzie, your new commanding officer. There are four things I want you to know. Four things I want you to remember. First, the Fourth Cavalry's assignment is to locate and defeat the Comanche, Kiowa, and Cheyenne tribes which have been raising so much hell. No easy task, I can assure you. Second, to accomplish this, you will be trained to fight them on their own terms. Tomorrow morning, that training will commence. Third, I will not order any soldier, any place, to do anything that I would not do myself. I lead only from up front. I expect you to follow. Fourth, when we have completed this assignment, we will be the envy of the U.S. Army. The Fourth Cavalry will have won great victories, and with the fewest casualties. It will be a regiment of which you will be proud to say, 'I served with the Fourth Cavalry.' It will be something you will tell your grandchildren about and history books will record your story for future generations of Americans." Mackenzie's words hung in the air. He turned to the officer of the day. "Lieutenant Carter, dismiss the men, please."

Later that evening a bull session was underway in the troops' quarters. Several troopers were stretched out on their bunks smoking their pipes. One was laboriously writing a letter, while another polished a belt buckle. Corporal Whit Davis was the center of attention. Trooper Ben Elias, a compact, wiry horse soldier, cuffed Davis playfully on the head. "Whit, you rascal," he said. "I knew you been in some fights, but I dint know you were buddies with old Mackenzie!" Davis preened in the limelight.

"Well, Eli, I'll tell you somethin'. I ain't exactly buddies with the Colonel, but I know him pretty good." Trooper Wayne Nolan, fair skinned and Irish, with a thick head of hair, joined the conversation.

"Hear him tell it, he's gonna work our butts off," he offered.

"Yup, expect he will," Davis replied. "For your own good." Nolan's face fell.

"For my own good! Last time I heard them words was when my Mama gave me sulfur an' molasses. 'It's for your own good,' she said. Darned near kilt me!" Nolan made gagging noises. "Terrible stuff!"

Davis chuckled. "Big difference here, Wayne. Your momma was givin' you that stuff for a spring tonic. Colonel is givin' you the works to save your sorry ass. Big difference!"

"Big-assed difference, you might say," Elias snickered. "Whit, this mornin' the Colonel told us that he leads from up front. That right?"

Davis nodded vigorously. "Damn straight, Eli. Lemme tell you somethin'. That man was wounded six times in the war. First time, he lay on the battlefield for twenty hours 'fore they found him. Took another bullet at Gettysburg. Then he had two fingers shot offen his right hand at Petersburg." Davis paused. His audience listened intently. "Then, at Winchester, he rode out front of our line with his hat on his saber. Horse got cut in two by shellfire, an' he got plugged in the leg, but wouldn't leave the battlefield. I seen that with my own eyes! Then, by thunder, at Cedar Knob, he got it twice in one day! He's a tough sumnabitch, I wanna tell you!" There was a brief silence.

"Then when he says he's gonna be out front, he ain't pullin' our leg?" Trooper Elias asked.

"He's gonna be out front all right, Eli. You can count on it!" Davis answered

"I can follow a man like that," Elias said quietly.

"Special kind of officer," Nolan added.

Trooper Elias brightened up. "Hey, bunky," he said to Nolan. "Did ya hear what he said about the regiment? I kinda like that! Bouncin' my grandson on my knee and telling him about the Fourth."

"Naw, Eli, you're prolly gonna be one of them 'fewest casualties' the Colonel was talking about!" Nolan replied.

Trooper Elias removed his hat, revealing his balding head. "Nope, not this hoss," he said rubbing his head. "No self-respectin' Comanche buck is gonna want my scalp. His friends would laugh him right outta their village. But you old bunky," he said, pointing to Nolan's thick hair. "You're fair game. Nice scalp! Look great hanging on some buck's war shield!" The barracks erupted in laughter.

At roll call and inspection two mornings later, Lt. Carter, as inspecting officer, moved through the ranks. Reaching Trooper Nolan, the officer halted, puzzled. "Trooper Nolan," he inquired. "What's the matter with your hat?"

Trooper Nolan looked blank. "Nothin', sir."

"Why is it so low on your head?"

"Prolly the haircut," Nolan replied solemnly. "In the interests of personal hygiene, like that, as the Colonel says, sir." Lt. Carter lifted the hat from Nolan's head, revealing a totally bald, gleaming scalp. There was a muffled, undercurrent of laughter from the ranks.

TWENTY

Fort Richardson, Texas
April 1871

A few months after his dispatch to Fort Concho, Mackenzie and the Fourth Cavalry were posted to Fort Richardson. To become familiar with the surrounding countryside, a small detachment of troopers formed up to leave on a reconnaissance patrol led by Lieutenant Carter and Colonel Mackenzie, who was riding his prized grey pacer. Four Tonkawa Indians, blood enemies of the Comanche, served as scouts. The officer of the day approached and saluted. "Good hunting, sir," he said. Mackenzie returned the salute.

"Thank you, Lieutenant. We're going to ride out and have a look at the country. Get the lay of the land." He turned in his saddle. "All right, Sergeant McSorley, let's move out."

At the sergeant's order the scouting party, two abreast, rode briskly from the fort.

"Music, Sergeant McSorley, if you please," Mackenzie ordered.

An Irish tenor, McSorley bellowed the first words of the regimental song. "Come home, John, don't stay too long. Come home soon to your own chick-a-biddy." The troopers joined him in song, and the detachment broke into a trot.

As the song ended, Mackenzie grimaced. "Sergeant, you were a little flat, weren't you?"

Sergeant McSorley bobbed his head. "Yes, sir, usually am goin' out. Comin' home though, I'm always on key. You'll see, Colonel."

"I'll look forward to that, Sergeant," Mackenzie said dryly.

Two uneventful days passed. The column had enjoyed a peaceful patrol. No sign of hostiles. Mackenzie had carefully noted the contours of the country, marking his maps and mentally filing his observations. As evening approached on the second day of the patrol, the column made camp on a hospitable site with plenty of firewood, water and grass. The troopers erected their tents and prepared for a leisurely supper.

From a promontory, Quanah and an older warrior, Red Bird, watched the camp intently. Flat on his belly, Quanah nudged Red Bird. "The horse soldier chief, he is 'Kinzie.' People say he is great warrior."

"They say he has many great wounds won in battle," Red Bird answered.

"Only three fingers on one hand. The People call him 'Bad Hand.'"

"Look," Quanah said. "He rides a fine horse. That big grey."

Red Bird smiled. "The grey would make a fine Comanche war horse," he suggested.

Quanah nodded. "Just what I was thinking!" The two Comanche bellied off the ridge and rejoined their raiding party.

A gentle night, brightened by starlight, caressed the camp. Men quietly lounged by the fires, smoking their pipes. The notes of a harmonica drifted softly over the encampment. The Tonkawa scouts were camped by themselves close by.

Mackenzie emerged from his tent. "Captain Boehm, have the horses been watered?"

Boehm, as chief of scouts, wore a white Stetson. "Yes, sir. They're all picketed. Guard's posted."

Mackenzie surveyed the camp. "Good stand of grass out there."

Captain Boehm smiled. "They'll be full of whiz-bang in the morning, Colonel."

"Very well. Good night, Mr. Boehm".

"Sleep well, sir." Mackenzie entered his tent as the camp fell silent.

At midnight, the tranquility was shattered as all hell broke loose. Eight screeching Comanche riders, firing guns and waving blankets, drove through the center of the camp. Four riders followed closely dragging buffalo hides, which collapsed tents, stacked carbines, supplies, and cooking gear into a huge tumult. As the troopers struggled to extricate themselves from tangled tent lines and canvas, the warriors, whooping and shouting, stampeded the detachment's horses into the darkness. Three troopers, clad only in their long underwear, fired wildly into the night.

Quanah had given the Civil War hero a lesson in frontier warfare. Mackenzie did not accept the teaching with grace. He struggled out from under his collapsed tent in a controlled fury. "Lt. Carter! Here on the double!" Lt. Carter arrived half-dressed, with a pistol in his hand. "Casualties, Lieutenant?" Mackenzie asked.

"None, sir. We were lucky! The Tonks say it was that damn half breed Quanah!"

"Quanah be damned. How many horses did we lose?"

"Can't tell yet, sir. They took some. We'll get an exact count at daylight."

"My grey?"

"Sorry to say, he seems to be missing, sir," Carter replied.

Mackenzie strained to hold his temper in check. "That's the final straw, Mr. Carter! The Fourth Cavalry has its horses stolen while on patrol, and the commanding officer loses his prize pacer, to boot!" He kicked a cooking pot savagely. "Get Captain Boehm here on the double."

Upon hearing his name, Boehm emerged from the darkness. "You want to see me, sir?"

"The Tonks are under your command, Mr. Boehm. How'd they know it was this Quanah person?"

"Heard a couple of riders call his name," Boehm answered.

"I see. Anything else, Captain?"

Boehm squirmed uncomfortably. "Well, ah, they said . . ."

"Spit it out, Captain. They what?" he asked brusquely.

"The Tonks said if we had cross-tied the horses and posted sleeping parties, this wouldn't have happened," Boehm answered awkwardly.

Lt. Carter tried to help. "'Cross-tie,' Colonel, is when you tie the horse's front foot to his diagonally opposite rear foot. And 'sleeping parties' are small groups of men scattered around the camp and the herd, sleeping on their weapons."

Mackenzie glared icily at Carter. "Thank you, Lt. Carter. I am familiar with those terms." He turned to Boehm. "Captain, at first light take six men and recover those horses. Take two Tonks with you. And don't take any unnecessary chances. Understand?"

"Yes, sir. Understood," Boehm replied.

Mackenzie examined the wreckage. "Now, Mr. Carter, let's put this camp back together."

At first light, several miles from the cavalry camp, Quanah and his raiders surveyed the stolen herd with satisfaction, bordering on delight. "A good thing," Quanah proclaimed. "Bad Hand must have a face like a thundercloud!"

To general laughter, Red Bird added, "And we have his grey horse!"

As the laughter subsided, Quanah sobered his riders. "The horse soldiers will come after their herd. So we must split into three groups. We will meet in three days where the Red River meets the Washita."

As the band of raiders dispersed, Quanah approached Mackenzie's prized mount. Impressed by this stunning piece of horseflesh, Quanah stroked the animal softly, murmuring soothingly. Ears up, the horse alertly watched him. When it had become accustomed to the Comanche, Quanah swung onto its back. Responding to knee pressure, the grey moved gracefully back and forth.

"That is a great horse," Red Bird said. "Bad Hand will miss him!"

Quanah slid from the grey. "Truly! So this is what we will do. . . ."

After Quanah outlined his plan to Red Bird, the raiding party rode off with the bulk of the captured herd. Quanah, Red Bird, a teenaged rider, Falling Water, and an aging warrior, Broken Bow, rode a circuitous route around the cavalry camp. Accompanying them was Mackenzie's fine grey pacer.

TWENTY-ONE

Indian Territory
Sunrise

After Captain Boehm's patrol had left camp in search of the herd, the camp itself was righted, and an accounting of the horses completed, Lt. Carter sought out Mackenzie. "Looks like we lost sixteen head, Colonel," he said.

Mackenzie snapped the fingers on his bad hand. "A damned disgrace, Lieutenant. Like taking candy from a baby."

"I know, Colonel. But I'll bet we get most of them back," Carter said soothingly.

"And I'll bet my grey won't be one of them," Mackenzie said darkly.

Lt. Carter looked uncomfortable. "Too early to tell, sir."

Waving excitedly, Trooper Davis approached the two men.

"Colonel, our pickets report two Indians riding towards us with a white flag!"

"Where, Corporal?" Mackenzie asked.

Trooper Davis pointed. "Off to the east, sir. You can barely make 'em out!"

Carter raised his field glasses. "By heaven, that's right! They're waving a white flag!"

Mackenzie studied the Indians through his binoculars. "Very well, Mr. Carter. Send Lieutenant Lee and Sergeant McSorley out to meet them with a white flag and an interpreter!"

There was a stir among the troopers, as all eyes were fixed on the two Indians, who sat their ponies atop a small rise. Under a white flag, with weapons cased, Lt. Lee led his little party out to meet them. There was speculation in the ranks.

"What you think they want?" Trooper Elias wondered.

"I dunno, but I'm some pleased I ain't ridin' out there with the Lieutenant," Trooper Nolan said.

"Yeah, fella could get kilt out there, white flag or no white flag," Eli added.

"Wouldn't mind if that sumnabitch Sergeant McSorley lost some hair. He's a real horse's patooty!" Nolan replied.

"Aw, don't wish that on no man," Eli said.

"Yeah, well, maybe if he just wets his pants a little," Nolan conceded.

As the troopers watched, the truce parties came face to face. Lt. Lee extended his palm upwards in the sign of peace. Red Bird returned the gesture, as Broken Bow gripped the white flag.

Red Bird waved his arms. "We Comanches have found something on the prairie and wish to return it to its owner." He paused, awaiting translation.

Lee looked puzzled. "Truly," he answered.

Red Bird waved his arms emphatically. "Truly. Our Chief, Quanah, believes the something found belongs to Bad Hand, chief of the Horse Soldiers."

"And what is this thing that Chief Quanah wishes to return to our chief?" Lt. Lee asked.

As the parties eyed each other, Red Bird turned in his saddle and called back over the ridge. In response, Water Falling appeared, leading Mackenzie's grey. He handed the lead to Red Bird. There was a prolonged silence as Lt. Lee tried to mask his astonishment. Red Bird signaled the interpreter.

"Quanah, Chief of the Quahadis, says that this is a fine pony. He is strong. Bad Hand will need him if he wishes to fight the Quahadi. Quanah does not wish to take advantage of Bad Hand by causing him to ride a poor pony. Quanah has spoken!" Red Bird handed the lead to the Sergeant. The three Comanche wheeled their mounts and cantered over the ridge and out of sight.

Sergeant McSorley was dumbfounded. "Well, I'll be teetotaly damned!"

"That about says it all," Lt. Lee agreed. "Let's go!"

As the truce party returned to camp, Mackenzie and Carter watched intently through their field glasses. "Colonel, isn't that your grey?" Carter asked in amazement.

Mackenzie adjusted his glass. "Just so, Lieutenant".

"What's this all about?" Carter wondered.

"We'll know soon enough," Mackenzie said calmly. The two officers cased their glasses as the truce party swirled into camp.

Lt. Lee led the grey triumphantly to his commanding officer. "Here's your horse back, sir," he said, flushed with success.

Mackenzie nodded. "So I see, Lieutenant. Your report please."

Lt. Lee tumbled his words. "Yes, sir. The Comanches we talked with were sent by Chief Quanah of the Quahadis. He said he wanted you to have your horse back because you would need him if you want to fight his people. He said he didn't want to put you at a disadvantage on a poor horse!"

Mackenzie looked at Lt. Lee as if he had just fallen out of the sky. "He said what?" As Lt. Lee started to repeat the message, he was interrupted angrily by his commanding officer. "Lieutenant, do you realize what's going on here? What this is all about?"

"Um, yes, sir. He's returning your grey," Lee said blankly.

"Wake up, Lieutenant! For God's sake!" Mackenzie fumed. "That Comanche, Quanah, he's playing with us! Taunting us! Humiliating us! Humiliating me! He must be laughing fit to die about now! His riders are probably wetting their pants they're laughing so hard!"

Lee looked confused. "But, sir, we got your horse back!"

"Damn the horse, Mr. Lee," Mackenzie raged. "What were you thinking when you accepted that horse? That was my decision, not yours!"

"But sir . . ."

"No *buts*, Lieutenant! Why do you think that Comanche gave back my grey? Out of the goodness of his heart? Because he had enough horses of his own? Of course not! He's way ahead of you, Mr. Lee. He did it because after stealing us blind he's added even more to our embarrassment. He's rubbing our face—my face—in it, damn him!"

Lt. Lee, having delivered his report and the grey to his commanding officer, hurriedly departed, chastened and confused.

Barely able to contain his anger, Mackenzie swept the countryside with his glass, focusing on the route of the Comanche messengers. As he watched, three riders were joined by a fourth, who, even at a great distance, could be seen astride an unusually large horse. As the truce party faded into the distance, a camp picket called the return of Captain Boehm's detail.

Boehm cantered into camp and joined his commanding officer.

"Your report, if you please, Mr. Boehm."

Boehm dismounted. "No luck, sir. They split into three parties and rode off in three different directions. One party seemed to be moving in this general direction.

"Thank you, Captain," Mackenzie said pleasantly, extending his glass. "Care to take a look? Look straight ahead to the west. See anything?"

Boehm adjusted the glass. "Yes, sir. Appears to be a dust cloud coupla miles out."

"That is indeed correct, Mr. Boehm," Mackenzie said. "That 'dust cloud' you saw is Quanah and his friends. Now, may I have my glass back?"

"What? Quanah? Comanches? Here?" Boehm was thunderstruck.

"Precisely, Captain," Mackenzie replied evenly. "He came bearing gifts. Mr. Boehm, are you familiar with the old saying 'Beware the Greeks bearing gifts'? If not, please remember it as your lesson for today!"

Boehm blinked. "Uh, yes, sir," he said blankly.

"Lt Lee will fill you in on all the excitement while you were on patrol. You're dismissed, Captain." The two traded salutes. Mackenzie stared out at the diminishing dust cloud. He took off his hat, smiled faintly, and shook his head. *Quanah, a master stroke, you rascal! I think I've underestimated you! Maybe some day we'll meet face to face. I'd like that!* As darkness fell and campfires glowed brightly, Mackenzie set his musings aside and rejoined his command.

The following day the scouting party struggled back to Fort Richardson in disarray, riding a variety of bedraggled horses and mules, some riding double.

TWENTY-TWO

Fort Richardson, Texas
October 1871

The officers of the Fourth Cavalry gathered in the post commandant's office for a briefing on the regiment's next campaign. The air was heavy with cigar smoke. Seated at his desk, Colonel Mackenzie surveyed his subordinates with satisfaction. "Gentlemen, a few things to keep in mind. I want to keep Quanah on the run. All the time. No let up. Always moving. We will not give him time to rest his horses or his men. No time to hunt. No time to put down winter meat. No time for the sick and wounded to recover. We will push, push, push, and push some more! I want Quanah to know that we're just one step behind him! Any questions?"

Lieutenant Lee raised his hand. "Are we to engage, sir, or just keep them on the move?"

"Good question. We will engage wherever possible. I expect they will try ambush and harassment, but I don't think they will want a major engagement. Quanah will be more concerned with moving his women and children to safety. Once he does that we can expect a major fight. I expect he will harass our horse herd constantly. So expect it and prepare for it. One last item, gentlemen. We will wear our summer uniforms. No need for winter clothing yet." He drummed his three fingers on his desk. "All right, gentlemen, let's go find him!"

The citizens of Fort Richardson turned out to bid the column and its supply wagons farewell. The women of the post gathered in little knots to wish their husbands and friends good luck, and to start counting the days until their return. A column of six hundred troopers, trailed by white-topped supply wagons, moved slowly out of the fort, amid bugle calls and scattered cheering. At the commanding officer's call, the men broke into their regimental song. Those musically inclined could detect that Sergeant McSorely was slightly flat.

After several days' march, the column was surrounded by a vast, migrating buffalo herd, seemingly unconcerned by the wagons. Taking every precaution to avoid panicking the animals into a stampede, the column slowed its march. By early evening, the last of the herd had passed, and soon after the column set up camp.

As the troopers erected their tents, started cooking fires, and secured their horses, Captain Boehm approached Mackenzie. "May I have a word with you, sir?"

Mackenzie looked up from a map. "Yes, Captain, what is it?"

"It's the Tonks, sir. They're some uneasy about that buffalo herd."

"How so, Mr. Boehm?" Mackenzie's interest was piqued.

"Stampede, sir. They're afraid if Quanah's any where near here, he might try to stampede that herd right smack through the center of our camp!"

"Yes, I see. And when do the Tonks think he might try this stampede?"

"They figure probably tonight. Sometime after midnight, maybe."

"I see. Thank you, Mr. Boehm," Mackenzie said thoughtfully. "And thank the Tonks for me, if you please. Pass the word. All officers and men to be on alert for a possible buffalo stampede!"

Boehm hesitated. "One more thing, Colonel. The Tonks say the best way to turn a stampede is for the men to wave their blankets at the herd. Really spooks 'em!"

Mackenzie nodded appreciatively. "Make sure everybody understands that, Captain. Tell the sergeants to pass the word. And, Mr. Boehm, your attention to duty is noted."

The chief of scouts saluted. "Thank you, sir," he said. " I'll pass the word."

In the dark of night, just past midnight, Quanah and a dozen Comanche riders quietly approached the tranquil buffalo herd. Positioned by the flank of the herd, the warriors rang cow bells, screeched, and waved blankets. The herd gradually started to move, jostling and crowding each other. Several animals started to run, and the movement became infectious. Soon, a few running buffalo became a thundering juggernaut, sweeping everything before it.

At the encampment, the pickets and nervous Tonk scouts were the first to recognize the distant rumble. The alarm was sounded, and sleepy-eyed soldiers tumbled from their tents, half-dressed and dragging their blankets. Some were without pants, some clad only in their long underwear, and two unlucky souls, stark naked, wore only their boots.

In the fading light of the campfires, the leaders of the buffalo herd were visible, heads down and running perilously close to the tents. A line of men, driven by cursing sergeants, held its ground, waving blankets and shouting in the face of a messy death. For several minutes, the outcome was in doubt, as the animals streamed past. Several men broke from the line in panic, only to be kicked back into place by bellowing sergeants. Gradually, as more men joined the blanket line, the buffalo began to veer away from the camp, to the great relief of the troopers. As the stampede subsided, a thick cloud of dust settled over the camp. Officers circulated among the troopers, patting backs and complimenting the men on their performance.

Mackenzie approached Corporal Davis, who was beating the dust from his clothing. "You all right, Corporal?"

Davis vigorously beat his clothes and flexed his shoulders. "I think so, sir."

"By thunder, Corporal, that was a close call! Those animals just missed us! Well done!"

"Thank you, sir. Ya know, Colonel, when I transferred to the Fourth, they never told me about no buffalo stampedes."

"No buffalo in Somers, Connecticut, Corporal?"

"Nope, never seen any. But I tell you, Colonel, this kinda thing does break the monotony, ya know?"

Mackenzie laughed. "There's something to be said for monotony. Especially after midnight!"

"Got a point there, sir."

Mackenzie walked back to his tent with Lt. Carter. "Things kinda quieted down, sir," Carter noted.

Mackenzie nodded. "You know, Mr. Carter, when I was a young cadet at West Point, they taught me about various military tactics. But somehow they never mentioned strategies to escape a buffalo stampede at midnight!"

Carter chuckled. "Why don't you write them and suggest that tactic be included in their next text book?"

"Maybe Quanah will help us write a new edition, Mr. Carter. Remind me to ask him someday."

"Now wouldn't that curl some hair in high places?" Carter replied. "Tell you what, Colonel. I'll buy the first copy!"

A week passed with no sign of the Quahadis. Wide-ranging patrols had only turned up old trails. Mackenzie called a meeting with Captain Boehm and two of his Tonkawa scouts, Job and Ethan. They conferred inside his tent with maps spread on a table.

"Sir, the Tonks think that maybe Quanah is heading for Palo Duro Canyon up on the Staked Plains. Safe place for the women and children," Boehm began.

"How so?"

"Winter coming quick," Job replied. Ethan nodded in agreement.

"Is this where Quanah goes every winter?"

"Most times he go there. Keep out of cold," Ethan explained.

"Have any of our people ever seen this Palo Duro Canyon?"

"Don't think so, sir," Boehm said. "But, Colonel, let me scout that area. Maybe we'll get lucky!"

Mackenzie turned to Carter. "Lieutenant?"

Carter nodded. "Certainly worth a try, Colonel."

Mackenzie snapped the fingers on his bad hand. "Permission granted, Mr. Boehm. Take six men. Travel light and travel fast. And get back here as soon as you can!"

Boehm stood up and saluted. "Thank you, sir. We'll pull out at first light. Give us two days and a little luck."

"Very well, Captain. Job, you and Ethan keep your eyes open. Good luck!"

Several days passed. The scouts moved cautiously through the canyons and cap rock bordering the Staked Plains. The Tonks scrutinized the ground for telltale signs, sometimes on foot, leading their horses. Job, at a distance from the detail, suddenly mounted his horse and swung his hat in circles. The detail joined him and discovered a virtual thoroughfare of tracks.

Job pointed. "Many, many lodges pass yesterday!"

Captain Boehm examined the sign. "What tribe?"

Job made the sign of the Comanche, a snake. "Comanche. Maybe Quahadi."

"We found them! Let's ride!" Boehm yelled exultantly.

Hours later, the detail swirled into the encampment. Captain Boehm pulled up at Mackenzie's tent. The post commander met him at the door flap. The scout saluted.

"We found them, Colonel! Big trail! Maybe two hundred lodges!"

"Good work, Captain! What direction are they moving?"

"Onto the Staked Plains, sir. Probably heading for Palo Duro Canyon!"

"Excellent! Please congratulate Ethan and Job for me. Now go get something to eat. You've earned it!"

Boehm saluted. "Yes, sir. Thank you, sir,"

Mackenzie turned to Lt. Carter. "All right, Mr. Carter, here's our chance. Pass the word. We leave immediately. Take what food and ammunition we'll need for seven days. Leave the wagons here. Detach the infantry and one troop of cavalry to stay with the wagons. Boots and saddles as soon as possible!"

"Yes, sir! On the double, sir!" Carter replied, exhilaration showing as he hurried off to brief his men.

With Mackenzie at its head, the column moved out quickly. As it approached the cap rock bordering the Staked Plains, dark clouds appeared, obscuring the sun. A biting wind whistled out of the north. Feeling the unexpected lash of the cold, the troopers added layers of clothing.

Climbing tentatively up the cap rock, the column entered the relatively unknown elevated plain, known as *Llano Estacado* to the Mexicans. The wind increased, bringing a cold rain with it. With their heads down against the frigid blasts, the Fourth Cavalry plodded on.

Captain Boehm returned from the column's perimeter and sought out his commander. "Comanche camp on the move just ahead, sir," he shouted over the roar of the wind. "Can just about make them out. They're moving pretty steady. They're throwing away anything that's heavy or that slows them down. A good sign, Colonel!"

"Any guards or sentries?" Mackenzie shouted back.

"Haven't seen any yet. Visibility's bad. But they're not going to leave their women and children unprotected!"

Before Mackenzie could speak, there was a burst of gunfire to the right of the column. A handful of warriors materialized out of the rain, fired a few shots, and disappeared back into the storm.

"Lieutenant," Mackenzie shouted into the wind. "Pass the word that nobody is to ride out after those forays! Understand? Nobody breaks ranks! Quanah is baiting a trap!" Boehm waved his understanding and rode off into the column.

As Mackenzie wiped rain from his face, another burst of gunfire broke out to the left of the column, as five warriors appeared, taunted the troopers, and vanished into the gathering darkness. During a momentary lull in the rain, fleeing tribes people could be seen in the distance—some walking, others mounted, and some leading a travois. As suddenly as they had appeared, they disappeared into the downpour.

The wind strengthened and brought a blast of stinging snow, blowing it horizontally to the ground. As the Comanche increased their harassing tactics, the ranks of the troopers closed up in an attempt to protect themselves.

Lt. Carter joined his commander in the fray. "It's a blue norther, Colonel," he shouted.

Mackenzie blew on his hands. "What the hell is a 'blue norther'?"

"Sudden blizzard out of the north. Bad wind. Low temperatures. Freezes animals stiff and stark if they're not protected."

"How long does it last?"

"Usually over pretty quick. One day. Two days sometimes."

Mackenzie shielded his eyes with his hand. "Mr. Carter, we'll pick up the pace and try to overrun the Comanche up ahead. Tell the men to expect more harassing attacks as we get closer." Carter saluted and rode off into the howling white.

The column, struggling with snow and bitter cold, found forward progress slow at best. Clothed in their soaking wet summer uniforms the troopers were preoccupied with their physical discomfort. A skirmish with an almost invisible enemy was not a priority. By now, visibility had closed to several feet, and isolated groups of warriors continued to worry the flanks. If a trooper strayed only a few feet from the column, he became disoriented, and found his way back only by the shouts of his fellows soldiers. The sky had turned prematurely dark, slowing the march even further, and hiding the fleeing tribes people.

Battered by the howling wind and driving snow, Mackenzie was faced with a decision: Pursue and perhaps overtake? Engage in a running battle with an enemy whose strength was unknown? Or break contact, go into camp, ride out the storm, and fight another day?

Mackenzie spurred his horse into the column. "Lieutenant Carter! Over here, Lieutenant! We halt right here! Make camp as quickly as possible! Protect the horses!"

Lt. Carter was surprised. "We're not going to try to take the village, sir?"

"No, Mr Carter, we're not," he shouted. "This is like fighting in a room full of feathers at midnight! No, Lieutenant, I am not going to risk the column!" A blast of icy wind rocked Carter in his saddle, as he acknowledged his orders. "The men can't pitch their tents in this mess," Mackenzie continued. "So have them lay out their canvas tents and crawl under them. Keep together for warmth. Post guards around our perimeter and change them every hour. And, Mr. Carter, I want the horses in a large circle." Mackenzie drew a diagram in the air. "Horses on the outside of the circle, held by their leads by troopers in the center of the circle. Understand? Each horse will be tethered to its rider!"

"Understood. But how about you, sir?"

Mackenzie was shivering violently. His rain-soaked clothing had induced muscle spasms, lingering effects from his six war wounds. Although in great pain, he maintained his dignity and stoicism. "I'll be all right, Lieutenant. Thank you."

Carter disappeared into the column, emerging shortly carrying a buffalo robe, which he wrapped around the shivering colonel. "Try this, sir. It's helped a lot of buffalo get through 'blue northers'!"

"Thank you, Mr. Carter. It should do the job," Mackenzie said, touched.

"I'm sure it will, sir. Now, if you'll excuse me, Colonel, I have to get back to the men."

Mackenzie pulled the robe around himself. "By all means, Lieutenant. I'm fine. See to the men."

At Lieutenant. Carter's orders, and after some initial confusion, a protective circle was formed. Each horse was tethered to its rider, who tried to stay warm under tent canvas and blankets.

As Mackenzie fought to stay warm, he was bumped in the semi-darkness by an ice-encrusted object. It was Corporal Davis, eyebrows and facial hair whitened with ice and sleet.

"Uh, sorry," Davis said numbly. He peered up. "That you, Colonel?"

"I think so, Corporal."

Davis wiped his nose. "Got a complaint, sir," he mumbled.

"A what?" Mackenzie asked incredulously.

"Got a complaint, Colonel," he repeated. "When I signed up for the Fourth Cavalry, they told me all about the nice, warm weather out here. They never told me about no blue northers! No, sir, they never did!" Davis brushed snow from his eyes. "Know what, Colonel?"

"No, Corporal, what?" Mackenzie answered, still incredulous.

"Colonel, I believe I've been bamboozled! And that's a fact!" Davis said seriously.

Mackenzie managed a smile. "Know what, trooper? They never told me, either!"

Davis's eyes watered in the cold as he wiped his dripping nose. "No! You, too?" he asked seriously.

Mackenzie managed a straight face. "Yup, me too! But I'll tell you something else, Corporal Whit Davis from Somers, Connecticut. I bet you could run a blue norther over those recruiting fellas, and they wouldn't know if it was pink, purple, or white! And that's a fact!"

Trooper Davis shivered. "You gotta point there, sir. Brrrr, cold enough to freeze the balls offen a brass monkey, as they say. Anyway, stay warm, Colonel," he added and disappeared into the whiteness.

Mackenzie swung his arms. "Sleep warm, trooper. At least we're not dying of thirst!"

As the night progressed, the wind howled incessantly, drifting the snow over the crude canvas shelters as troopers of the Fourth Cavalry huddled together in their wet, sodden summer clothing.

By the next morning the storm had abated, leaving a blanket of wet snow over the encampment. Mounds of white revealed haggard, wet troopers clinging to their horses' leads. Cooking fires coaxed from the snow were quickly circled by cold, shivering men. The morning sun burst out and the temperature soared to its seasonal level. The Staked Plains was a sea of white, as far as the eye could see.

The Comanche had vanished, as if by magic. An entire village had slipped through Mackenzie's fingers, cold and stiff as they might be.

As the shivering troopers were rousted from makeshift shelters by their grizzled sergeants, Mackenzie, wrapped in his buffalo robe, trudged through the snow, giving encouragement to his men. "Reveille, boys! Reveille! Be the first to see the sun. At least we're not dying of thirst! Let's see to the horses. First things first! Take a piss and feed your horse! Let's move, troopers. It's a bright, new day!" Gradually the camp came alive.

Lieutenant Carter plodded through the snow toward Mackenzie. "Coffee, sir, and your breakfast," he said, handing his commanding officer a steaming cup of black liquid and a piece of hardtack

"Thank you, Mr. Carter. How are the men?"

"Few cases of frostbite, Colonel. Dr. Kosack is looking at them right now. All in all, we made out pretty well considering."

"And you, Mr. Carter? You appear to be in one piece."

"I'm all right, sir. How are you?"

Mackenzie smiled wanly. "Let's just say that I'm functioning, Lieutenant". He handed the buffalo robe to Carter. "Here's your robe back, Lieutenant. It did the job just as you said it would."

As Carter took the soaking wet robe, the warmth of the sun caused it to steam.

Carter chuckled. "Look, Colonel, it has a life of its own!"

"And may it have many more, Mr. Carter. After rations, all officers here for a brief meeting, if you please."

The officers of the Fourth Cavalry straggled together for a briefing by their commander. Disheveled and in disrepair, they nevertheless maintained some semblance of military decorum. Mackenzie surveyed the group. "Well, gentlemen, you really do not look as if you could pass inspection," he said, smiling faintly. "But neither could I, gentlemen. So I assume you are all well and we shall carry on. We will form up and return to Fort Richardson. The Comanche managed to give us the slip this time. But there will be another day, I can assure you. I want an orderly line of march. Captain Boehm, your scouts will proceed ahead and flank the column as well. If there are no questions, gentlemen, that will be all. Boots and saddles as soon as possible please."

The camp bustled with activity, as the troopers prepared to depart. Within a few minutes, the column moved out, leaving the plateau of the Staked Plains, and entered the cap rock canyons of its border.

As the column wended its way through the maze of rock walls and boulders, there was a burst of gunfire ahead. Mackenzie joined Boehm near the front.

"What's the firing all about, Mr. Boehm?"

Captain Boehm pointed ahead. "Our scouts jumped two Comanche who were observing us from that canyon, sir!"

"Very well. Take eight men and flush them out," Mackenzie ordered.

"Right away, sir." Boehm wheeled his horse back along the column. "Sergeant, seven men and you dismounted as skirmishers. Carbines and pistols. Follow me!"

The troopers quickly formed up, and, with Captain Boehm leading, entered the canyon, which soon rattled with gunfire. The two warriors were dug into a canyon wall, and Boehm ordered his detail to attack and flush them out.

Mackenzie, true to his word, rode into the canyon. "Easy, Captain, your men are overly exposed," he cautioned.

"If you say so, sir," Boehm answered.

"Yes, Mr. Boehm, I do," Mackenzie said flatly. "Have your men rush the enemy in twos. One breaks and runs, two covers him. With four teams, you're less likely to have any casualties."

"Sergeant," Boehm shouted. "Four units of two! One man goes, two man gives covering fire! When you're ready!" The men, working as teams, dipped and ducked up the canyon as the Comanche fired at suddenly elusive targets. The gunfire swelled into a crescendo, and Mackenzie, impatient to finish the firefight, rode deeper into the canyon, drawing a shower of arrows, one of which sliced into his upper thigh. Grimacing in pain, Mackenzie gripped the shaft.

"Colonel, how bad?" Boehm asked, alarmed.

"Hellsfire, Captain, it struck meat!" Mackenzie gritted through clenched teeth. As he spoke, there was a sudden burst of gunfire, followed by a ragged cheer, signaling the death of the two warriors.

"Can you ride, sir?" Boehm asked.

Mackenzie, grunted in pain as blood seeped through his pant leg. "Goddamn it, Captain, of course I can ride!" he cursed irritably. "Go clean up that mess and see to your men! I'll be all right."

As the commanding officer returned to the column, the skirmishers reached the canyon floor with the bodies of the two Comanches. Trooper Elias nudged one with his foot. "Put up a pretty good fight!"

Trooper Nolan wiped his dripping nose. "Yup. An' they dinged old Mackenzie to boot!"

"Ya know, Wayne, that's his seventh hurt. Six in the war. Another one today!"

"Yeah, seven times in the wrong place! But I tell you, he was up front like he said. Man ain't afraid, Eli, man ain't afraid!"

The troopers shared a plug of tobacco, and methodically stripped the bodies for souvenirs.

Back at the column, the surgeon and the ambulance wagon had been summoned. The doctor inspected Mackenzie's latest wound, which bled profusely.

"Have to cut the arrow head out, Colonel. Lucky it's not embedded in the bone," the surgeon observed.

Mackenzie glared at him. "Damn it, doctor, be quick about it! We're holding things up!"

Dr. Kosack laid out his instruments. "As you wish, Colonel. This is going to smart a little!" After swabbing his upper thigh with disinfectant, the surgeon proceeded to cut the arrow head from Mackenzie's leg. Averting his eyes as sweat dripped from his face, he bit the sleeve of his uniform in silent agony. Lt. Carter shooed other officers away, allowing his commander to suffer in privacy.

Mackenzie looked at Carter. "Casualties, Lieutenant?" he asked in a strained voice.

"None, sir. Just the two Comanches." Mackenzie grunted his approval.

Dr. Kosack straightened up from his labors and handed his commander the blood-stained arrowhead. "That should do it, Colonel," he surmised. "You may want to save that for your grandchildren."

Mackenzie shook his head. "I keep going like this, I won't have any grandchildren. Doctor, you keep it."

"Sir, the dressing on your thigh has to be changed frequently," the surgeon noted. "Keep that leg as quiet as possible. Don't want to irritate the wound. You probably should ride in the ambulance wagon."

"I'm the one who's irritated, doctor!" Mackenzie snapped peevishly. "Goddamn it! The Commanding Officer of the Fourth Cavalry is not going to return to Fort Richardson in a damned ambulance wagon! And, doctor, one more thing. I do not wish for this episode to appear in your medical report. Understand?"

"Of course, Colonel, if that's what you wish," Dr. Kosack replied awkwardly.

"That's what I wish. And that's also an order," Mackenzie said grimly. Dr. Kosack looked at Lt. Carter in astonishment. Standing behind Mackenzie, Carter raised his eyebrows and shrugged.

"Of course, sir, I understand. No report," the surgeon replied.

Mackenzie stood up shakily with the help of a makeshift crutch. "Now, Mr. Carter, let's move this column out."

As their commanding officer was helped onto his horse, a bugle sounded "Boots and Saddles," and the column resumed its slow return to Fort Richardson.

TWENTY-THREE

At the close of the Civil War, Kansas and Texas teemed with all kinds of drifters who set out to make a few quick dollars hunting buffalo. The mighty Kansas herd, of some five million animals, had been reduced to one million, and that number was diminishing every day. As a result, impatient hunters turned to the relatively untouched Texas herd, violating forbidden Indian Territory boundaries. Adding insult to injury was the profitable collection and sale of buffalo bones, which were ground into fertilizer. Alarmed and infuriated as they watched their food supply melt away, the Comanche, Kiowa, and Southern Cheyenne turned their warriors loose on the hunters. Added emphasis was given to those trespassing on Indian lands, supposedly set aside by the Medicine Lodge Treaty.

Dodge City, Kansas
May, 1874

Dodge City was nooning when a bull train moved slowly down Main Street with its cargo of hides and bones. At the railroad siding, large ricks of buffalo bones bleached in the sun. As their oxen toiled through Dodge, their drovers provided a show for bystanders, cracking their bull whips in a noisy demonstration. Standing on the steps of a building marked "C. Myers' General Store," Billy Dixon and Charlie Myers enjoyed the show.
"Well, Charlie, looks like more business for you," Dixon said.
"Appears so. Business is slowin' down, though."
Dixon nodded. "Yeah, Kansas herd about gone."
"It's a fact. Texas herd ain't been hunted much though."

Dixon shook his head. "Too risky, that bein' Indian land and all. A fella could get kilt down there."

Myers laughed. "Seriously, Billy, I've been thinkin'. I just might send a bunch of hunters down there. Maybe a wagon train. Set up a trading post. Like that. Buy hides on the spot. Sell stuff right there—guns ammunition and such. Get enough hunters there, the Feathers will think twice about botherin' us. Whaddya think?"

"Yeah, would save luggin' our hides all the way back to Dodge. Get more time to hunt. Yeah, I like that idea," Dixon added.

"That's about the size of it."

"Where you thinkin' of settin' up?" Dixon asked.

"Probably at the ruins of that old Adobe Walls fort that Kit Carson built. Probably have to rebuild some."

Dixon snapped his fingers. "Yup. Know the spot. Good water and grass. Some timber, too."

"That's the place. Like to come along?"

"When you leavin'?" Dixon asked.

"Soon. Five to six days, maybe."

Dixon dug into his pants pocket and produced two coins. "These two fellers need some company, Charlie. Count me in!"

Myers shook Dixon's hand. "Glad to have ya, Billy. Don't spend them two dollars all in the same place!"

Dixon slipped the coins back into his pocket. "Stay right there, friends. Don't go away. Help is on the way!" he muttered.

Several days later, a wagon train of merchants and hunters moved slowly down Main Street. A large, noisy, high-spirited crowd had assembled to wish the train good luck. Two small boys raced down opposite sides of the street, poking their heads into saloons and stores. "The wagon train is leavin'!" they shouted excitedly. "Hurry up or you're gonna miss it! Goin' after them Texas buffalo!"

The stores and saloons emptied out, and citizens lined the street to cheer on the train. Several Ladies of the Evening appeared at windows and balconies, blowing kisses and waving. Somewhere an enthusiastic but discordant band produced appropriate sounds.

Amos Chapman watched the proceedings with interest. He shouldered his way through the crowd and walked beside Dixon. Billy looked down from his horse. "Hey, Amos! How are ya? Comin' with us?"

Chapman frowned. "Nah, Billy. Can't. Scoutin' for the Army now."

"That a fact?"

"Yup. Anyway, too many Kiowa an' Comanche down where you're goin'."

"Maybe, but there's a big herd down there!".

Chapman grinned. "That's why the Comanche and Kiowa are there! Anyway, good luck, Billy. Keep yer hair on!"

Dixon laughed. "Have so far, Amos. Same to ya!"

Amos dropped back into the crowd. The wagon train creaked and jingled slowly ahead, raising an immense cloud of dust.

Dixon turned to the rider next to him, a darkly handsome youth "Pretty nice send-off," he commented.

"Yeah, seems so," the young man replied.

Dixon's horse shied at the sound of a discordant tuba. A pretty painted lady waved frantically from a balcony. "Hey, Bat, that lady on the balcony is callin' you!" Dixon exclaimed.

Bat, a handsome man of twenty who signed on to Dixon's hunting party as second skinner, waved his hat to the ladies. "Be good, Selma. I'll be back soon. Gonna wait for me?" A wave of derisive laughter erupted from the wagons.

"Bat Masterson, you know I'll wait for you!" Selma called out over the uproar. Just don't stay away too long, Sweetie!" she added coyly. "A girl can't wait forever, you know!"

The train took up the refrain in unison, "Selma, oh, Selma, gonna wait for me?" Then, in falsetto, "Oh, Bat Masterson, a girl can't wait too long! Oh, sweetie!" Masterson turned beet red, much to Dixon's delight, as the train moved out of voice range of Selma and her friends.

To the pop of bull whips and the cursing of teamsters, the train rolled out of Dodge City.

As the wagons lumbered into Indian Territory, their progress was carefully monitored by Comanche riders.

It was early in a Texas June when the wagons arrived at the old Adobe Walls. The ruins of the old trading post lay on a wind-swept plain dotted with sage brush and sloping gently to a small creek.

The latest arrivals set to work immediately building Jim Hanrahan's

Saloon. Hanrahan, a prominent businessman in Dodge, was a prime mover in the illegal expedition to Adobe Walls, in utter disregard of the Medicine Lodge Treaty. Bob Wright and Charlie Rath, both from Dodge, partnered in a new sod supply house, while Charlie Myers and Fred Leonard supervised the construction of the trading post to deal primarily in buffalo hides. Brothers John and Wright Mooar, meanwhile, cautiously sought after the Texas herd, trading with hunters from several supply wagons. The restaurant, run by Hannah and Bill Olds, was last, together with the stable and corrals. Horses dragged timbers from the stream banks, sod was cut and fitted into walls and roofs, a well was dug, and pickets sunk in the ground as a corral. Gradually, the outpost known as Adobe Walls took shape.

And, fittingly, a celebration was held in Hanrahan's saloon, where beer and whiskey flowed freely. There was no piano, but there was a Jew's harp and fiddle. An occasional piece of roof sod cascaded over the bar and its patrons.

Dixon encountered Hanrahan behind his bar.

"Looks like you're kinda busy, Jim."

"Appears so, Billy. Here," Jim said as he slid a beer across the bar. "Have one on me."

Dixon sipped appreciatively. "Thanks. Tastes better out here than it did in Dodge."

Hanrahan glanced up at his roof. "Tastes even better if you can keep that damn dirt from fallin' into your glass!"

Dixon appraised the huge ridge pole that supported the sod roof. "It should settle down pretty quick. Anyhow, Jim, ain't you s'posed to eat a peck of dirt afore you die? Ain't that the sayin'?"

"It says 'eat.' Don't say nothin' about 'drinking' no peck of dirt," Hanrahan said sourly.

Dixon laughed. "Gives your beer a little body." He paused and took another sip. "Anyways, I'm ridin' out in the mornin'. See if I can find the herd. Should have been movin' though here by now."

"Never know about them animals. Migration's late this year," Hanrahan commented.

"Gonna travel light and fast. Maybe get lucky," Dixon said.

"When an' if you find 'em, hustle back. That kinda news is worth a few free beers!"

Dixon downed the last of his beer. "Take you up on that!"

He turned to leave as a large piece of sod dropped onto the bar, splashing precious beer and whiskey over three scruffy customers. One, an old, ragged hunter, wiped muddy beer from his face. "Hanrahan!" he bellowed. "Your damn roof don't work! You owe me two beers!"

Hanrahan slid two beers down the bar. "Sorry," he said contritely. "Have a couple on the house."

Early the next morning, Dixon rode out, searching for the first signs of the Texas herd. By midday, he met small groups of buffalo traveling north at a steady pace. Elated at these signs, he rode further south for several hours. Topping a low rise, he saw, for the first time, the enormous Texas herd, stretching from horizon to horizon, a sea of brown movement under a boiling cloud of dust. Overwhelmed by the vastness of one of the West's most spectacular sights, Dixon sat in reverent silence for several moments, then wheeled his horse and headed for Adobe Walls at a gallop.

As the sun dipped below the horizon, he cantered into the outpost. Swinging his hat and yelling, he slid from his horse in front of the saloon. "Yaaaah! Buffalo on the way!"

A crowd of hunters burst from the saloon.

"You seen 'em, Billy?"

"Where? How far? How many?"

"Think it's the Texas herd?"

Dixon wiped dust from his face. "Texas herd, all right. Biggest herd I ever seen! Should be here in a coupla days!"

The hunters cheered. "Billy Dixon for mayor of Adobe Walls!"

"Back to work, boys. Buffalo steaks, here we come!"

"C'mon, boys, let's buy old Billy a beer!"

"Hellsfire, fellas, we'll buy him a barrel!"

At the crowded bar, Billy Dixon recounted the details of his discoveries to a now bleary-eyed audience until the early morning.

The long-awaited announcement threw the post into a frenzy of excitement. Wagons were loaded, guns and ammunition were checked and packed. Food and supplies were purchased at the stores, which remained open well into the night. The little outpost, located deep in outlawed Indian Territory, was about to serve its purpose.

TWENTY-FOUR

Indian Territory, West Texas
June 17, 1879

A ramshackle wagon, drawn by four mules, rattled noisily up a gradual slope covered with buffalo grass. Billy Dixon rode ahead of the wagon with his Sharps rifle across his saddle. Riding alongside him was Bat Masterson. Frenchy, the party's cook, drove the wagon. Seated next to him was Cranky McCabe, a veteran first skinner. Tagging along, skittering hither and thither was a pretty pinto filly, whose mother was tied to the wagon. Fanny, a vagrant English setter who had adopted Dixon in Dodge, searched busily for prairie chickens.

The wagon topped the rise, and spread out as far as the eye could see was a vast herd of buffalo. New calves jumped playfully by their mothers, while young bulls butted heads. Several thousand animals were lying down, while the old bulls, in small groups quietly chewed their cud. Others, more belligerent, pawed the dust petulantly, or ground their horns into the dirt. The hunting party stopped. Dixon took off his hat and wiped sweat from his eyes.

"Ain't that a sight, Bat?" he said.

Bat looked up. "How many, you reckon?"

"Dunno. Coupla hunnert thousand maybe. Best enjoy it while we can."

Bat waved his hand towards the horizon. "I hear we ain't never gonna run outta buffalo."

Billy smiled and shook his head. "Heard wrong. Dodge City shipped a million hides last year. Can't last."

Bat looked at Billy skeptically. "Aw, I dunno about that."

Dixon shaded his eyes. "Well, I'll tell ya something, them Comanche and Kiowa, they know. An' they ain't so damn pleased about us hunters wipin' out their buffalo, neither."

Bat hesitated. "I s'pose."

Dixon continued. "And I'll tell ya somethin' else. Them Comanche ain't gonna roll over and say 'uncle.' Neither are them Kiowa. There's gonna be some trouble. In a way, can't blame them."

"You sidin' with the Feathers?"

Dixon smiled and shook his head. "Naw, not really. But they've been the Big Dogs around these parts for a long time. They ain't about to change."

Bat cocked his head. "Hope you're wrong."

"I ain't wrong. Count on it," Dixon said flatly.

Dixon playfully lifted Bat's hat and mimed a scalping. "Nice head of hair you got there. Hope you can keep it!"

Bat swatted Dixon with his hat. "Looks better on me than on some Comanche's war shield!"

Dixon became all business. "Awright, boys, we'll make a shoot here. Frenchy, you set up camp by that creek down hill. We're burnin' daylight. Let's get a move on." As the skinners unloaded their gear, Frenchy moved toward the creek, humming off-key to his mules. The trailing mare was untied from the rear of the wagon, and the nursing filly nuzzled close to her mother.

On the ridge Dixon set up his shooting sticks, arranged a handful of cartridges by his side, and bellied down in the grass. He tossed a handful of dust into the air. "Wind's about right," Dixon muttered to himself. Gauging the distance to the nearest bull, Dixon adjusted the windage and range on the telescopic sight of his rifle. Slipping the large cartridge into the rifle's chamber, he squeezed off his first shot. There was a thunderous *boom*, a cloud of powder smoke, and a bull, some two hundred yards away, dropped abruptly. The surrounding buffalo milled about uneasily, then resumed grazing. Dixon reloaded, fired, and another bull fell. After some thirty minutes of firing, Dixon crawled off the ridge.

"You done?" Bat asked.

Dixon shook his head. "Naw. Barrel's too hot. Hand me that canteen."

He poured the contents of the canteen over the barrel of his rifle. There was a hissing sound, and a cloud of steam rose from the cooling barrel. "That oughta do it. Sit tight, boys. Few more shots."

He crawled back to the top of the ridge, and after several more shots, the herd gradually moved out of gunshot range. The ground in front of Dixon was strewn with dead animals. He stood up stiffly, brushed the dirt from his clothing, and beckoned to his skinners. "Let's go, boys. Runnin' outta daylight."

The skinners waved in acknowledgement and approached the first carcass. Bat expertly rolled the animal onto its back, cut along its belly with a razor-sharp skinning knife and then made a cut up each leg. Cranky hitched their horses together, connected another hitch to the side of the buffalo's hide, then urged the horses ahead, ripping the hide from the carcass. Having set up camp, Frenchy arrived with the wagon, and the men loaded its bed with fresh, dripping hides. Far off, the sound of gunfire reverberated.

Bat cocked his head, listening. "Sounds like another outfit's doin' some business," he said.

Cranky nodded. "Sound of them Sharps is a comfort, I tell ya. Helps keep them Feathers away."

Bat strained with a carcass. "Maybe. Gimme a hand here, Cranky."

The huge bull was rolled onto its back.

"Hear tell two other outfits out yonder," Cranky said conversationally.

"Could be. Everybody's gettin' their share an' then some," Bat grunted.

Fresh hides were loaded into the wagon. The mules shied at the smell of blood.

"Frenchy, quiet them mules, for Gawd's sake," Bat said irritably. He finished loading the wagon and wiped his hands on the grass.

Cranky cleared his throat. "Ya know, Bat, them buffs are my only wages. My beans 'n' bacon, you might say."

Frenchy chuckled. "And yer whiskey supply. Don't forget that! While yer at it, Bat, how 'bout cuttin' me a bunch of tongues and some ribs?"

Bat smiled. "Because you're a good feller, an' can cook a little, I'll throw in a coupla livers." The young skinner fingered his knife and plunged back into the blood.

Frenchy had pitched a good camp for the night. Two, white canvas tents were surrounded by hides, pegged out on the ground, hair-side down. A small fire flickered, casting dancing shadows. The shallow creek meandered close by. A pot of molten lead simmered by the fire and Billy Dixon, in his sweat-stained clothing, sat cross-legged by the fire with his bullet moulds, casting the heavy bullets needed for the next day's hunt. At his elbow were empty cartridge cases. The powder, for the re-loading process, was placed a safe distance from the fire. Bat very deliberately honed two skinning knives on a treadle-operated whet-stone. Frenchy puttered about with his pots and pans, having cleaned up after supper, while Cranky stretched out on a tarpaulin, contentedly smoking his pipe. The filly nursed fitfully on her mother. Asleep by the fire, Fanny twitched fitfully as the night birds overhead chirped softly.

At sunrise the next morning, Dixon broke camp.

"Damnation!" Cranky McCabe grumbled. "These skins so stiff a man kin hardly handle 'em." He shoved a hide onto an already overloaded wagon.

"Dollars in yer pocket, friend," Frenchy said.

"And they stink, too," Cranky added.

"Life is tough," Frenchy said sardonically. "How long kin you hold yer breath?"

Cranky bridled. "Come to think of it, yer cookin' don't smell so good either, Frogface!"

Dixon intervened. "C'mon, boys. Get a move on. Still a good poke back to the Walls."

"Now, Hanrahan's saloon, that's gonna smell good!" Cranky interjected, wanting the last word.

Bat lashed down the last few hides. "Awright, boss, we're ready to roll."

"Everything lashed down tight?" Dixon asked, as he mounted his horse. He scanned the camp one last time. "Where's Fanny?"

"Yeah, we're all set," Bat said. "Fanny? She's around here someplace. She's a smart dog. She'll catch up."

As the hunting party departed for Adobe Walls, there was the boom of other buffalo guns in the distance. Fanny, the absent English setter, dashed from the brush and was hoisted aboard the cook wagon by Frenchy.

After traveling all day, the hunting party returned to the walls. Frenchy halted the wagon at Myers' store, where hides were stacked in towering piles. Charlie Myers had been a busy buyer.

"Hold it right here, Frenchy, while I find Charlie Myers," Dixon said.

Frenchy wiped his mouth expectantly. "Shake a leg, Billy. Hanrahan might run outta whiskey!"

"Yeah, or maybe beer!" Cranky added.

"No chance. Back in a minute," Dixon said.

As Dixon entered the store, Myers was doling out ammunition to a scruffy hunter.

He looked up. "Hey, Billy, how'd your hunt go?"

"No complaints," Dixon said. "Wagon's over by the hide yard."

"Be with you in a minute," Myers replied. He turned to his customer. "That'll be six bits, friend."

"You've got a real pile of hides out there!" Dixon marveled. "What're you paying?"

"Two bucks a hide. Three if it's prime," Myers said matter-of-factly.

"Sounds about right. Go have a look at my wagon."

"Don't have to," Myers replied. "Gimme an hour. Settle up then." He paused. "You see any Feathers out there?"

Dixon shook his head. "Nope. Not a sign. But that don't mean nothin'. You know an' I know that they're out there somewhere."

"Yeah, it's been pretty quiet," Meyers said.

"Here, maybe," Dixon said. "But I heard that a couple of skinners named Dudley an' Wallace went under over to Plummer's camp. And somebody said that Blue Billy and Antelope Jack lost their hair a coupla days ago. Only about a day's ride from here."

"Heard that, too," Myers replied. "Next coupla nights gonna be a full moon. Comanche moon. Keep yer eyes peeled, son!"

"Count on it,' Billy responded. "You want me, I'll be over at Hanrahan's helpin' Cranky spend his wages."

"Wet yer whistle, Billy. You've earned it!"

"Now that you mention it, was kinda dry out there!"

"That's why Jim opened a saloon," Myers said.

Dixon laughed and turned to leave, then hesitated. "Charlie, you got plenty of cartridges in stock?"

"Hell's fire, yes! Got enough to fight a war!"

"Good. Save me a case," Dixon said. Charlie Myers nodded and scribbled a note on his order pad.

TWENTY-FIVE

Angered by the hide-hunters' invasion of their Treaty lands, the Quahadi Comanche called for a Sun Dance to seek the help of the Great Spirit. Led by Quanah and a young medicine man named Isa-Tai, the Indians desperately sought a solution for the violations of the Medicine Lodge Treaty. Isa-Tai claimed he could raise the dead and possessed a magic yellow paint that provided protection from the white man's bullets. He was said to have risen into the heavens to talk to the Creator, who promised the Comanche His help if they went to war with the Whites. Impressed, the Quahadis sent Quanah to the neighboring tribes of Kiowa and Cheyenne asking for their help. He was received with open arms. The pipe was smoked. War was agreed upon. But first, said the tribal elders, the buffalo hunters must be dealt with. After they are wiped out, the Tejanos will be next. Rumors of an attack began to circulate among the reservation Indians at Fort Sill.

Adobe Walls, West Texas
June 24

As the blazing red orb of a setting sun cast long shadows across Adobe Walls, a small detachment of two bluecoats, troopers Ben Elias and Wayne Nolan, led by scout Amos Chapman, trotted into the compound. While the troopers watered their horses, Chapman sought out Charlie Myers at his store.

"Mr. Myers, got a message for you and Mr. Hanrahan," Chapman said.

"What kinda message?" Myers inquired.

"It's sorta private," the scout answered.

"I see. I'll get Hanrahan. How about Rath an' them Mooar brothers?"

Chapman nodded. "Yeah, maybe best get Mr. Wright and Mr. Leonard, too."

Myers rounded up his fellow merchants and led them back to his store. "You fellers all know Amos Chapman?"

"Sure do. What's up, Amos?" Rath asked.

Chapman lowered his voice. "Fort Sill just sent word over to us at Camp Supply that you're gonna get hit by a huge war party the day after the next full moon. That's two days from now!" There was a stunned silence.

"What?" Rath said in disbelief.

Chapman nodded. "Yup. Comanche, Cheyenne, an' Kiowa!"

"You serious?" Myers asked.

"Damn straight, I'm serious," Chapman replied. "Rumors started in the reservations. Fort Sill looked into it. Sent me to warn you?"

Leonard flushed. "How big a war party?"

Chapman shrugged. "Heard big. Maybe four, five hundred!"

"Five hundred! We don't even have thirty people here! One woman, a bunch of clerks, and a few hunters," Myers said incredulously. "We're sittin' ducks!"

"Army thinks maybe you should pull out!" Chapman offered.

Hanrahan exploded. "Leave? No way! My life savings are wrapped up in this here saloon! Rest of you, same as me. All our money's invested right here in these stores! We leave, we lose everything!"

"Army knows that," Chapman continued. "But the Army can't do nothing. Can't help you! You're in Indian Territory. Medicine Lodge Treaty land! Army won't set foot in here!"

Myers motioned to Hanrahan. "Jim close the door. We gotta come up with some kinda plan." Hanrahan slammed the door shut, and almost immediately there was an insistent banging on the closed door as several hunters sought to buy supplies.

"We're closed. Come back in an hour," Myers shouted. The banging stopped. "Awright, boys, what are we gonna do?"

Rath squirmed uncomfortably. "I'm gonna pull up stakes. Leave the store with my clerk and hope for the best!"

"Ain't you gonna tell him? What if he wants to leave, too?" Myers asked.

Rath grimaced. "I'll pay him extra to stay."

"We hafta keep this between us," Myers said. "If it gets out, the whole damned kit and kaboodle, all them hunters will pull out. We'll lose everything!"

"I'll be going with Rath," Bob Wright said lamely. "We're partners."

Hanrahan's temper flared. "Ain't none of you gonna stand and fight? You're gonna leave a woman here to help fight this place?"

"Brother John and me gotta get back to Dodge. Business matter," Wright Mooar said nervously.

"Jim, I'll stay," Dave Leonard said quietly.

"Look, Hanrahan," Myers said. "There's a bunch of hunters hanging around here. They shoot purty good and they don't scare easy. You'll be awright."

"Maybe," Hanrahan answered. "But I ain't leaving!"

"Your choice," Rath said. "I'm outta here at first light with Bob Wright!"

Hanrahan turned to Rath. "That couple who run your restaurant, Bill and Hannah Olds. Take them with you."

Rath nodded. "Yeah, I'll ask them."

Hanrahan put his hands on his hips. "So! Upshot is you four go. Dave Leonard and me stay. For God's sake, keep this under your hat. Somehow me and Dave have gotta figure a way to keep everyone from gettin kilt." There was an embarrassing silence. Hanrahan continued. "When you get back to Dodge, send some riders out here quick. And keep your fingers crossed!" He paused. "C'mon, Amos, Let's you and me get a drink." The gathering broke up, and Myers reopened his store in a last-minute effort to make a few dollars.

After the meeting, Myers and Amos Chapman entered the saloon, where they surprised Billy Dixon.

"Amos! What're you doing way out here?" he asked.

Chapman smiled and shook Dixon's hand. "Army business, Billy. Me and a coupla bluecoats are trailin' some horse thieves."

"Ain't you a long way from home?" Dixon inquired.

"Sort of," Chapman said casually. "Still got yer hair, I see"

"Amos, if you need a place to spread your bedroll, you're welcome down by my wagon."

"Thanks, Billy," Amos replied. "But we're movin' on tonight."

Dixon clapped Chapman on the shoulder. "C'mon, Amos, buy you a drink afore you leave."

Chapman brightened. "That's two offers! Take you fellas up on both!"

Whiskey in hand, the three men leaned on the crude bar in Hanrahan's. Close by, two half-drunk hunters started to taunt Chapman's trooper escort. A fight was in the offing. Hanrahan, wise in the ways of bar fights, beckoned his bartender. "Keep the lid on things, Oscar."

"Tryin' to, Mr. Hanrahan," Oscar replied. "These hunter fellas think them soldier boys are snoopin' around here looking for horse thieves . . . or deserters, maybe."

Hanrahan turned to the hunters. "Howdy, boys! Them Johnnies there just escorted my friend here through some rough country," he said pleasantly.

One of the hunters swayed and looked closely at Chapman. "Ain't he the one who lives with them Injuns?" he snarled.

The other hunter squinted blearily at the scout. "Damned if it ain't," he mumbled. "Prolly spyin' for them heathen!"

His companion dribbled whiskey down his greasy shirt. "You ain't welcome, here, squaw man. Go back to yer Injun friends!" He lurched menacingly towards Chapman.

"Hold on there, hoss," Hanrahan said angrily. "Amos Chapman here is my friend. And I'm gonna buy him and his friends a drink. And then they're gonna be on their way. Ain't that right, fellas?" Oscar slid a bottle toward Chapman and another toward the troopers. Nodding their appreciation, the troopers poured their drinks, hitched up their pants deliberately, and swaggered enticingly past the hunters.

Trooper Elias sniffed the air dramatically and turned to Hanrahan. "Much obliged for the drink, Mr. Hanrahan." He sniffed the air again. "Hellsfire, somethin' musta died in here! Phew! What a stink!"

Trooper Nolan grimaced. "Naw, it ain't that! Smell like that would give a skunk a bad name! It's them hunters! I smelt skunks back home that smelt better than them!"

One of the hunters rose to the bait. "Who you callin skunks, soldier boy," he snarled, fumbling for his skinning knife.

The fight ended as soon as it began, as Hanrahan and Oscar expertly dropped the two hunters with bar mallets. Stepping over and around the inert hunters on the floor, Chapman and his escort drained their glasses. Oscar sloshed the groggy hunters with a bucket of water. "Prolly the first time in six months them fellas had a bath," he commented, wrinkling his nose.

Having delivered their somber message, Chapman and the troopers mounted up and rode out of Adobe Walls, bathed in the white light of a full Comanche moon.

TWENTY-SIX

Comanche Village, West Texas
June 24

Scores of the finest fighting men of the Kiowa, Cheyenne, and Comanche assembled in preparation for the upcoming battle. Summoned to a war council, they faced Quanah and Isa-Tai in a huge half circle. Quanah spoke first.

"Hear me, my brothers! It is a good thing that you have come. My heart is full. Our brother, Isa-Tai has great medicine. He has done wondrous things. I wish for you to hear him."

Isa-Tai, wearing a wreath of sage, extended his arms toward the heavens. "Brothers! Quanah will lead us to a great victory over the white hunters! The Great Spirit told me so when I spoke with him up in the clouds. He gave me this powerful medicine!" He held a bowl over his head. "Bullets will not harm you if you use this medicine!" He smeared yellow paint from the bowl across his arms and face. "We will kill the Whites in their sleep, and our buffalo will return again to us in even greater numbers! But, my brothers, heed my words! Do not harm any living thing on our path to the hunters' camp! To do so will destroy my medicine! I have spoken!" The warriors responded with a roaring acclamation.

Quanah raised his arms to the sky. "Brothers! Make your hearts strong! We have waited for this Day! We have longed for this Day! And our Day is almost here!" The warriors raised their weapons in joyous salute.

In the early hours of the following day, the huge war party rode slowly from the village, with extra ponies and pack animals trailing at the rear. The village women formed two facing lines, stretching out of the village, and, as their warriors rode out between the lines, the women ululated in quavering crescendos in an eerie farewell.

The five hundred riders raised a large dust cloud as they moved purposely toward Adobe Walls. A number of teenaged riders, determined to prove themselves in battle, rode with their elders. Two of them, riding at the rear of the war party, detected movement in a patch of tall grass and, upon investigation, discovered a skunk digging for insects. The boys quickly shot it with an arrow, pleased that they had acquired a revered skin for ceremonial use.

In late afternoon, the war party halted and scouts were sent forward. After several hours, they reappeared in the distance, making circles to their right, telegraphing a successful scout. Quanah and a group of war chiefs rode to meet them.

"Tell me what you saw," Quanah said.

"Truly, we saw four lodges made of dirt and wood. We saw horses moving around. We did not see many Whites," the scout reported.

Quanah turned to the chiefs. "Good! Very soon we will kill some white hunters. We will ride until dark. Then we will rest and make our hearts strong." The war party reassembled and moved quietly toward Adobe Walls.

When darkness gradually overwhelmed the riders, Quanah called a halt. "We will rest here. Hold your pony's lead in your hand. No fires. Tomorrow will be our day!"

A full moon, so bright that it bathed the compound in near daylight, made the warm June night conducive to sleeping in the open, an option several whiskey-soaked hunters and freighters preferred. Awake and worried, however, were Dave Leonard and Jim Hanrahan. An Indian attack was imminent, and they had yet to determine how the personnel of the Walls could be warned without casting suspicion upon themselves, as having been forewarned. The two men conferred in low tones inside the saloon.

"There hasta be a way to do this!" Hanrahan said.

Leonard lit a cigar. "I know! I know! You're right! But time is runnin' out! If these fellas ever learn we were warned and didn't tell them, it's gonna be our ass and then some!"

Hanrahan paced back and forth. "Well, maybe we could fire a shot. Wake everybody up! Tell them a wolf was pestering the stock!"

"Yeah, just before daylight! Get everybody up!" Leonard, added, newly confident. "If the Feathers come at sunrise, like they usually do, we'd at least be half-ready!"

"Damn, it might just work!" Hanrahan said enthusiastically.

At that moment, a large piece of sod pulled loose from the roof and dirt cascaded down upon the bar "Again?" Leonard said angrily. "Next thing we know that ridgepole will let go and there'll be hell to pay!" The two men looked at each other as realization dawned.

"That's it, Jim! The ridgepole!"

"Yeah! If that ridgepole snapped, would sound just like a shot!"

"And it's high enough so nobody could really tell if it busted or not!" Leonard added.

Hanrahan warmed to his task. "It needs to be braced, right? Somebody's gotta cut a pole for a brace, right? Takes time. Everybody's gotta help! Lots of noise! Everybody up! It's perfect!"

"You want to fire the shot?" Leonard asked.

"Should. It's my saloon!"

Leonard stretched. "Whew! Feel better already! Don't mind tellin' you that! Gonna get some shut-eye. Be over at Myers' store if you need me." The two men shook hands. Hanrahan was left in the silent saloon, eyeing the ridgepole speculatively. Outside, the Comanche moon shone brightly in the peaceful Texas sky.

TWENTY-SEVEN

Adobe Walls, West Texas
June 25

At the restaurant, Hannah and Bill Olds were busy serving lunch to a handful of hunters. Seated at a crude table, the customers drank their coffee from tin cups and speared bacon from a platter with their skinning knives. A tame crow flitted back and forth near the tables, snatching scraps from the dirt floor and cawing raucously.

Billy Tyler, a young freighter with a pock-marked face, waved his knife at the bird. "Get outta here, you black rascal!"

Cranky expertly skewered the last biscuit on the platter. "Hear them crows are smarter than most people."

Billy Tyler chewed determinedly. "Meanin'?"

"Meanin' he's prolly smarter 'n you," Cranky said politely.

Tyler bridled. "Is that so?"

"Yup."

"Well, if he's so all-fired smart, he better not crap in this here dining room!" Tyler replied.

"Now, now, boys!" Hannah intervened. "Billy's right. My goodness, our restaurant is no place for that bird!" She shooed the crow away with a broom. "There, that's better. How about some more coffee. fellas?"

"Yes, ma'am, if you please," Tyler said smugly.

Ignoring her, Cranky shouted to the cook. "How about some more biscuits, old man? Be nice if they wuz hot for a change!"

Old Man Keeler, presently a cook, but an old frontiersman well known to the Cheyenne, squinted at Cranky from the kitchen. "You had enough, Cranky. An' besides, you dint say please!"

"Only time I'll say please is when they're hot, which they ain't most times."

"Don't make no difference, no how. Plumb outta biscuits," Keeler said smugly.

"Dint want no more, anyhow," Cranky muttered under his breath.

As the argument ended, a sizable dog entered the restaurant and made the rounds, cleaning scraps from the floor. Tyler snapped his fingers. "Here, Fanny. C'mere, girl," he said. Fanny sidled up to Tyler, waggling furiously. "That's a good girl," Tyler said.

"Sorta looks like she's gonna be a Mama."

"Does at that," Cranky said. "Who you think is the Daddy?" Old Man Keeler spoke up. "Prolly my old dog, Duke, here. He's a real devil with the ladies!" He reached down and patted Duke. "Ain't cha, boy?"

"Where'd Fanny come from?" Tyler asked.

"She adopted Billy Dixon in Dodge," Cranky explained.

"Looks sorta like a bird dog, don't she? Maybe keep that crow outta here," Tyler said.

Hannah Olds laughed. "That would be nice!"

Cranky stood up. "C'mon, Fanny, let's you an' me go find Mr. Billy Dixon. Got better things to do than lissen to some old foolish cook." He tossed a silver coin on the table. "That's for lunch, Mrs. Olds."

Old Man Keeler angrily threw a biscuit at Cranky. "Here's yer biscuit, you horse's patooty!" He turned to Hannah Olds. "Sorry about the language, ma'am. Cranky's an old friend but I hafta keep him in line!"

Rath entered the dining room. "Hannah, you and Bill got a minute?"

"Sure do, boss. What's going on?" Bill answered.

"I'm leavin' for Dodge in a coupla hours. Thought maybe you'd like to come along. Get back to town, so to speak."

"Who'd take over the restaurant?" Hannah asked.

"Old Man Keeler could take over," Rath answered.

"It's up to you, Hannah," Bill said softly.

"Well, Hannah, what do you think?" Rath asked.

"We need the wages, Mr. Rath," Hannah replied. "I think we'll stay. Not much for us in Dodge."

"You sure? You're the only woman out here. What if you need a doctor or dentist or something?" Rath persisted.

"I'll be all right." Hannah said. "The boys watch over me. We'll stay for the summer. Maybe go back after the fall hunt. Is that alright with you, Bill?"

Bill Olds nodded. "Fine with me, Hannah." He turned to Rath. "Guess we'll stay, Mr. Rath. But thanks for thinkin' of us."

"I . . . well . . . it's up to you," Rath said reluctantly. "If you change your mind, let me know." As he spoke, the crow fluttered back into the restaurant, cawing loudly.

"Tell you what, Mr. Rath," Olds said. "Instead of us, take that damned bird with you!"

The crow settled on a table and stared suspiciously at Olds. Attracted by the glitter of Cranky's silver coin, the crow waddled across the table, picked up the coin, and flapped out of the building.

"Come back here, you thievin' sumnabitch!" Olds shouted. "Damn! That was two bits!"

"Don't you fret," Hannah replied. "He'll hide it somewhere inside here. We'll find it."

"We'd better!" Olds grunted. He turned to Old Man Keeler. "You ever cooked a crow?"

The cook shook his head. "Not yet, I ain't."

Unable to sway the Olds, Rath quietly left the restaurant, eager to head back to Dodge and be out of harm's way.

In another corner of the dining room, Billy Dixon, Bat Masterson, and Willie Ogg were finishing their lunch.

"Willie," Dixon began. "We're gonna take another crack at that Texas herd. We'll pull out at first light. Get your stuff together if you're comin' with us. Bat, you seen Frenchy?"

Bat nodded. "Yeah, over at Hanrahan's."

"He got the flour and bacon supplies?"

"Dunno. I'll go see."

"Willie, tell Frenchy and Cranky to bring their bed rolls down to the wagon tonight. Get a fast start in the morning," Dixon said.

Ogg produced a toothpick. "Sounds reasonable to me."

Bat pushed back from the table. "I'll go find Frog Face."

Humming to herself, Hannah stacked the dirty dishes and wiped their table clean. Dixon pushed his chair back. "How's it feel to be the only woman out here?"

Hannah smiled and brushed her hair back from her face. "I don't mind. Nice to be out of Dodge for a spell."

"I s'pose," Dixon answered. "Nice for us out here to see a lady now and then. Keeps us a little civilized, you might say."

Hannah smoothed her skirt. "Nice of you to say so, Billy."

"Mean it," Dixon said as they watched Billy's pretty filly frisk about its mother.

Hannah shaded her eyes. "Isn't she the prettiest thing?"

Dixon smiled. "Sure is. Full of ginger. Gonna be a very pretty pony some day. Maybe call her Ginger."

"I've always wanted a filly like her," Hannah said wistfully.

"Really?"

"Yes, maybe some day I'll get one," Hannah said.

"Tell you what, Mrs. Olds," Billy said. "You like her, she's yours!"

"No! Really? Are you funnin' me?" Hannah said in disbelief.

"Nope. She's yours if you want her."

Tears welled in Hannah's eyes. "Oh, Billy! I don't know what to say!"

"Just say you want her!"

"Oh, yes! I want her," Hannah said fervently. "She's so beautiful! How can I ever thank you?"

Dixon laughed. "You just did! I figger you'll take better care of her than I will when I'm out huntin' somewhere. Look at it this way, Mrs. Olds. Now you got another female out here to keep you company. And both of you are right pretty!"

Hannah blushed. "Glory be! I just remembered! I have a fresh-baked apple pie out in the kitchen and it's yours if you want it!"

"Apple pie? Sounds like a good swap to me," Dixon allowed.

Hannah walked out to the corral, fondled the filly affectionately, and fed her an apple from the kitchen. Pie in hand, Dixon watched the budding love affair before returning to his wagon.

Outside of Adobe Walls, two large freight wagons pulled by tandems of oxen plodded slowly toward the outpost. Laden with supplies, each wagon was emblazoned with SHADLER BROS. FREIGHT on its side. Reaching Hanrahan's saloon, the wagons halted, and their owners, Ike and Shorty

Shadler, began unloading.

Jim Hanrahan sauntered up to the wagons. "Got some freight for me?"

"You Mr. Hanrahan?" Ike asked.

"You got it," Hanrahan replied.

"Do indeed," said Shorty, sweating profusely. "Soon as we get unloaded, got some papers for you to sign." He worked unabated as he talked.

"Good," Hanrahan said. "Why you bustin' yer backsides? I ain't in no all-fired rush for my stuff."

Ike paused. "Mr. Hanrahan, we gotta get unloaded, take on a load of hides, and get outta here 'toot sweet,' as the Frenchies say."

"What's the rush?" Hanrahan asked innocently. "Lay over a day or two. Treat you to a coupla free beers!"

Shorty grunted under a heavy barrel. "Appreciate that, Mr. Hanrahan. But we run into some fellas two days ago who told us about some killings hereabouts. Four, five hunters cashed in!"

"Who?"

Shorty wiped the sweat from his eyes. "One was a fella called Blue Billy. Another was called Antelope Jack. Know 'em?"

Hanrahan nodded. "Yeah. The Jack fella was from England, and Blue Billy was from Germany."

"That right?" Ike said. "Prolly wished they'd stayed home! They say it was Comanche or Kiowa."

"Anyways, we're gonna load up tonight, sleep right here, and pull out at daylight," Shorty explained.

"Up to you. Drinks on the house when you're done," Hanrahan said.

"Much obliged," Ike replied. "A nice, foamy beer would slide down pretty good about now."

Shorty mopped his face with a grimy bandanna. "No argument from me."

As Hanrahan turned to leave, he noticed a huge black Newfoundland asleep in the shade of the wagons. "That your dog? Looks like a small horse!"

Shorty stopped working. "Yessir. That's old Bonaparte! Good size, ain't he? Nobody messes with our wagons when old Bonaparte's around!"

"Expect so!" Hanrahan marveled. "Ain't never seen a dog that big!"

"Yeah, well, he eats a ton! Good thing buffalo meat's free!" Ike added.

"I bet!" Hanrahan said as he knelt down to pet the dog. Bonaparte promptly growled and showed his teeth.

Shorty chortled. "What'd I tell ya? Ain't he somethin'?"

Hanrahan backed away. "Yeah, see what you mean! When you fellas come up to the saloon, best leave old Bonaparte here."

Ike nodded. "Sure enough, Mr. Hanrahan. Old Boney, he don't care much for beer, do you, Boney?" Ike reached inside a wagon and produced a huge, whitened buffalo bone. Boneparte accepted the bone gently, laid down with it between his paws, and showed his teeth to Hanrahan. The saloon keeper looked at the dog with respect.

"Bonaparte, I wouldn't think of takin' your bone. I ain't armed," he muttered, as the unloading resumed.

TWENTY-EIGHT

Adobe Walls
June 27, 1874—Sunrise

Several hours before sunrise, Hanrahan slipped out of his saloon and fired a shot into the air. He rushed back into the saloon. "Everybody up! Get outta here! Ridgepole busted! Out! Everybody out!" Three hunters, sleeping on the floor, scrambled out the door. The cry was taken up throughout the outpost. Sleepy-eyed men in long underwear, some wearing only their pants, milled about the saloon.

"You men!" Hanrahan directed. "Get up on the roof and tear the sod off. Lighten the load! Get that damned sod off!" Two men scrambled up a ladder, mysteriously placed nearby, and tore at the sod. By this time, the compound was in an uproar. Hanrahan pointed at the ridgepole. "You men! Cut a brace for that ridgepole! Quick! Before it cracks some more!" There was a scramble to the woodpile where a suitable pole was found. Two men shouldered the brace into the saloon where Hanrahan directed its placement. Positioned beneath the ridgepole, it was wedged into place.

As the emergency repairs were completed, Hanrahan glanced to the east. No sign of sunrise yet.

"Great work, boys!" Hanrahan said boisterously. "Drinks on the house! C'mon everybody! Belly up!" The ploy worked to perfection. Even those not involved with the repairs crowded the bar.

"Now, this is the way every day should start," Billy Tyler observed, glass in hand.

"Too damn early, if you ask me," Cranky said sourly.

"Didn't ask you!" Tyler answered tartly.

"Cranky, why you always hafta be such a pain in the patooty?" Billy Ogg asked.

"Jus' the way my Momma raised me," Cranky said blithely.

"Well, she didn't do you no favors," Ogg added as Dixon approached.

"Thought I might find you here," Dixon said.

Ogg drained his beer. "Here I am."

"Seein' we're all up, we can get an early start. Willie, shake a leg and round up our horses. I'll be at the wagon."

Ogg banged his empty glass on the bar and wiped his mouth. "That beer's gonna hafta last me a while, I expect. I'm on my way, Boss."

"Cranky, find Bat and tell him to meet me at the wagon," Dixon said. He shouldered his heavy Sharps and started for the wagon, parked several hundred yards outside the compound. Bat joined him, carrying his bedroll. Nearby, the snoring of the Shadler brothers marked their freight wagons, and the black mass sprawled beneath was the sleeping form of Bonaparte.

Three miles to the east of Adobe Walls, to a brightening eastern sky, the huge war party, having rested for several hours, became increasingly restive. An air of expectancy permeated the camp as blankets and saddles were stored in trees, extra ponies hobbled, war bonnets and shields uncovered, war horses painted and feathered, and, most importantly, the magic yellow paint that would turn aside the white man's bullets was liberally smeared on warriors and their ponies. Within minutes the war party became a thing of savage beauty, breathtaking in its decorative splendor.

Stripped to the waist, Quanah wore two feathers in his hair. Large brass earrings contrasted with his face, painted half black and half scarlet. A streak of yellow paint slashed across his chest. His braids were tied with red ribbon and fell down his back. His horse was decorated with colored ribbons in its tail and mane. His fourteen-foot lance and war shield were adorned with feathers. He carried a pistol, tucked into his breechclout.

Astride his war horse, he addressed the warriors. "Today we will kill some white men in their sleep! Our medicine is good. The Great Spirit has shown us the way! Our Cheyenne brothers have asked for the honor of leading our charge! It will be so! Brothers, hear me ! This is our day!"

Quanah turned to his war chiefs. "Walk your ponies. Make no noise. Before we attack, form a long line. Keep your young men from going ahead. I will give the sign to attack." They nodded in understanding, and quietly one of the largest war parties ever seen in the Southwest moved toward Adobe Walls.

Just below the crest of a low hill, the long line of warriors waited, poised and ready. At a signal from Quanah, the line leaped ahead at full gallop, spearheaded by the best of Cheyenne fighting men. As the eager line broached the ridge, there was a wild, throaty battle cry that drowned the thunder of hooves.

Dixon and Masterson were busy greasing their wagon's axles when out of the corner of his eye Billy saw something moving. From the sound of hooves, he thought it was buffalo, but when he heard the battle cry, he froze, as a line of the finest warriors in the Southwest thundered towards him, feathers flying, lances and shields held high, scalps fluttering from bridles—a supreme moment of beauty, courage, and terror. Willie Ogg, tending the horses, whirled and sprinted for his life. Dixon snapped off one shot with his rifle and raced for the compound with Masterson. Reaching the saloon, they found the door shut and pounded desperately on it with their rifle butts. When the door opened, they fell inside. Willie Ogg was close behind as arrows zipped into the sod walls and bullets kicked up dust at his feet.

The warriors quickly overwhelmed the compound and surrounded Myers' store, the saloon, and Rath's. In the center of the compound, milling horsemen encircled the Shadler brothers' wagons. In a deep sleep when the Indians attacked, the Shadler brothers, hoping to be overlooked, were crouched silently inside one of the wagons. Several warriors dismounted to investigate, and were savagely attacked by Bonaparte. Ears back, and growling ferociously, the huge dog mauled one of the warriors and slashed another's legs in a bloody frenzy. Impressed by the dog's courage and ferocity, a mounted Comanche killed Bonaparte with a rifle shot. As the dog quivered in death, the rider slid from his horse and cut a scalp from the dog's side, a tribute to a valiant enemy.

Another warrior cautiously approached the wagons and lifted a corner of its canvas top, only to be met by a shotgun blast. Once discovered, Ike and

Shorty Shadler were quickly killed. The brothers were scalped, their wagons looted, and their prized oxen riddled with arrows.

Inside Myers' store, lances and arrows smashed through windows. Out front, Quanah backed his horse up to the saloon's door where it lashed out with its rear hooves, pounding the door repeatedly. A Kiowa, standing on his horse, vaulted onto the roof of the store, which bent under his weight, raining dust and dirt onto its occupants.

"Watch the roof! Watch the roof!" Cranky shouted, as he fired two shots into the ceiling. The Kiowa leaped to the ground and zigzagged to safety. By this time, the store was filled with gun smoke streaming from its broken windows. The hunters knocked chinks of sod out of the walls for gun ports.

At Rath's, several young warriors beat on the doors with their rifle butts. Firing through the wooden doors, the hunters pushed the Indians back, carrying several wounded with them. A crumpled Kiowa, marked by his black legs, was plucked from the dust by two warriors who drove through the compound at full gallop, snatching the wounded man under his arms on either side and carrying him to safety.

At the saloon, Hanrahan was in command. "Them grain sacks over in the corner," he shouted to several hunters. "Pile 'em against the door. Them tables and chairs, too! Hurry up!"

Outside, Hanrahan could see the Indian's gathering for another attack. At the sound of a bugle, they charged. "Watch it! Keep yer heads down, here they come!"

"Hear that?" Bat shouted. "Sounds like a bugle!"

Dixon reloaded his Sharps. "Soldier boys?"

Bat peered through the smoke. "Don't see none here? Any sign over there?"

"Nothin' but Comanche over here," Dixon answered.

Hanrahan joined them. "Seems like I heard that some Kiowa had a bugler. Used him like the Army does, to signal *rally* and *charge*."

"Makes it easier for us, long as we know the calls," Bat said, ducking from window to window.

"My guess is he ain't Kiowa at all. Prolly an Army deserter," Hanrahan offered.

Dixon sipped from a canteen. "How much ammunition we got, Jim?"

"Not a helluva lot. Most of it's over at Rath's."

"Wonderful," Dixon said wryly

"When we get a little lull, I'll make a run for some," Hanrahan said.

"If we get a lull," Dixon replied.

"Yeah, well, I'll go anyway!" Hanrahan said.

As the next wave of riders surged past the saloon, a brilliantly garbed warrior slid from his pony and jammed a pistol through a gun port, pouring six shots into the saloon at point-blank range. There was a frantic scramble for cover, and when the gun smoke subsided, miraculously, nobody had been hit. When the Indian dashed for cover, Willie Ogg killed him with a single shot.

"Jumpin' Jehoshaphet! That was close!" Bat exclaimed, crouched behind a table.

"Too close!" Ogg replied. "Everybody all right?"

"Yup. For now anyway," Dixon said. "Wonder how things are over at Rath's and Myers'?"

"Don't know," Hanrahan replied. "But they seem to be shootin' pretty steady."

Inside Myers' store, grain and flour sacks were stacked against the door. A heavy pall of gun smoke caused fits of coughing. Eleven men crouched at the gunports, most of them hunters with Sharps rifles. As they braced themselves for yet another charge, Old Man Keeler noticed a dead Cheyenne warrior on the ground outside. "Uh oh," he said. "There's trouble!"

"What, now?" Cranky inquired. "We got enough trouble!"

Old Man Keeler pointed. "See that dead Cheyenne over there?"

"So what? Just another dead Indian."

"So what?" Keeler answered. "That's the son of Stone Calf, chief of the Cheyenne. He ain't gonna like this one little bit!"

"I ain't so crazy about this, myself!" Cranky observed. "You know him? The kid, I mean?"

Keeler spat into the dust. "Yep. When I lived with the Cheyenne a spell. Know a bunch of them."

Cranky looked pained. "Well, I'll tell you somethin', Old Man. That don't speak so damned good of the company you been keepin', present company excepted, of course!"

"They prolly don't know I'm here."

"Wouldn't bet on it if I was you. Watch it! Here they come again!"

At the sound of the bugle, the Indians made another charge. But by now the hunters were prepared, and their deadly fire took its toll on the war party. A Comanche went down in a burst of gunfire close to the saloon. As the riders fell back, there was a furious burst of covering fire from the Indians, and a Comanche, riding low on his horse, swooped in and lifted the body of his friend from the ground. Clinging to the side of his horse, protected from the hunters' bullets, he carried the fallen warrior from the field.

Billy Tyler watched in awe. "Frenchy, didja see that?"

Frenchy was reloading his Colt. "Looked like that half breed, Quanah Parker!"

"Dunno about that, Frog Face, but if that was me lyin' out there, would you come back for me?"

Frenchy looked up. "You think I'm daft? Course not!"

"Yeah, well, bet Bat or Billy Dixon would," Tyler said.

"Then why don't you go out and get your sorry self shot," Frenchy said sardonically. "Then you'll find out!"

"Don't think so," Tyler answered. "How's our water?"

Dave Leonard checked the water barrel. "Almost gone."

Tyler dipped a cup from the barrel. "Tell you what, Dave. Soon as it quiets down, why don't you and me make a run for the well?"

"Fine by me. I'll cover you while you fill the buckets," Leonard agreed.

As the gunfire gradually subsided, the Indians withdrew. Taking advantage of the lull, Tyler and Leonard cleared the barricaded door and raced across the post. As they neared the well, several warriors hidden behind the pickets opened fire. The two men hesitated, and then with bullets snapping around their heads, turned and scrambled back to the store. Leonard sprinted through the door to safety, but Billy Tyler, several steps behind, was hit twice in the back. He slumped through the doorway, blood bubbling from his mouth. Frenchy carried him tenderly into the room and laid him on a table.

"Awful thirsty," Billy whispered.

Leonard dipped the last of the water from the near empty barrel. "Here you go, Billy. Drink as much as you want."

"Frenchy, you there?" Tyler whispered.

"I'm here, Billy."

A faint smile crossed Tyler's bloody face. "Well, at least you dint hafta go out and get me."

Frenchy wiped his eyes. "You know I would have, Billy! You know that don't ya?"

Tyler licked his lips. "I know that, Frenchy. I know you too good, Frog Face. Any more water?"

As Frenchy raised a cup of water to Tyler's lips, his head slumped to the side and he died quietly in the smoke-filled room. The hunters wiped the blood from his face, closed his eyes, and covered him with a dirty blanket.

Old Man Keeler grabbed two water buckets determinedly. "Gimme them buckets! Open that door when I say," he ordered.

Leonard blocked the door. "Are you crazy? You ain't got a chance in hell of makin' that well!"

"I'll make it!" Keeler said stubbornly. "Don't worry 'bout me none. I know some of them people out there! If anybody's gonna make it, it's gonna be me!" He called over to his dog, who was huddled in a corner. "C'mon, Dukie, old dog. You an' me is goin' for a walk!"

The terrified dog pressed tightly to Keeler, staying between his legs, as they emerged from the store. Keeler, affected by a chronic limp, made his way slowly toward the well, talking conversationally to his dog. "Good boy, Dukie! Just a nice walk in the sun! Gonna get you a nice drink of water! How'd you like that, old friend?" By the time he filled both buckets, a shot had yet to be fired.

Two Cheyenne warriors watched Keeler intently from behind the pickets. "That Old One, he lived among us once?" one warrior asked his companion.

"Truly, he limps from a Kiowa arrow long ago."

"The dog I do not know," the warrior responded. "The dog has no Cheyenne past."

"There is no honor in killing one so old," his fellow warrior said. "But he should know we are not pleased that he fights with those stinking Whites!"

"The dog, then!" they said in unison.

As Keeler limped back towards the store, the Cheyenne fired a volley of shots at Duke, killing him. Stricken, Keeler bent over his old friend. "Dukie! You poor little fella! You old friend!" He straightened up and shook his fist in a fury. "Damn you for this! You gonna shoot me, too? Go ahead, damn you, cuz I'll kill you if I get a chance!"

The door to the store quickly opened and Cranky rushed out, grabbed Keeler, and dragged him back inside, his water buckets still filled.

Cranky held out his hand to Keeler in admiration. "Damn! That was a brave thing you done!"

Keeler refused the extended hand. "Brave, my ass! Them sumnabitches!" he snarled. "They kilt ole Dukie right in front of me! On purpose! They knew who I wuz, them bastards! They dint have to shoot ol' Dukie! My best friend! Damn them!" He snatched a rifle and limped to the door, but was restrained by two hunters. "Lemme go, damn it! I got a score to settle!"

"C'mon, hoss, you're gonna get yourself kilt. Then who am I gonna pester about hot biscuits and all?" Cranky reasoned.

Keeler's anger abated. "Yeah, well, Cranky, you know I grudge pretty easy. And I tell you what, I ain't never gonna forget this day! No, sir! I'm gonna get even somehow, you'll see. Poor ol' Dukie! What am I gonna do without him?"

"You kin adopt that crow over at Rath's," Cranky said, attempting to lighten the moment.

"Not funny! No dumb bird is gonna take Dukie's place."

"Yeah, you're prolly right," Cranky said contritely.

After the two friends paused briefly in remembrance, Cranky peered out a smashed window and saw another wave of riders bearing down on the compound. "Uh oh, hold everything! Here they come again!" he shouted.

At the saloon, Hanrahan peered at Dixon through the gun smoke. "It's quieted down some, Billy. Maybe a good time to make a run for Rath's."

"We that low on ammunition?" Dixon asked.

"Yeah, pretty low. Looks like the coast is clear, though."

Dixon hefted his Sharps. "I'm ready." He turned to Bat. "Cover us. Dust up them pickets." The two men opened the saloon door cautiously and then sprinted out into the compound, dipping and ducking. A hail of bullets greeted tham at Rath's. The door opened quickly and slammed shut. Breathing hard, the runners leaned against a wall to catch their breath. A chorus of voices greeted them.

"You awright? Anybody hit over to the saloon?"

"Pretty fancy runnin', fellas!"

"How many guns at Myers'? Anybody go under at Myers'?"

"Billy, you ever seen so many Feathers?"

"We . . . we . . . need more ammunition at the saloon," Hanrahan panted.

"Myers need any?" Bill Olds inquired.

"Don't think so. They should have plenty."

Olds handed Hanrahan a cup of water. "Anybody kilt at your place?"

Hanrahan nodded. "The Shadler brothers and that monster dog of theirs, they all went under. And we heard that Billy Tyler's dead."

"Oh, poor Billy. He was such a nice young man," Hannah Olds said softly.

"Yes ma'am, he sure was. How about here?" Dixon asked.

"So far, so good," Bill Olds said. "But we need a coupla more guns. Only seven of us here includin' Hannah."

Dixon glanced at Hannah, who clutched a rifle. "Tell you what, Jim. I'll stay here an' help. You got eight guns without me."

"Good idea," Hanrahan agreed, as he filled a sack with ammunition. "Now I gotta get the hell outta here while I can! Everybody keep yer head down! And good luck!"

The door was cracked open and Hanrahan zigzagged back to the saloon unscathed. As he left, the crow flitted through the open door and alighted on a grain sack, cawing loudly.

"Looky there!' Dixon exclaimed. "He's still in one piece!"

"That damned bird lives a charmed life!" Bill Olds observed.

Dixon nodded. "We all do. So far!"

As the attack continued, Hannah Olds fought doggedly beside her husband, flinching at the recoil of the big rifle on her shoulder. In the lulls between attacks, she provided cold coffee and stale biscuits to the dirty, sweating men.

Although unspoken, her fate, should the restaurant be overrun, weighed heavily on the hunters. During a pause in the fighting, Dixon called Bill Olds aside. "How's Hannah doin', Bill?"

"Fine. She's doin' fine. Proud of her!" Olds replied.

"You got a good woman there," Dixon said. "Take care of her."

"Best I can."

Dixon reached into a pocket. "Uh, why don't you take this, just in case."

"What is it?"

"It's my bite," Dixon answered.

"Your 'bite'?"

"Yeah, you know. In case you get grabbed by the Feathers. All us hunters carry one," Dixon explained .

"I don't follow," Olds replied.

"It's a cartridge case, only filled with cyanide, not powder," Dixon explained patiently. "You get taken, you bite the case and its all over!"

Olds blinked several times. "Oh, yeah. I think I have heard about them."

"Well, Hannah, she's a nice lady. We—the boys, I mean—we don't want no harm to come to her," Dixon said awkwardly.

"Appreciate this, Billy. I'll explain it to her."

Dixon shook hands with Olds. "Hope she don't never need it."

As the two men parted, several hunters nodded at Dixon affirmatively.

"You fellas seen Fanny?" Dixon asked.

"Nope. Prolly hidin' some place. If she's smart, she's a far piece from here!"

Dixon chuckled. "That makes her smarter than you 'n' me."

TWENTY-NINE

Adobe Walls
June 27, 1874—Afternoon

On a promontory out of rifle shot, Falling Water, a young Comanche, was participating in his first major battle, an opportunity to prove his bravery and skill. The first-time warrior sat on his pony, overlooking the battle ground.

"Those buffalo hunters don't scare me!" he announced to his fellow warriors.

"Big talk from one so young!" a rider answered. "Their big guns scare me!"

"Remember what Isa-Tai said," Falling Water said, pointing to his chest. "This yellow paint is strong medicine!"

"If that is so, why do we have dead and wounded?" asked another.

"Maybe they did not use the yellow paint," Falling Water argued." Maybe they did not believe!"

"Does Falling Water believe?"

"Of course I believe. See? I am wearing the medicine paint!"

"Well?" a warrior said.

"Well what?"

"Well, show us how much you believe," the rider teased.

Falling Water straightened his shoulders. "And do what?"

The rider pointed to the fray. "Count coup on the dead wagon men down there!"

"By the hunters' lodges?" the boy asked.

The warriors nodded. "Just ride in and touch them with your lance. A very brave thing! All the great warriors of the Comanche, Kiowa, and Cheyenne will see you do this thing! You will bring great honor to your lodge!"

"I could do that," Falling Water said hesitantly.

The warriors smiled derisively. "You could. But will you?"

"Yes! I will do this thing," the boy said, having convinced himself. He smeared more yellow paint on his pony.

"And we will watch you so we can truly say you did this great thing!" one of the warriors said condescendingly. They exchanged knowing smiles.

Falling Water extended his arms to the heavens. "Grandfathers, watch over me. Make my heart strong!"

Gripping his lance, Falling Water urged his pony forward, and resplendent in full war paint, drove down the slope at full gallop towards Adobe Walls. A break in the fighting focused all eyes, both friendly and hostile, on the lone horseman as he thundered towards the hunters' barricades. It was a savage and splendid spectacle. One against many. Incredible bravery in the teeth of almost certain death.

Inside the saloon, Bat maintained a close watch on the battlefield. Falling Water caught his attention. "Hey, boys," he shouted. "Looky here!"

"Some kid tryin' to make a name for hisself," Hanrahan observed.

"He sure as hell is comin' in!" Ogg exclaimed.

"Hold up! Don't shoot!" Bat shouted to the three buildings.

At Rath's, Dixon echoed Bat. "Hold up, boys. Keep an eye on him!"

Inside Myers', Dave Leonard joined in. "Don't shoot, fellas. Hold your fire!"

The young Comanche circled the outpost at full gallop, searching for the bodies of the Shadler brothers. Not a shot was fired. After two circles he returned to the shelter of the hill from where his fellow warriors watched him.

Falling Water reined in his pony. "See? Did I not say so? Isa-Tai has strong medicine!"

"But you did not count coup on the wagon men," a rider said, hiding his astonishment.

Falling Water patted his pony. "This time I will do so!"

"This time?" the rider repeated incredulously.

"Yes, this time," the boy said nonchalantly. He quirted his pony and galloped determinedly back toward Adobe Walls.

The defenders could hardly believe their eyes. "Damn! If this ain't a sight to behold!" Dixon muttered.

"The kid's got more guts than brains," Bill Olds added.

"If he ain't careful, some of them brains are likely to be scattered on the ground!" Dixon said.

"Easy, boys. Enjoy the show!" Bat shouted from Hanrahan's.

From the window of Myers' store, Cranky centered his Sharps on the young rider. He fingered the double trigger. "He's comin' in again! Pushing his luck a little, I'd say!"

Old Man Keeler watched the youngster as he rode from warrior to legend. "Ain't he somethin', Cranky? Almost too pretty to shoot!"

The young rider whirled into the compound and reined in at the bodies of the Shadler brothers. Piled on top of each other, their bloody remains flanked that of Bonaparte, sprawled on his side. The young warrior touched each body with his lance. As a last flourish, he circled the compound one more time, proudly brandishing his lance.

Willie Ogg trained his Sharps on the young rider as he flashed past Hanrahan's. "Got him dead center in my sights, Bat!" he said, squinting down the barrel.

Bat reached over and depressed the barrel of Willie's rifle. "Naw, Will, let him go! Let the kid be a hero! Got more sand than most us, I'd say!"

"Had him dead center, too," Ogg grumbled.

Falling Water, now the stuff of legends, rejoined his friends, accepting their shouts of approval. He defiantly smeared more of the yellow paint on his chest, applying it to his lance and the forehead of his pony, preening in the sudden admiration of his fellow warriors. Stories of his bravery would be told and retold around tribal campfires for generations to come.

As the day drew on, Isa-Tai, the Medicine Man, sat his white pony on a hilltop overlooking the outpost. His pony was painted with yellow stripes, and Isa-Tai, naked except for a breech clout, was painted entirely yellow. He wore a wreath of sage in his hair. He was joined by Quanah and Stone Calf and several warriors.

Quanah spoke first. "Isa-Tai, we lose too many young men!"

Isa-Tai sat, eyes closed. "I am told a Cheyenne killed a skunk on his way to this place despite my warning! Did I not say no living thing could be killed as we rode here? My medicine was taken from me by that deed!"

Stone Calf, infuriated, raised his quirt to slash Isa-Tai. "Yah, polecat medicine! You are nothing! My son lies dead down there! Killed by a bullet that mocked your medicine!"

Eyes closed, Isa-Tai remained silent. Stone Calf continued. "If your medicine is so strong, you ride down there under the white man's guns and bring me back his body!"

Quanah intervened. "Stone Calf, nothing comes of such talk"

Stone Calf studied Quanah's face. "You are right. But Isa-Tai, from this day, among the Cheyenne people you will be known as 'Coyote Droppings,' and that is what you are! Coyote droppings!" As if to emphasize his words, there was a loud smack as a heavy Sharps bullet struck Isa-Tai's pony in the head. The animal staggered and fell, victim of an errant, long-range shot.

Stone Calf pointed at the dead pony. "See? Your pony covered with your medicine paint, see how dead he is!" He flung his quirt at Isa-Tai in disgust. Quanah beckoned to Stone Calf and the two chiefs rode off the hilltop.

"Stone Calf, this fight does not go well for us," Quanah said sadly. "The Whites' big guns kill us at great distances."

"Starve them," Stone Calf said curtly. "All their horses are dead. They cannot run. Starve them. Cut off their water!"

"We do not have that much time," Quanah answered. "Other hunters will come soon. More big guns!"

"Truly. We did not catch them in their sleep, as we planned," Stone Calf agreed.

"But I need one last charge, to rescue the body of my son."

Quanah nodded. "So be it. One last charge! I will ride with you!" The two warriors touched hands in respect, and rode off to organize the final attack.

Some forty Cheyenne riders formed a long line, and at the sound of the bugle, whipped their ponies into a headlong assault on the outpost. Two seasoned warriors swept close to the barricades and snatched the body of Stone Calf's son off the ground, riding in tandem, with his limp body dragging between the two ponies.

In the vanguard of the assault, Quanah had his pony shot out from under him, throwing him heavily to the ground. Surrounded by gunfire, Quanah scrambled behind a large stack of hides. As he hunkered down, a heavy Sharps bullet, ricocheted off a nearby rock, striking him squarely in the back, below his right shoulder blade. While scarcely drawing blood, the impact of the flattened bullet slammed Quanah to the ground, stunned and disoriented. Red Wolf, a lifelong friend, glimpsed his leader in the dust, whirled his pony, and dragged Quanah up and across his saddle. Bent low and riding double, the two Comanche retreated to the safety of the hills.

Unnerved by the sight of their wounded war chief, the tribesmen moved aimlessly about, beyond the field of fire. Faced with the reality of their dead and wounded, and the unmasking of Isa-Tai's ineffective medicine, the Indians resorted to long-range sniping. It had become apparent that the attack on Adobe Walls had failed. In an effort to reorganize the failed effort, a groggy Quanah, Stone Calf, and two other chiefs rode to a promontory overlooking the Walls. The firing subsided, as they pondered their strategy.

As the afternoon wore on, the hunters at Myers' store relaxed at their posts. Cranky, chewing on a stale biscuit, noticed movement in the wreckage of the Shadler's wagons and cocked his Sharps. He watched and waited. Suddenly, partially shielded by the wreckage, a running figure, carrying two large coffee cans, scuttled for cover. Squeezing the trigger gently, Cranky dropped the running man with one shot. As he crumpled to the ground, a blood-splattered U.S. Army bugle broke loose and rolled in the dust.

Meanwhile, Bill Olds was standing watch at a transom window on a ladder inside Rath's. "Hey, Billy," he called "Come take a look at this."

Dixon came to the foot of the ladder. "Look at what?" he asked.

Olds pointed. "Way out there. Bunch of Feathers. Look like chiefs, maybe."

"Feathers all over the place, Bill," Dixon replied.

Olds shook his head. "These fellas look special. How far away, you think?"

Dixon picked up a Sharps fitted with a telescopic sight and focused on the gathering. "Mile. Maybe a little less. Why?"

"Some folks say that you're the best shot in the Territory, Billy," Olds said. "This a possible shot?"

"Dunno. It's a hell of a long way."

"No wind to speak of," Olds persisted.

"Might be worth a try."

Olds slapped his hands. "Stand back, boys. Billy's gonna dust a Feather."

"Make that *try* to dust a Feather," Dixon said.

"Oh, c'mon Billy! You can do it!" Olds insisted.

Dixon studied the distance and the wind, and adjusted his sights. "We'll see."

Dixon carefully rested his Sharps on a window sill. Squinting through his sights, he dry-fired the double triggers and rechecked his sights. Satisfied that he had compensated for wind and elevation, he slid the heavy cartridge into the rifle's chamber and gradually squeezed the trigger. There was a thunderous boom and a choking cloud of gun smoke.

On the promontory, Stone Calf struggled with his emotions. "My heart is like a stone," he said somberly. "My son is dead and we have little to show for his sacrifice."

"You speak the truth," Quanah said sadly.

"The stinking white hunters, they . . ." As Stone Calf spoke, a nearby warrior threw up his hands, a surprised look on his face. An ugly wound blossomed on his chest, and he slid slowly from his pony. The chiefs looked at each other in disbelief, then scattered from the high ground. Two warriors on foot dashed out and carried the wounded man to safety. Bewildered, Stone Calf turned to Quanah. "They hurt us from too far away, Quanah! I will take my young men away from here. They cannot fight the big guns! We will fight another day, another place!"

"It has not gone well for us," Quanah said bitterly. "We did not catch the Whites in their beds. The yellow medicine was weak!"

"The horse soldiers will come soon," Stone Calf said. "I will send my young men away in small parties."

"Truly," Quanah added. "Tell your warriors that the Cheyenne stood tall today. The Comanche will be honored to fight beside them any time!"

Stone Calf nodded, touched. "The honor was ours, Quanah." He raised his rifle in salute. "Until we meet again!"

The shattered war party broke into small bands and rode off disconsolately. Overhead, ominous looking thunderheads gradually obscured the sun, and a distant rumble of thunder spoke of a coming storm.

At Rath's store, the hunters peered through the smoke of Billy Dixon's shot. When the unfortunate target crumpled from his pony, there was a raucous cheer and exuberant back-slapping.

"Yeah, Billy! You done it!"

"Damndest shot I ever seen!"

"Listen, boys, that was just dumb luck!" Dixon answered.

"Dumb luck, my ass!" Olds marveled. "That was the greatest shot ever made!"

"Well, maybe it will make them Feathers back off," Dixon said, grinning.

"What's all the hollerin' about?" Hanrahan shouted from the saloon.

"Billy just plugged a Feather a mile out!" Olds shouted.

"What?" Hanrahan asked incredulously.

"Yup! One mile! We all seen it!" Olds repeated.

"Who shot what?" Cranky asked from Myers' store.

"Billy Dixon just shot a Feather a mile away!"

"Naw, not a mile?" Cranky answered.

Bill Olds shook his head and laughed. "Yes, sir, you bet! One mile!"

As the afternoon waned, it became apparent to the outpost that the attack had failed. The defenders slowly cracked their doors and moved cautiously outside. The Shadlers' twenty-six oxen lay dead, bristling with arrows. All the horses and mules had either been run off or killed. Hannah Olds's pretty filly was huddled against a wall of Rath's store, as if seeking protection. Two arrows were buried up to the feathers in her lifeless body. The bodies of the Shadlers, Bonaparte, and several Indians were sprawled in the dust. The dead bugler, daubed with yellow paint, was found with a large hole in his back and proved to be a deserter from the Tenth Cavalry. Flies had already discovered the bodies of the horses. It had been a long day.

As the hunters collected souvenirs from the battlefield, there was a gunshot, followed by a woman's scream. Rushing into Rath's store, the hunters found Bill Olds on the floor with a gaping head wound. His rifle lay nearby. Hannah, crying hysterically, knelt by his side.

"What happened?" Dixon shouted.

"Bill was climbin' that ladder there to get a better look at them hills. He musta slipped or somethin'. He fell off the ladder and his rifle touched off!" a skinner said.

It was evident that Bill Olds was dead, but Hannah refused to allow the hunters to touch his body. She was crying hysterically.

"My gawd," Bat said to Dixon. "He goes through the whole day fightin' for his life and then gets kilt when it's all over!"

"Don't seem right." Dixon answered. "Poor Hannah! What's she gonna do?"

"She'll be all right," Bat said. "The boys will take care of her."

"Know that. But it ain't gonna replace her husband! He was a good feller."

"Yeah, an' now she's a good widow," Bat concluded.

As the sky grew dark and cloudy, small groups of hunters gathered in the center of the outpost, comparing notes and swapping stories of the fight. Thunderclouds rumbled with the promise of a refreshing rain, as lightning flickered in the distance. The pet crow, cawing loudly, hopped happily about in the desolation.

"Long day," Bat said, looking older than his twenty years.

"Lucky we're all not under," Dixon added.

Cranky spat with difficulty. "Damn! Mouth tastes like an old boot!"

Old Man Keeler stroked his stubble. "Lucky you can still taste!"

Cranky nodded. "Know it. Think them Feathers pulled out?"

"Expect so. Maybe a few still around," Keeler explained. "Them Cheyenne, I know 'em! They expected to take us in their first rush! Dint expect no fight worth mentioning. Way it turned out, wasn't their kind of fight. Don't think we'll see no more Cheyenne."

"If Stone Calf pulls out, the rest should follow," Dixon added.

Keeler produced a well-gnawed plug of tobacco. "Yup. You're right. Might be a few kids still hangin' around, tryin' to make a name for themselves."

A noise in the brush caused Bat to stiffen. "Somethin's moving in the brush over there!" Rifles readied, the hunters scanned the brush intently.

"I see it!" Keeler shouted. "It ain't a Feather!"

"Wolf, maybe? Smells them dead animals?" Cranky replied.

The brush parted and Fanny appeared, wagging her tail. Bat shook his head. "No .Don't think so. Hey, it's Fanny!"

"Fanny?" Dixon said elatedly.

"Yes, sir, by Gawd, it's Fanny!" Cranky echoed.

Dixon whistled. "C'mere, Fanny! C'mon, Fanny girl!" Fanny dashed to Dixon and leaned against his legs, licking his hand and waggling furiously. Both parties were delighted to see each other.

"Where you suppose she's been?" Cranky asked.

"Prolly hidin' in the weeds," Keeler replied. "Shootin' must have scared the bejeebers outta her." Fanny turned and trotted back to her hiding place in the brush.

"Where's she goin'?" Bat said

"Beats me," Dixon answered. He whistled again. "Fanny! Here, girl! C'mon, Fanny!"

Unmindful of his calling, Fanny disappeared into the sagebrush. By now, everyone was aware of the dog and joined the chorus. "Here, Fanny! Good girl! C'mon little girl!" As they shouted and whistled, the brush parted and Fanny reappeared, carrying something in her mouth. Picking her way across the compound, she approached Dixon, her tail wagging, and laid a newborn puppy at his feet. She looked up at Dixon and whined expectantly. He knelt and cuddled the newborn, its eyes tightly closed. The puppy cried softly, and Fanny, ears up, whined in response.

"Looky here! She had her pups right smack in the middle of our fight!" Dixon said. "Ain't you somethin', little fella'!" He patted Fanny. "You done just fine, little lady. I'm real pleased to see you!"

Fanny whirled and disappeared again into the brush, reappearing shortly with a second puppy in her mouth. Fanny repeated her retrievals until she had delivered five squirming puppies to Dixon and his delighted companions. The timely introduction of new life to the field of death and carnage was not lost on the hunters, who took turns cuddling the newborns as Fanny maintained a maternal watch.

"Damn! If this don't beat all!" Bat exulted, stroking a puppy.

Dixon patted the dog affectionately on the head. "Fanny, you've earned a big dinner tonight! Cranky, do me a favor and fix a nice bed for this girl and her kids someplace in the back of Rath's store."

"Good idea. Why Rath's?" Cranky asked.

"Because Hannah's there. She's gonna need somethin' to keep her mind offen her husband, and Fanny needs a woman's touch, what with them puppies and all," Dixon replied.

"Proud to know ya', Billy," Cranky said.

Old Man Keeler squatted down and fondled a squirming puppy. "Hello, little thing," he whispered hoarsely.

Cranky watched the old man and the puppy. "Well, hoss, you just found him."

Keeler looked up. "Found who?"

"Found your new Dukie, that's who!"

Keeler blinked back tears and picked the puppy up gently. "He's right ya know," he whispered to the puppy. "You'll be Duke the Second, little feller!" He rolled the puppy over to confirm its sex.

Cranky looked at the puppy and grinned. "Guess you'd better call him 'Duchess'!" The crowd of onlookers burst into laughter as a light rain began to fall.

The inability of five hundred of the Southwest's best fighting men to overwhelm the tiny outpost of twenty-nine Whites was a bitter disappointment to Quanah and his allies. In frustration, the tribesmen struck into Texas with retaliatory raids. In an effort to distinguish between "hostile" and "friendly" Indians, the Commissioner of Indian Affairs ordered all "friendlies" to enroll at their reservations and to be accounted for by daily roll call. Although many complied, others bitterly resented such regimentation and disappeared into the hills. Now all bets were off.

PART FOUR

TEDDY

THIRTY

Fort Concho
September 1874

An early morning meeting in the Commandant's office found the Fourth Cavalry's officers and Billy Dixon, a newly enrolled scout, crowded around Colonel Mackenzie listening intently to his plan of operations. Captain Boehm and Lieutenant Thompson, as Chiefs of Scouts, were particularly attentive. A large map rested on a table.

"Gentlemen, we will be one of five columns that will take the field against the hostiles. We will march west to the Staked Plains, the *Llano Estacado.* Familiar ground to the Fourth. The other columns will flush out the hostiles, wherever they may be. We are authorized to enter Indian Territory, even the reservations, if necessary."

"So much for the Medicine Lodge Treaty," Lt. Carter said somberly.

Mackenzie snapped his three fingers. "Precisely, Mr. Carter!"

"The hostiles, sir. Any idea how many?" Carter inquired.

"Hard to say, Lieutenant. Maybe as many as two thousand."

"How large is our force, sir?" Captain Boehm asked.

"About three thousand, Lieutenant. Mostly cavalry. About thirty-five scouts including Mr. Dixon here, and our Tonks, under the command of Mr. Thompson and Mr. Boehm."

Mackenzie snapped his fingers again. "I expect results, gentlemen."

Boehm exchanged glances with Thompson. "Yes, sir, Colonel. You'll get them!"

"Good. I'll hold you to that," Mackenzie said. "Now, gentlemen, any further questions?"

"How long can we expect to be in the field, Colonel?" Lt. Carter asked.

"For as long as it takes, Mr. Carter. For as long as it takes! We come home when the hostiles come in!"

"Dead or alive, sir?"

"Preferably alive, Lieutenant," Mackenzie answered. "But it's their choice. If there are no further questions, gentlemen, please see to your posts. Dismissed."

As the officers left the room, Mackenzie beckoned Dixon to remain. Mackenzie studied Dixon for a long moment. "Mr. Dixon, I have heard of your exploits at Adobe Walls and your heroics at the Buffalo Wallow fight."

"I'm lucky to be alive, Colonel."

"Perhaps, Mr. Dixon, but from what I've heard luck didn't have much to do with it."

"Thank you, sir. But of the six of us that got jumped by the Kiowa and Comanche at Buffalo Wallow, five of us got wounded and one got kilt."

"And you, Mr. Dixon?"

"Plugged in the calf of my leg. But Amos Chapman, who was scoutin' with me, he lost his left leg."

"How is he," Mackenzie inquired.

"He's good. Was ridin' coupla weeks after they cut off his leg. Don't seem to bother him none."

Mackenzie shook his head in admiration. "General Miles tells me that he recommended you and Chapman for the Congressional Medal of Honor!"

Dixon looked uncomfortable. "Yeah, but, Colonel, Amos an' me was just tryin' to keep our hair on."

"Just so, Mr. Dixon. Have you received your medal yet?"

"Yeah, well, General Miles passed them out last month," Dixon replied self-consciously.

Mackenzie smiled. "My congratulations, sir! I am pleased that you will be scouting for me. Your experience and judgment will be of great value to the regiment. Please feel free to give us your opinions and concerns."

"Do what I can, Colonel," Dixon answered, as the two men shook hands.

"Any words of wisdom before we part?" Mackenzie asked.

"Well, Colonel, Amos Chapman has some of them wise words."

"And they are?"

Dixon grinned. "Keep yer hair on!"

The following day, a large column slowly departed the fort. The scouts, Tonks, and a handful of Seminoles in brightly colored clothing led the column. Behind them marched eight cavalry troops and four companies of infantry, followed by a supply train. Post residents, wives, and children lined up to wish them well. The post band struck up the Fourth Cavalry's Regimental song, "Come Home, John."

Colonel Mackenzie, riding with Lt. Carter, returned the salute of the fort's guards.

"Well, Lieutenant," he said, "I have a very positive feeling already about this campaign."

Lt. Carter waved to the crowd. "I share your feeling, Colonel. We know what to expect from Quanah and his people."

"He's no ordinary opponent, Mr. Carter. Matching wits with him is a challenge."

"We sure know a helluva lot more about his tactics than we did six months ago," Carter replied.

Mackenzie smiled. "And he about ours, Lieutenant. Think about that!"

"Yes, sir, that's right. But five columns in the field against him should limit his choices."

"Don't underestimate the man, Mr. Carter. He's playing a losing hand, and I'm sure he realizes that."

"That's true, Colonel. But he's fighting for his native land, for his people. Pretty basic stuff!"

Mackenzie paused, staring across the vast prairie. "And that's the tragic part of all this. If we were in his moccasins, we probably would do the same thing!"

Carter shook his head. "It doesn't seem right sometimes."

Mackenzie shifted in his saddle. "It strikes me as downright wrong! But, we're just soldiers. Let's leave the politics to someone else."

"I know, sir. But I bet that Quanah has no misgivings about what he's doing. I'm sure he's doing what he thinks is right. And I'm not so sure that I disagree with him!"

"Now, now Lieutenant, that sounds almost seditious!" Mackenzie said sardonically.

"You know what I mean, sir," Carter said lamely.

Mackenzie smiled. "I believe I do, Mr. Carter. But let's get on with our job, shall we?"

For the next three months, the Fourth Cavalry pursued hostile bands of Comanche and Kiowa, sometimes making contact, but mostly keeping the tribesmen on the run. Whether in the baking-hot sun, bitter-cold rainstorms, or battered by the howling winds of the open plains, the search was unrelenting. They had learned to live with the land, sometimes without food or water for days. They once had to slit the veins of their horses and drink their blood to survive. These hardships made the troopers become tough and confident. And then one day, a relatively insignificant event led to a major breakthrough in the campaign. . . .

On a routine patrol, Lt. Thompson's scouts correctly identified several sets of wagon tracks as those made by a small band of Comancheros. Pushing ahead, the patrol soon sighted their white-topped wagons jolting across the prairie. At the sight of the soldiers, the wagons halted in confusion. As Lt. Thompson and his patrol approached, a man was seen to leap on a horse and gallop off. The patrol gave chase and eventually overtook the rider, seizing his reins and forcing him to a halt. Feigning nonchalance, he averted his gaze from the patrol.

"What's your name?" Thompson asked.

"No sabe," he replied.

"Can you speak English?"

"No sabe."

Thompson took off his hat and wiped his forehead. "You, amigo, look guilty as hell about something!" He motioned to his patrol. "We'll bring him in. He sure looks guilty of something, don't he?" The patrol cantered back to the column and presented their new prisoner to Mackenzie.

"This gentleman tried to give us a run, Colonel. We believe him to be Comanchero," Lt. Thompson said.

Mackenzie was very interested in the Comancheros. He knew their reputation and how they traded and lived in the *Llano Estacado*. He examined the captive; the small, thin man appeared Mexican, with a dark complexion and a black moustache. Needing to know more, he sent for his scouts.

When his scouts arrived, Mackenzie exhibited the prisoner. "I need your help. This man was seen riding hell-bent away from his Comanchero wagons. Seemed suspicious. Do any of you know him? Ever seen him before?"

A scout stood up and walked around the man, scrutinizing him closely. "I seen this feller afore. Big dog Comanchero. At least he was when I seen him. Name is Jose Tafoya."

Several scouts nodded in assent. "Yup, that's him alright. Don't look so big now!"

Mackenzie walked up to the man. "So, Mr. Jose Tafoya, you have lived in these parts for many years?"

The captive looked steadily at the officer. "No sabe," he muttered.

"Mr. Tafoya, have you and your friends traveled throughout the Staked Plains in your business dealings?"" Mackenzie inquired mildly.

"No sabe."

"Colonel, this fella knows the Staked Plains like the back of his hand," a scout offered.

"He knows every trail, creek, and canyon up there."

"Ah, sir, you have read my mind," Mackenzie replied to the scout. He turned to Tafoya. "Now sir, I have a proposal for you. Guide us through the Staked Plains, the *Llano Estacado*, if you will, and we will release you to your people." A scout translated the message into Spanish.

"No sabe."

Mackenzie grew impatient. "We are wasting precious time. We need to know more about those damned Staked Plains! Mr. Thompson, you and your scouts talk some sense into Mr. Tafoya. Report back to me in one hour please." He turned to Lt. Carter. "Mr. Carter, we will make camp here. Pass the word please."

Lt. Carter nodded. "Right away, sir."

As white tents blossomed on the prairie and cooking fires were lit, Thompson, his scouts, and Tafoya met with Mackenzie. "Report, please, Mr. Thompson."

"Sir, no luck. We think he knows English, but only thing he says is 'no sabe.'"

Mackenzie smiled faintly. "I see. Mr. Thompson, see that wagon over there with the large tongue? Have your people roll it over here, please."

The wagon was brought to Mackenzie's tent. Tafoya looked mildly interested.

Mackenzie snapped his three fingers peevishly. "Mr Thompson, throw a rope over the tongue please after you raise it. Fashion a noose at the end of the rope." Tafoya's expression quickly changed from interested to distraught. At the officer's order, the Comanchero was placed at the base of the tongue, and the noose placed around his neck. The rope was tightened over the top of the tongue, until Tafoya's toes barely touched the ground. His expression turned from distraught to distressed.

Mackenzie spoke in measured tones. "Jose Tafoya, either you agree to our terms or we will tighten that rope several turns. Your choice!"

Tofoya gagged. "No sabe! No sabe!"

"Another turn on the rope please, Mr. Thompson!" Tafoya's toes lifted from the ground. His eyes bulged.

"Si, si, Capitan! I speak the English!" he choked.

Mackenzie smiled. "I thought he'd see it our way. Mr. Thompson, release Mr. Tafoya and get him something to eat and drink. You want to take good care of your new scout!"

Three days passed uneventfully. Scouts and trackers ranged far ahead of the column, seeking telltale signs. In early evening of the fourth day, Lieutenant Thompson, Captain Boehm, Dixon, and Jose Tayofa cantered back to camp and swung off their horses at Mackenzie's tent. Their commanding officer stepped from his tent, clad in pants and boots, with suspenders over his long underwear. He wiped the sweat from his face with a bandanna and looked up expectantly. "Your report please, gentlemen."

Lt. Thompson beat the dust from his white hat. "Scouts cut a big trail, sir. Many horses. Got jumped by a coupla Comanches. Think they were concerned about us cutting their tracks!"

"Mr. Tayofa, what do you make of this?" Mackenzie asked.

Tayofa took off his hat respectfully. "Seen other trails, too. All goin' the same place."

"Going where, Mr. Tayofa?"

"Palo Duro Canyon."

Mackenzie turned to Dixon. "And you, Mr. Dixon. What do you think?"

Dixon took a drink from his canteen. "It's September, Colonel. Winter's comin'. Hear that Palo Duro is their wintering-over ground. S'posed to have good grass, water, and timber. Out of the wind. I agree with Jose. That's where they're headed."

Mackenzie turned to his Lieutenants. "Mr. Boehm and Mr. Thompson, what do you think?"

Boehm nodded. "I agree with the scouts, sir."

"And you, Mr. Thompson?"

"No question in my mind, Colonel," Thompson agreed. "It's Palo Duro."

Mackenzie snapped the fingers on his bad hand. "Your old stamping ground, Mr. Tafoya. Can you take us there? How far is it?"

Tafoya nodded. "Si, Capitan, I can do that. The canyon is very deep, very wide. Eight-hour ride from here."

Deep in thought, Mackenzie paced about. "Very well, gentlemen. Job well done!" He entered his tent and emerged with a handful of cigars. "Cigars all around, gentlemen, with my compliments! Now, go get something to eat and some rest. Busy times ahead!

Mr. Thompson, please ask Lieutenant Carter to join me immediately."

Mackenzie retired to his tent. Within minutes, there was a scratching on the tent flap. "You wanted to see me, sir," Lieutenant Carter inquired.

"Yes, Robert, come in and sit down. Our scouts have brought interesting news."

Carter sat down on a cot. "'Interesting,' Colonel?"

Mackenzie produced a bottle of whiskey. "Very interesting, Robert. But first, have a cigar and a little snakebite remedy with me." The men clinked glasses. "To the Fourth Cavalry."

"To the Fourth," Carter echoed.

"Now the news, Lieutenant. We may have hit the jackpot. A very large trail—many lodges, the scouts think—is headed towards Palo Duro Canyon, their wintering-over ground."

Carter pored over a sheaf of maps. "When do we start?"

"Tomorrow morning. First thing. We'll leave one cavalry company here with the infantry and supply wagons. Load the pack mules with seven days' rations. Every trooper will carry extra ammunition. Close check on horses and equipment!" Mackenzie drummed his three fingers on the table. "By thunder, Robert, this is what we have been waiting for!"

"Hallelujah, Colonel! It's been a long wait!"

"We can assume that Quanah's scouts will be watching us. So tomorrow we'll march west, away from Palo Duro. Make them think we missed their trail. When it gets dark, we'll swing around and hope to be at Palo Duro by sunrise. That's assuming Tafoya can take us there!"

"By Jupiter, we may be ahead of Quanah this time," Carter exclaimed. "Anything else, Colonel?"

"That's all for now, Lieutenant. Please have Sergeant McSorley report to my tent."

Mackenzie immersed himself in his maps. A scratching on the tent flap announced Sergeant McSorley. "Sergeant McSorley reporting as ordered, sir."

Mackenzie looked up. "Enter, Sergeant."

Sergeant McSorley entered the tent and saluted.

"At ease, Sergeant." He surveyed McSorley from his camp stool, placed a bottle on the table, and reached into a canister for a cigar. He handed the cigar to McSorley and poured two drinks. "Join me, Sergeant?"

McSorley was flattered. "Don't mind if I do, sir. But beggin' the Colonel's pardon, sir, I'm still on duty."

Mackenzie waved his cigar dismissively. "I declare you off duty."

Sergeant McSorley beamed and held his glass up. "Well, sir, in that case, here's to me sainted mother, to the old sod, to the Fourth Cavalry, and to you, me dear Colonel!" He downed the whiskey in one gulp, wiped his mouth on his sleeve, lit his cigar from a lantern, and puffed expansively. He twirled the cigar in his fingers. "A fine leaf, Colonel."

"Thank you, Sergeant. You're obviously a man who enjoys the finer things in life!"

McSorley preened. "I do indeed, Colonel. And I thank you for noticin'!"

Mackenzie became serious. "Sergeant, tomorrow at sunrise, we move out on a forced march. I want you to keep a close eye on the new men. Hard ride coming. Probably a good scrap, too. I need to count on my sergeants!"

McSorley drew himself up to his full height. "Not to worry, sir. The Fourth is ready. On that you have the word of Patrick Aloysius McSorley!"

"Aloysius?" Mackenzie repeated.

McSorley's embarrassment showed. "Beggin' the Colonel's pardon, sir, but can we just keep that between us?"

"My lips are sealed, Sergeant!" Mackenzie said solemnly. "Now, report to Lt. Carter for your orders. Thank you, Sergeant."

McSorley came to attention and saluted. "Thank you, sir."

Left to himself, Mackenzie drew thoughtfully on his cigar, and put the bottle away. It had served its purpose.

Quanah, he mused, *I know you're out there. Are your scouts going to believe our march to the west? Maybe. Maybe not. Are you really in Palo Duro Canyon?*

Can we find it? How do we get into the canyon? Ah, the joy and comfort of command!

Deep in thought, he snuffed out the lantern and lay down on his cot, fully dressed, removing only his boots.

Deep in the heart of Palo Duro Canyon, hundreds of lodges had been erected, grouped by tribe. Surrounded by good vegetation, a free-flowing creek, and large mesa walls that protected against cold winter winds, the huge canyon floor was an ideal spot to settle their villages.

At the back of the chasm, the Quahadis were camped. Near the foot of a ridge, Quanah stepped from his lodge and met two scouts as they descended a trail into the camp.

"You saw Bad Hand?" he asked.

Sees Everything, a veteran scout, nodded. "Truly, he is one sleep from here. But he has never found this place."

"Yes, he may pass by again," Quanah replied, tapping his head. "But my heart is troubled. Bad Hand is a great warrior. He fights with his head as well as his heart! Do not underestimate him!"

"You speak the truth," Sees Everything agreed. "I will ride out and watch to see where he goes."

"I will ride with you," Quanah said. He called to a young guard of the herd. "Bring me my white pony."

"You do not ride your big black this day?" Sees Everything asked.

Quanah shook his head. "No, he needs some rest and good grass. He will stay with the herd."

The two Comanche rode slowly up the rear of Palo Duro Canyon to begin their personal scout of the Fourth's column as it wended its way westward, apparently leaving the canyon secure and its camps unmolested.

Quanah and Sees Everything were bellied down on a knoll watching the Fourth Cavalry pass below. Two other scouts slithered on their bellies to join Quanah. The four Comanche watched in silence.

"Bad Hand moves toward the setting sun," one scout noted.

"Same path since sunrise," commented another. "He has many horses. Maybe we should take some?"

"No, I want him to leave this place quickly," Quanah said. "Taking his horses would only slow him down."

"Bad Hand left many wagons and Bluecoats behind," the scout said. "They have not moved."

"The wagons carry many good things," said another. "Blankets, food, guns."

"Perhaps Bad Hand baits a trap," Quanah said.

"Let us ride and see these wagons," Sees Everything suggested. "Maybe it is not a trap."

"Yes." Quanah turned to the scouts. "You follow Bad Hand. Sees Everything and I will go and look at the wagons."

The Fourth Cavalry moved west at a steady pace. Corporal Whit Davis rode with troopers Elias and Nolan.

"I tell ya, Whit," Elias said. "I got so much ammunition on me, I could start my own war."

"Don't hafta. Already got one," Davis replied.

"Looks like we're gonna find out soon enough," Elias answered.

Trooper Nolan swigged from his canteen. "I ain't in no rush to find out, I can tell ya that!"

With the approach of evening, Machenzie waved Lt. Carter to his side. "Mr. Carter, we'll halt for supper. Make it appear that we are preparing our night camp. Light some cooking fires. As soon as it's dark enough to hide our movements, we'll remount and pull out."

"Yes, sir. Anything else, Colonel?"

"Muffle all gear. As little noise as possible. When its completely dark, we'll turn and head for Palo Duro."

"Any estimate of our time of arrival?" Carter asked.

"Scouts think about first light."

"On my way, sir," Carter said, as he wheeled his horse and headed down the column to relay Mackenzie's orders.

Darkness fell quickly on a moonless night. After a quick meal, the column was on the move again, wheeling and changing its course. The scouts rode in advance. The Tonkawa and Seminole, often on foot, searched for telltale lodge pole ruts that would signify tribal movement.

At midnight, the column came to a halt. The trackers had lost the faint vestiges of the trail. Mackenzie fretted in the darkness. "Damn it, Lieutenant, we've got thirty-five scouts and trackers out there. How the hell can they lose the trail?"

"Don't worry, Colonel," Carter said soothingly. "Those Tonks can find a needle in a haystack!"

"Wonderful!" Mackenzie said sarcastically. "I need them to find the trail, and right now! We'll leave the haystacks to another day."

"Good chance to rest the men, Colonel," Carter suggested. "They've been in the saddle for about eleven hours."

"You're right, Lieutenant," Mackenzie acknowledged. "Have the men stand to and rest the horses."

In the darkness, the troopers gratefully dismounted and sprawled on the ground.

"My ass is plumb wore out," Trooper Elias moaned.

"You have plenty to wear out," Trooper Nolan offered.

"I'm gonna' be so bow-legged after this that I'm gonna be walkin' on my ankle bones," Corporal Davis added.

Sergeant McSorley patrolled the ranks. "Awright, keep it down! My ass is as sore as yours, but you don't hear me cryin' about it!"

"Your sorry Irish ass ain't worth cryin' about!" said an anonymous voice.

Sergeant McSorley bristled. "Who said that? Who said that?"

There was a muffled snickering in the darkness. The sound of approaching horses quieted the ranks. Dixon, Tayofa, and two Tonks answered a sentry's challenge and joined the column.

"Colonel Mackenzie?" Dixon called out.

"Over here. Over here. Report, please," he answered from the darkness.

"The Tonks found the rim of the canyon, Colonel!"

"Excellent!" Mackenzie exulted. "Great work, Mr. Dixon! How far?"

"Four, five hours, maybe."

"Mr. Carter." Mackenzie ordered. "Let's get to work. Mount up on the double!"

Rejuvenated by the report, the column resumed its march. By the time the first streaks of daylight appeared in the eastern sky, Colonel Ranald Mackenzie and the Fourth Cavalry found themselves at the brink of the canyon.

The view was magnificent, if not overwhelming. Palo Duro Canyon stretched far into the horizon, and appeared much wider than it was deep. Its majestic pillars and pinnacles glowed in soft shades of red and beige as the early sun's rays crept across the landscape. Steep, precarious rock walls lined the rim, without a trace of a trail in sight.

It was a violent piece of landscape—a gaping rift in northern Texas that was too wide to travel around, and too daunting to travel down.

Mackenzie took a deep breath. "Judas Priest!" he exclaimed to his officers. "It has to be four miles wide, maybe more!"

"All of that, sir," Carter agreed. "Look at the number of lodges down there! Must be hundreds!"

Mackenzie nervously drummed his three fingers on his saddle horn. "Lt. Thompson?"

"Here, sir."

"Have your scouts discovered a way in?"

"No sir. They're still looking."

"Not good enough, Lieutenant," Mackenzie snapped. "We're running out of time!"

Lt. Carter pointed to a nearby ridge. "Colonel, there seems to be a faint path about a hundred feet to the east, down that wall over there. See it? It zigzags back and forth!"

Mackenzie studied the precipitous trail that twisted and turned among the boulders and outcroppings. It was scarcely wide enough to allow passage. Loose gravel and crumbling rock suggested treacherous footing for the horses. The troopers exchanged uneasy glances.

"All right, it will have to do," Mackenzie said urgently. "Lieutenant Thompson! Take your men down that path and open the fight!" He paused. "Captain McLaughlin, you will take the First Battalion and guard the top of the path. Captain Beaumont, you and I will follow Lieutenant Thompson down that trail with the Second Battalion. This, gentlemen, is the chance we have been waiting for! Good luck!"

THIRTY-ONE

Palo Duro Canyon
September 28, 1874

The descent into Palo Duro Canyon was a military nightmare. Leading their reluctant horses down the narrow path, slipping and sliding across steep rock walls, the troopers were exposed and defenseless. Loose rock and debris cascaded down into the canyon. Gradually, as the path descended, patches of vegetation afforded some protection from discovery. A lone Indian sentinel sighted the approaching column and was shot before he could alarm the sleeping tribesman. Miraculously, the sound of gunfire was ignored.

Eventually, Lt. Thompson and his scouts reached the canyon floor, undetected and unscathed. They formed a battle line, then Thompson led a thunderous charge through the encampments. The second wave, companies A and E, came close behind, crouched in their saddles with pistols cocked and sabers unsheathed. The third wave, led by Mackenzie, responded to the bugler's charge call, and companies H and L galloped headlong down the canyon floor. Racing through the awakening villages, the shouting horse soldiers made a shambles of lodges, robes, cooking fires and utensils, creating a chaos that sent the Indians fleeing for their lives, as wave after wave of the Fourth Cavalry washed over them.

In the turmoil Mackenzie shouted out his orders. "Captain Beaumont! The pony herd, Captain!" He pointed down the canyon. "Down there, Captain! Their ponies!"

Captain Beaumont waved his acknowlegement. "Company A, follow me!" he bellowed.

Company A drove for the pony herd at full gallop in a race with several Indians. Beaumont reached the herd first, and pushed it through the canyon to Mackenzie. A scattering of rifle fire rattled off the canyon's walls.

"Well done, Captain!" Mackenzie shouted. "How many animals you estimate?"

"Quite a few, Colonel. Twelve to fifteen hundred, maybe!"

"Excellent, Captain! Take Captain Boehm and Companies A and E and secure that miserable trail we just came down." Beaumont and Boehm waved in understanding and thundered off. Mackenzie turned to Lt. Carter. "Mr. Carter, take as many men as you need and burn the villages! Everything! Especially food supplies. Blankets, lodges, weapons! Everything!"

"On my way, sir!" Carter replied. He stood in his stirrups. "Sergeant McSorley! Twenty-four men here on the double!"

Carter's detail set the canyon ablaze. Black smoke boiled from the canyon as anything flammable was torched. The winter's supply of food for the tribesmen was incinerated.

As the fires roared, Troopers Whit Davis and Ben Elias discovered cases of the latest model Winchester rifles within several lodges. Davis picked up a Winchester. "Look at this! he snarled. "Brand-new Winchesters! Better rifles than ours! Prolly got 'em from them damned Comancheros!"

Trooper Elias smashed a Winchester on a rock. "That one ain't gonna work so well," he said. He threw a case of rifles into the fire. "And neither will these!" he added angrily as they proceeded to destroy the Comanche arsenal.

Late in the morning, Indian resistance had ceased. The tribesmen, carrying only what they could pack on a pony, slipped away from the canyon, leaving behind their winter supplies, clothing, and necessities. The rout was complete; the surprise overwhelming. Mackenzie's only casualty was a wounded bugler and several horses. Indian casualties were unknown.

As the cavalrymen drifted back to the access trail, heavy clouds of smoke billowed from the canyon. "Captain Beaumont," Mackenzie called out. "Start the herd up the access trail, please."

"The whole herd, Colonel?" Beaumont asked incredulously.

"Yes, Captain, the entire herd," Mackenzie said pleasantly. Then angrily, "Or would you prefer, Captain, that the Comanche and Kiowa get their ponies back? Maybe prolong the fight for a few more months? Of course, damn it, the whole herd!"

Chastened, Captain Beaumont, with the scouts leading the way, led the herd up the steep trail to the rim of Palo Duro Canyon. It was a chaotic scene, as the animals scrambled and slipped, kicking and crowding each other, while exhausted troopers drove them relentlessly. Hours later, as evening approached, the last horse and trooper reached the canyon's rim. To protect the herd as they moved across the plains, a square was formed with the horses in the center and the troopers guarding the perimeter. Twenty miles later, just after midnight, the herd arrived at the supply train where Lieutenant Lawton and his personnel took over. The exhausted troopers, without sleep for thirty-three hours, gulped down cups of scalding coffee and biscuits before collapsing into a deep sleep.

As the day brightened, Mackenzie ordered a late breakfast for his weary troopers, who lingered by the fires, regaling each other with tales of valor, both real and imagined.

Inside his tent, coffee in hand, Mackenzie conferred with Lieutenants Carter and Thompson. "Mr. Thompson, I need an accurate count of the captured herd. When you have done that, give Mr. Tafoya first pick of the herd. He's earned a bonus. No more than forty animals maximum. Rest of the scouts, Tonks, Seminoles, and Whites, ten horses apiece. Report back when they've claimed their animals, please."

Lt. Thompson saluted. "Very well, sir."

Lt. Carter and his commanding officer watched as the scouts selected and roped their bonus ponies. They were unaware of Lt. Lee, who approached, leading a handsome black stallion. He cleared his throat noisily.

Mackenzie turned. "Oh, Lieutenant Lee. I was watching the roping."

"Quite a sight, sir," Lee replied. That's why I'm here."

"How so, Lieutenant?"

"Well, sir, I figure I owe you."

"Owe me? Owe me what?"

"A favor, sir," Lee responded. "Remember when I accepted your grey from Quanah and the Comanche?"

Mackenzie smiled. "It's hard to forget, Lieutenant."

"Yes, sir, I know," Lee said awkwardly. "Anyway, in that herd we took yesterday ..."

"Go on, Mr. Lee. Go on," Mackenzie said, intrigued.

"Well, sir, when Jose Tafoya cut out his bonus animals this morning, he took a good lookin' black horse."

"One of many, I should guess," Mackenzie observed.

"Not really, Colonel," Lee persisted. "You see, Tafoya has seen that horse before. It's got unusual white markings on both hind feet. Looks different."

"What's different about a black horse with white markings on its hind feet?" Mackenzie asked.

"The horse belongs to Quanah, Colonel, It's his war horse. Tafoya saw it a coupla times when he was riding with the Comancheros!"

Mackenzie was stunned. "Well, I'll be damned! Are you sure?"

"Yes, sir," Lee answered. "Anyway, Colonel, I bought the animal from Tafoya. I want you to have him. Sorta makes me feel better, if you know what I mean!"

Mackenzie was touched. "Well, Mr. Lee, I am both pleased and amazed! I thank you for your consideration!" He stroked the horse gently. "Heaven help us, you are a beauty! Quanah will surely miss you!" He turned to Lt. Lee. "Lieutenant, would you be kind enough to tell Mr. Thompson that I'd like to see him?"

Lt. Lee saluted. "Glad you like him, sir," he said, relief showing as he departed.

Mackenzie turned to Carter. "What's that old saying, 'what goes around, comes around'?"

Lt. Carter smiled. "Sounds about right."

"Quanah. What was that message he sent when he returned my grey?" Mackenzie ruminated.

"The grey is a great horse and you will need him if you choose to continue the fight aganst the Comanche. He does not want to put you at a disadvantage," Carter answered spontaneously

"By causing me to ride a poor pony!" Mackenzie added. "By Jupiter, Robert, as they say up in New England, 'If this don't beat all'!"

"So! Quanah was here!" Carter exclaimed.

"Possibly."

"Possibly?" Carter asked.

"Yes, Robert. The Indians' lack of fight, their confusion—not like Quanah."

"Good point," Lt. Carter answered. "But his horse?"

Mackenzie shrugged as Lt. Thompson appeared. "Can't explain it."

"You wished to see me, sir?" Lt. Thompson said.

"Yes, Lieutenant, I do. How many horses remain in the herd after the bonus selections?"

"Before we gave the scouts their pick, sir, there were about fifteen hundred head. The scouts took about four hundred. Leaves us with about eleven hundred head," Thompson replied.

"Thank you, Mr. Thompson," Mackenzie said. "Shoot them!"

Lt. Thompson was thunderstruck. "Shoot them?"

"Yes, Mr. Thompson," Mackenzie said evenly. "Shoot them!"

Thompson had trouble finding his words. "Shoot eleven hundred ponies?"

"Lieutenant, we cannot take the risk of having those animals regained by the hostiles! We have robbed the Comanche of their mobility, Mr. Thompson! They realize this! They will make every effort to recover their herd! Lieutenant Thompson, shoot them! Now! That's an order!"

"I . . . if you say so sir," his voice quavered. Lieutenant Thompson was near tears.

Mackenzie relented slightly. "Lieutenant, I am not ordering you personally to shoot the animals. Sergeant McSorley will organize that. Please send him to me immediately. You are dismissed, Mr. Thompson."

Thompson turned and stumbled away. Carter looked searchingly at Mackenzie, who met his gaze.

"We have no choice, Robert."

"I know. I know. But . . ." Carter mumbled

"No *buts*," Mackenzie said coldly. We've destroyed their lodges and winter supplies. The herd is no different."

"I know, Colonel. I know. You're right, of course," Carter said miserably.

Sergeant McSorley approached and saluted. "Reporting as ordered, sir," he said briskly.

"Sergeant, I want you to organize firing squads and shoot the captured herd," Mackenzie said matter-of-factly.

"But, sir. There's over a thousand," McSorley said, open-mouthed.

"Eleven hundred to be precise, Sergeant."

"You're not serious, Colonel, sir?" McSorley asked half-smiling.

"Do I look like I'm joking, Sergeant?" Mackenzie replied, frowning.

"But eleven hundred head, sir!" the sergeant exclaimed, appalled.

Mackenzie was nettled. "Sergeant! You will carry out my orders! Now!"

Tears glistened in McSorley's eyes. "Colonel, sir, for twenty years I've been a cavalry man. Horses are my life sir! They've saved my life three times, sir! Eleven hundred horses! I can't do it! Meanin' no disrespect, Colonel,

I just can't do it!" Tears flowed down his cheeks. "I know you can court
martial me, sir. But I can't do it! I'm Fourth Cavalry, Colonel! A horse
soldier! I'm a horse soldier!" Lieutenant Carter watched intently. "Colonel,
may I have a word with you?" he said softly.

"What is it, Lieutenant?" Mackenzie said petulantly.

"Colonel, your men have been riding and fighting for forty-eight hours
without much sleep and only one meal. They're stretched pretty thin, sir,"
Carter said earnestly.

"And?"

"And this firing squad duty—cavalry men shooting eleven hundred
horse—is a pretty heavy burden about now," Carter said.

"I realize that, Mr. Carter," Mackenzie said wryly.

Carter persisted. "On the other hand, Lieutenant Lawton and his infantry
have been guarding our wagons, eating and sleeping pretty regularly."

"Your point, Mr. Carter?"

"My point, sir, is that Lieutenant Lawton might be the right man,"
Carter concluded.

Mackenzie's bad hand twitched convulsively. "Quite so, Lieutenant," he
said decisively.

"Sergeant McSorley, ask Lieutenant Lawton to report to me on the
double. You can stand down, Sergeant. You're off the hook."

Sergeant McSorley blew his nose loudly and left hurriedly.

Lt. Lawton, an officer who performed brilliantly in the world of supply,
hurried to join his commanding officer. "You wished to see me, sir?"

"Lieutenant, I want you to organize firing squads and shoot the entire
captured pony herd. We will not break camp until you have carried out
your orders," Mackenzie said.

"Very good, sir," Lawton said smartly. "Firing squads will shoot the
Indian ponies."

"And, Mr. Lawton, use only your infantry men. The troopers have
earned a rest."

Lt. Lawton saluted. "Right away, sir," he said as he departed.

Mackenzie nodded at Carter. "Thank you, Mr. Carter. I commend your
resourcefulness."

Lt. Carter flushed. "Thank you, sir."

Lieutenant Lawton proceeded in a business-like manner. Eight-man
firing squads were formed. The horses were led to a shallow depression,

where they were summarily executed. As the body pile of animals increased, the horses, spooked by the relentless gunfire, became frantic with fear. With the smell of blood heavy in the air, the herd thrashed about in blind confusion among their wounded and dead. Making the scene even more surreal, an autumn thunder storm burst briefly, yet violently, overhead. The cavalrymen watched in shocked disbelief, and many turned away, sickened by the slaughter.

In his tent, Mackenzie uneasily paced its length time after time, as the killing dragged on, hour after hour. The sounds were overwhelming. Heartbreaking. Mackenzie was indeed paying the price of leadership. Finally, unable to retain his composure, Colonel Ranald Slidell Mackenzie pressed his hands over his ears in a futile effort to block out the screams, and doubled over, broke into choked sobs.

THIRTY-TWO

Fort Sill
April 25, 1875

Mackenzie's surprise attack and rout of the tribes at Palo Duro was a crushing defeat for the Indians. The loss of their winter supplies and lodges was devastating, but the loss of their horses was catastrophic. Scattered, hunted, and unable to rest or care for their sick and wounded, the Indians were pursued relentlessly by the Fourth. With the onset of winter and the prospect of starving women and children, many demoralized tribesmen drifted into the reservations, glumly accepting the white man's ways. Quanah and the Quahadis, however, clung doggedly to their freedom. His resolute leadership held his diminishing band together through that terrible winter.

Spring had finally arrived at Fort Sill. The warming sun was welcomed as a harbinger of summer and the greening of the grass gave evidence of kinder days ahead. On a soft, sunlit morning, Mackenzie called a meeting in his office. Invited were Billy Dixon and Dr. J.J. Sturms, post physician and interpreter. Married to a Caddo woman, he was respected by both friendly and hostiles.

Mackenzie gestured toward a map spread on his desk. "Gentlemen, I need your help. Quanah Parker and his Quahadis are the last remaining force of any size left out there. When, and if Quanah surrenders, any serious fighting will be over."

"He's s'posed to be up on the Staked Plains, ain't he?" Dixon asked.

Mackenzie nodded. "We think so, Mr. Dixon. But where on the Staked Plains? There's a good chance he might be over on the western edge. But nothing is certain."

"Prolly at a good waterin' hole," Dixon commented.

"Possibly. It's like the proverbial needle in the proverbial hay stack," Mackenzie answered.

"And you want us to find him?" Dixon asked.

Mackenzie smiled. "You're getting ahead of me, Mr. Dixon. Dr. Sturms here is known throughout the reservations as a fair man. He has an Indian wife. He knows their ways." He turned to Sturms. "I would appreciate you volunteering for this scout, Doctor. We need a man of your capabilities, and you speak the Comanche tongue."

Sturms shifted uneasily in his chair. "But Colonel, I haven't the faintest idea where to look for Quanah!"

"I appreciate that," Mackenzie said soothingly. "We have two reservation Quahadi Comanches who say they know where to find Quanah. If Mr. Dixon agrees to go along, you should have no problems. I want you personally to deliver my message to Quanah, and to wait for his reply."

"I see," Sturms said. "And the message, Colonel?"

"That I want him and the Quahadis to surrender their arms and to ride peacefully into Fort Sill. We will take good care of them. My word on that. However, if he fails to surrender, I will exterminate his band." Mackenzie said grimly.

"Tough message, Colonel," Dixon said softly.

"Yes and no, Mr. Dixon," Mackenzie replied. "Quanah is an intelligent leader of his people. I'm sure he's known that this message was only a matter of time."

"I'll need a day to get ready," Sturms said.

Mackenzie shook Sturms's hand. "I am in your debt, sir," he said. "And, you, Mr. Dixon?"

Dixon nodded. "Count me in!"

Mackenzie rolled up the map. "Thank you both, gentlemen," he said warmly. "Our supply people will provide whatever you need." They shook hands all around. "And, gentlemen," the Colonel said, "God speed!"

Two days later, a party of four—Dixon, Sturms, and the two Comanche scouts, Watebi and Toviah—rode out of Fort Sill, leading two pack horses, in search of Quanah and his band. After six days of riding, Toviah recognized two Quahadi scouts, and after a friendly meeting, the party was escorted to Quanah's sweet water camp. To the great delight of the Quahadi, the visitors had thoughtfully bought large quantities of coffee and sugar, which was quickly divided among the tribesmen.

Having survived a bitter, cold winter of howling winds and relentless hunger, the Quahadis refused to surrender their independence. The protuberant ribs of their famished ponies were proof of the winter's agonies. With increasing concern, Quanah kept a close watch on the children and the Old Ones—those the Hunger struck first. As the first signs of spring appeared and ice turned to mud, the tribesman gradually came to the realization that their world was changing. After numerous anguished councils between the Quahadis and Dr. Sturms, it was agreed that the band would break camp and join the reservation at Fort Sill.

The night before departure, greatly disturbed by the imminent loss of freedom for his people, Quanah retired to a nearby hilltop. With a blanket over his head, he spent the night in meditation and prayer. At dawn, an eagle flew overhead in the direction of Fort Sill. Reassured by this omen, but nonetheless saddened, Quanah rejoined his people and made ready for the journey to Fort Sill and a new way of life.

While camped out a day's ride from Fort Sill, Dixon conferred with Sturms. "You stay here with Toviah and Watebi," Dixon suggested. "I'm gonna ride out and let the Colonel know we're comin' in."

"Good idea, Billy." Sturms turned to Toviah. "He goes to tell Bad Hand the Quahadi come in peace."

Toviah nodded. "I go tell Quanah," he said.

In late afternoon, Quanah sought out Sturms. "I have talked with Toviah. I am ready to meet with Bad Hand."

"He is a fair man, Quanah," Sturms said reassuredly. "His word is strong. The Quahadis will be treated like warriors. They have won the respect of Bad Hand. Hear me!"

Quanah listened attentively. "There is much to learn, I think. It will take some time."

"Truly! You have made a wise decision for your people," Sturms replied.

"It is not an easy thing," Quanah said softly. "But the grandfathers came to me in my sleep and counseled me to take my people to the reservation."

Sturms nodded gravely. "The grandfathers are wise, Quanah. You will see!"

The Comanche hesitated briefly, then nodded.

In late evening, Dixon trotted into camp and swung off his horse. "How did things go?" Sturms asked. "You talk to the Colonel?"

Dixon poured himself a cup of coffee. "Yup. Expects us about midday. Won't have no trouble."

"Good!" Sturms said in relief. "I'll tell Quanah. His people are a little uneasy."

"Can't say I blame 'em," Dixon said. "Their dealings with the military ain't exactly been what you might call 'pleasant.'"

"Weapons!" Sturms asked. "What about their weapons?"

"All arranged," Dixon answered. " When we get to the signal station outside the fort, they'll turn their weapons in there. Then a cavalry escort will take us into the fort."

Sturms shook Dixon's hand. "Excellent! Appreciate what you've done, Billy!"

Dixon emptied the coffee grounds from his cup. "My pleasure, Doctor. Now, it's time for this hoss to hit the hay. See you bright an' early!"

In the quiet camp, the Quahadi Comanches, legendary warriors of the Southwest, spent their last night as free men under an endless canopy of stars. The tribes people, once feared and respected throughout the Southwest, grieved quietly for their fading way of life.

THIRTY-THREE

Fort Sill
June 2, 1875

In early morning, Fort Sill was bustling with activity as preparations were completed for the long-awaited surrender of the Quahadi Comanches. Mackenzie met with Lieutenants Lee, Carter, and Lawton on the parade ground. "Gentlemen, I want everything to go smoothly this morning. Spit and polish. Don't forget, we're taking the surrender of a valiant enemy. They deserve our respect. I want the best possible from our bugler when Quanah enters the fort. I want the band to play on key, if possible. Mr. Lawton, I want the infantry at attention and to give a hand salute. No 'present arms,' please. Mr. Carter, the troopers will be in review formation with hand salutes. No sabers. Let's not ruin a good thing! Understood?"

"Yes, sir," the officers responded in unison.

"Very well, gentlemen, you're dismissed," Mackenzie said. "Oh, Mr. Lee, may I see you for a moment?"

"Of course, sir," Lee answered.

"Mr. Lee, do you recall the day you returned my grey to me? The one that Quanah's riders ran off," Mackenzie asked solemnly.

"Hoped you'd forgotten that, sir," Lee said in embarrassment.

"No, not yet, I haven't, Lieutenant. But if you follow my instructions today, it will go a long way in helping me forget!"

Lee brightened. "Just say the word, Colonel."

"I thought you might say that, Mr. Lee," Mackenzie said wryly.

In the distance, the Quahadi Comanche could be seen. A palpable tension pervaded the parade ground as the column neared the fort. The bugler sounded off, announcing its arrival, and the troops fell into formation, with boots shined and brass polished.

Quanah led the column, dressed in his finest clothing, somewhat battered by winter's wear. Other warriors rode to the fore and rear, as guards, women, children, and the old ones rode in the center. As the Comanche entered the parade ground, the bugle sounded again and the band blared forth. The troops snapped to attention and saluted. Sitting rigidly in his saddle, Quanah gave no sign of recognition. His warriors followed his example. The column came to a halt in front of Mackenzie.

Astride his grey, Mackenzie saluted in unison with his officers. "Mr. Sturms! Be kind enough to translate for us, please." Sturms waved in agreement. "Please tell Chief Quanah how pleased I am to see him and his people."

After Sturms's translation, Quanah regarded Mackenzie in dignified silence. "The things Bad Hand has promised, we Quahadis accept. We know him to be a fair man. An honored enemy."

"We will take good care of your people. My word on that," Mackenzie replied. "Your young men can be proud of their strong hearts and bravery! Your warriors have won the respect of the Bluecoats!"

"I accept your word," Quanah answered. He recognized Bad Hand's grey and nodded slightly. "A fine horse! I seem to remember him!"

Mackenzie smiled. "You found him once, somewhere, and gave him back to me. I owe you my thanks."

A trace of a smile creased Quanah's face. "Yes, I remember."

"And now, let me return that favor," Mackenzie said. He turned to Lt. Lee. "All right, Lieutenant. Now." Lee left hurriedly and returned moments later, leading Quanah's black stallion. He had been groomed meticulously, and rubbed down with prairie grass. His coat gleamed in the sun. Stunned, Quanah covered his mouth in astonishment. Mackenzie savored the moment. "Quanah, I found this great horse somewhere, and wish to return him to his owner. To learn the ways of the white man, a man must have a fine horse, and I do not wish to put you at a disadvantage!"

Quanah smiled. "The words are familiar, Bad Hand. We are even, you and me. Maybe we know each other better than we thought."

The two warriors studied each other. Mackenzie smiled faintly. "Yes," he said quietly, "I have often thought that. But there is much to learn between us."

As the troops were dismissed to assist in the surrender proceedings, the two warriors nodded at each other in parting, but did not touch. Honored enemies, not yet friends.

Several weeks passed, and the Comanche, little by little, adjusted to their new life. The Old Ones and women were posted to a campsite beyond the fort, their ponies and mules attached by the cavalry. A number of warriors were imprisoned in the post ice house, but later released as better accommodations were provided.

Colonel Mackenzie, at the window of his small office, stared thoughtfully across the parade ground. A knock on the door announced Doctor Sturms. "Morning, Colonel," he said. "I spoke to Quanah and he'll join us shortly."

"Thank you, Doctor. Please have a seat. Your Comanche is better than mine."

There was a muffled sound from the hallway and Quanah entered the room without knocking. Sturms rose. "Quanah, the Chief of the Bluecoats welcomes you here and would make talk with you." Quanah was impassive, but his eyes flickered over the room, noting all its details.

"Tell him that I trust his people are comfortable, and that they are being treated well," Mackenzie said. "Ask him if there is enough food, enough coffee and sugar."

As Sturms translated, Quanah listened intently. "Tell Bad Hand that, at first, it was not good. But it has gotten better. Bad Hand is living up to his word."

Mackenzie drummed his three fingers on the table as he listened to Sturms's translation. "I am pleased to hear that," he said. He paused. "Tell him the reason we make the talk is that I am looking for a man who has the respect of his tribesmen, who has the respect of the Whites, his old enemies." He paused again. "Does Quanah know of such a man?"

As Sturms translated, Quanah fixed his gaze on Mackenzie. "If he found such a man, what would Bad Hand want of him?"

Mackenzie met Quanah's gaze. "I would ask him to be Chief of all the Comanche people, not just one band."

"Why?"

Mackenzie continued. "The People need a courageous and honest man to lead them. To tell their story to the White Chiefs in Washington. I need such a man to help me, to counsel with me, to help make the path smooth for the People who have come in from the plains."

Several moments of silence were broken only by the nervous drumming of Bad Hand's three fingers. Mackenzie broke the silence. "Would you know of such a man?"

Sturms finished his translation as Quanah stared icily at Mackenzie. "No," Quanah replied.

Bad Hand acted as if he had not heard the answer. "I have asked several ranchers to give some breeding cattle to your people. The buffalo are almost gone. Cattle will take their place."

Another silence. "I might know of such a man," Quanah said softly. Sturms and Mackenzie exchanged glances at the translation.

The Colonel raised his voice. "Private Wirth, bring us some coffee, please. Three cups and a lot of sugar." Private Wirth hurried into the office with coffee cups filled to the brim. Mackenzie smiled. "Here we are. Coffee all around," he said. Doctor Sturms added one spoonful of sugar to his cup. Mackenzie follwed suit. Quanah, however, ladled four spoons of sugar into his coffee. As he added the fifth spoonful, he noticed that the others had used only one. He hesitated, spoon in midair, and looked questioningly at his hosts. Mackenzie noticed Quanah's hesitation. "It's all right. Take as much sugar as you like." Quanah looked at Sturms for his translation.

"Bad Hand says to take as much sweetness as you want," Sturms said.

Quanah looked at Mackenzie, who nodded in agreement. But Quanah pushed his coffee cup aside, and motioned for another cup.

"Colonel, he wants another cup," Sturms said.

Mackenzie raised his voice again. "Private, another cup, please." Private Wirth returned with another cup and handed it to Quanah. Mackenzie solemnly filled the cup. Quanah carefully measured one teaspoon of sugar and added it to his cup. Sturms and Mackenzie exchanged glances, then looked at Quanah and nodded approvingly. Quanah took a noisy sip from his cup. There was a moment of silence as Quanah finished his coffee and wiped his mouth on his sleeve.

"I will speak to the man you seek tonight in his lodge," Quanah said. "He will speak to you tomorrow, when the sun is high." He rose and departed quietly, leaving three empty cups on the table, and a fourth cup, which had overflowed and rested in a black puddle.

The next day, precisely at noon, Quanah entered Mackenzie's office. Doctor Sturms promptly poured three cups of coffee from a battered pot.

"I am happy to see you, Quanah," Mackenzie said. Quanah said nothing, but his gaze settled on the sugar bowl. "Doctor Sturms, tell Quanah we would be pleased to have him drink coffee with us." Sturms passed the coffee cups, and each man took one spoonful of sugar. Stone-faced, they took their first sip, and nodded gravely at each other.

Quanah broke the silence. "Tell Bad Hand I have found the man he seeks," he said.

"Truly! How is this man called?" Bad Hand asked.

The Comanche drained his cup. "He is called Quanah Parker."

Mackenzie covered his mouth, feigning astonishment. "Truly! An honored enemy! My heart is glad to hear this!" Quanah remained silent. "You can do many good things for your people, Quanah, and I will help as much as I can."

Three weeks later, Mackenzie, leading his big grey across the parade ground, greeted Quanah, astride his black stallion. Mackenzie motioned to his interpreter. "Tell him I wish him to ride with me for a while."

"Yes," Quanah replied through the interpreter. Then, in newfound English, "Where?"

"*Where?* Good! You're learning," Mackenzie answered in surprise.

"Good! Good!" Quanah repeated.

Mackenzie swung into his saddle, and as the two men rode slowly from the fort, the officer explained their mission. "I want you to meet some men," he said through the interpreter. "Cattlemen. Ranchers."

Quanah looked puzzled. "What do these men want of me?"

"They have a problem and have asked for your help."

"Truly." Quanah said warily. "How can I help such men?"

"They wish to talk to the Chief of the Comanches," the Colonel replied.

Quanah studied Mackenzie's face. "These men. They are Tejanos?"

"Yes, they are."

"Did you know that the Tejanos have a law which says that no Comanches can come upon their land?" Quanah asked pointedly.

"No, I did not know that," Mackenzie answered. "But I can tell you, these Texans are good men. You have my word on that."

The little party of three rode in silence. Topping a rise, they saw several thousand cattle spread out below them being herded for the night amid the whistles and shouts of the drovers.

Two fires flickered by a chuck wagon. One was a cooking fire, crowded with cow hands, and the other was a smaller fire set apart, where three men were crouched on their haunches drinking coffee. As the riders started down the slope into camp, the three stood up, hitched their pants, settled their hats, and brushed dust from their clothing.

There was a noticeable stir around the cooking fire as the drovers recognized Quanah. "Hey! Ain't that Quanah Parker?" the cook asked.

"Sure as hell is!" the foreman exclaimed.

"It's him all right!" a cowhand said. "Last time I seen him, I was squintin' down a gun barrel!"

"Looks like you missed him!" the cook said mockingly

"Hope old Quanah dint bring none of his friends with him!" the cowboy said fervently.

"Them days is just about over, thank the Lord," the foreman replied. "Anyhow, boys, the boss invited him. It's all right."

"Looks like old Mackenzie, old Iron Pants hisself, is with him," the cook said.

"Appears so," the foreman replied. He turned to the cook. "Hey, Cookie, looks like three more for supper. Better add more water to the stew," he said laughing.

As the riders approached, they were welcomed at the small fire. Mackenzie dismounted and shook hands with the ranchers.

"Quanah, I want you to meet Burk Burdette, Dan Waggons, and J.D. Stubbs."

Quanah shook their hands. "Burrrk . . . Wagg . . . Subbs."

Burdette spoke through an interpreter. "Welcome, Quanah Parker, we are pleased to see you."

Stubbs reached for the coffee pot. "Belly up, boys, get her while she's hot."

Quanah carefully measured one teaspoon of sugar into his cup. He glanced at Mackenzie, who nodded ever so slightly. Their cups filled, the men sipped the hot liquid noisily and settled onto their haunches around the fire.

"Good! Coffee! Good!" Quanah said in English. The cattlemen nodded approvingly.

"You learn our language. That's fine,"Waggons said. "Burk here speaks your tongue."

"Not much, Quanah. Only a few words," Burdette said in Comanche.

"We are even, you and me," Quanah replied. "You in my tongue, me in yours."

"Truly," Burdette said. "Quanah, there are things we would say to you." He motioned to the interpreter. "The Comanche people live among great lands. And the grass grows thick and green on these lands." Quanah, impassive, poked the fire gently with a stick. "These grasses are food for the buffalo. They become fat from their grazing. But the buffalo are almost gone, and the grasses grow green in the spring, and wither away in the fall. And nothing eats them. The grass is not used. It is wasted."

Quanah raised his head from staring into the fire. "The buffalo, our brothers, are almost gone. Yes, that is true. But there are some of my people who say that they will return, will become like leaves in the forest again, will provide for their brothers, the Comanche, like they did for our grandfathers."

"What do you believe, Quanah?" Stubbs asked softly.

Quanah stared at Waggons. "I do not believe the white man will stop killing our buffalo. The only time he will stop is when there are no more buffalo to kill."

Stubbs bobbed his head. "Yessir, I agree with that! It ain't right, but that's the way it is."

Burdette persisted. "On the other hand, Quanah, cattle, the white man's buffalo are increasing like snowflakes in the winter. And they need grass. You have seen this. The Comanche people have some cattle of their own. They see how those cattle grow fat upon the grass."

"That is the truth," Quanah acknowledged.

"My cattle need more grass," Burdette continued. "More grazing space. Your people have much grass and grazing space that is not being used. Can we make a treaty? The Comanche and the cattlemen?"

Mackenzie spoke for the first time. "Don't mean to butt in, gentlemen, but *treaty* is a dirty word to the Comanche. Our side has yet to live up to its word and its treaties!"

Waggons grimaced. "That's a shameful fact, Colonel. But you're right. Maybe *contract* is a better word."

Burdette responded emphatically. "Bad Hand speaks the truth. But these men right here are not from Washington. We are people who live on the plains, as you do. We are men of our word!"

Quanah turned to Mackenzie. "But these men are Tejanos!"

"Yes, they are from Texas. But I trust in their word. I think you can, too," Bad Hand replied.

Quanah studied Mackenzie's face for a long moment, and then turned to Burdette. "What would you say to me?"

Burdette glanced appreciatively at Mackenzie. "If you allow us to graze our cattle on Comanche lands, we will give your people money."

"How much of the money?" Quanah asked, suddenly interested.

"Whatever is agreed upon by the Comanche people and the cattlemen," Burdette said.

Quanah turned to Mackenzie. "Will you counsel with me on this thing?"

"I would be honored," Mackenzie replied.

"Good. Then we must make the talk, you and me," Quanah said.

Waggons clapped his hands. "Sounds good to me! Sooner the better!"

Quanah raised his hand. "One thing . . ."

"Sure. What is it?" Burdette asked.

Quanah waved his arms expansively. "Some cattle people drive their herds across our lands going to the iron road. They just pass through, but they use our grass, too."

"The trail herds drivin' to the railroad?" Stubbs asked the interpreter. Quanah and the interpreter nodded.

Mackenzie shook his head in admiration. "Gentlemen, he's talking about toll fees!"

"For each animal?" Burdette asked.

"I should think it would be written into the contract," Mackenzie said.

Quanah stood up. "Bad Hand, we must go. We have much talk to make."

The men shook hands and the little party rode off into the evening. Stubbs gazed reflectively after them. "I'll be damned! Don't nobody ever teach that Quanah to play poker! He'd own us lock, stock 'n' barrel!" He spat into the fire. "Yessir, damned if he wouldn't!"

After extensive negotiations, a contract was agreed upon. The cowmen enjoyed good grass, and the Comanche, money. Everybody benefited. And the agreement gained the respect of both Whites and Comanche. Even President Theodore Roosevelt learned of the arrangement and sent his congratulations.

THIRTY-FOUR

Indian Territory
Washita River

A large cattle herd, driven by the Charlie McKnight outfit, entered Indian Territory, the land set aside by the U.S. Government, for the exclusive use of the Comanche. Because a drive across the Territory was the shortest route to the railhead, cattlemen had come to an agreement with the Indians that would protect their herds and the lives of their drovers. Quanah, as the titular head of the Comanche, had shrewdly suggested a toll fee for each animal.

The McKnight herd raised an immense cloud of dust, as it entered a modest alley, with low hills bordering the trail. The day was dark with rain clouds. A few drops pattered in the dust. As the herd plodded along, lines of menacing, mounted Comanche appeared on the ridge tops, feathers and decorations fluttering in the wind. The drovers pointing up the herd rode swiftly back to the gray-bearded McKnight.

"Washita River ahead, Mr. McKnight!" the point man said. "And it looks like we got company!"

Bose Ikard, the trail boss, joined them. "They're Comanche, sir," he said.

McKnight scratched his beard. "Yup, reckon they are," he replied.

The point man looked incredulous. "You expectin' them, sir?"

McKnight shifted in his saddle. "Sort of," he answered.

Bose nervously watched the ridge tops. "Well, they sure as hell are here!"

"Just take it easy, boys," McKnight cautioned. "Just calm down. Bose, ride out and tell our riders to keep their guns cased. You hear me?"

Bose nodded. "I hear you, Boss!" he said as he spurred his horse.

A single rider detached himself from the line of warriors and picked his way down the rocky slope. Dressed in buckskins, his braids fell down his back. He wore no paint. Bells attached to his coal-black horse jingled as it walked. It was Quanah.

McKnight spurred ahead to meet him, passing several concerned cowhands. "It's all right, boys," he yelled. "Just stay where you are. This ain't no war party!"

"How's he know that?" a young drover asked.

"Cuz they ain't wearin' no war paint, that's how!" Bose said condescendingly. "Open your eyes!"

The drover was visibly relieved. "Yeah, yeah, that's right! No paint!"

The herd moved slowly ahead, pushed by apprehensive cowhands. Nearing the herd, Quanah raised his hand in the sign of friendship.

"Jumpin' Jehoshaphat! Ain't that Quanah Parker?" the young drover exclaimed.

"Sure as hell is," Bose answered.

"Coupla years back, I betcha we'd have smoked him!" the youngster speculated.

"Coupla' years back, them Comanches would have run your sorry ass right outta here," Bose said sardonically." He pantomimed scalping. "Prolly lifted your hair, to boot!"

"You think so, huh?" his companion said truculently.

"I know so!" Bose answered. He spat tobacco juice. "They'd of had you for breakfast!"

"I dunno about that!" the youngster replied indignantly.

"I do," Bose said solemnly. "And the worst part is that they'd have planted me with you!"

"Aw c'mon," the drover said. "The both of us?" He started counting the silent warriors. ". . . Twenty-two, twenty-three, twenty four. Um, I see what you mean!"

"Damned straight!" Bose replied. "Let's you an' me keep these beeves movin'."

As the drovers rode off into the herd, they cast anxious glances at the lines of silent, watchful Comanche.

McKnight cantered up to Quanah and raised his hand in peace. "Quanah, how goes your life?" he asked in Comanche.

Quanah nodded. "Well, Gray Face. And you?"

"The same."

"Good!" Quanah gestured toward the herd. "And all this?"

McKnight quieted his horse. "The white man's buffalo are also well."

"I see that," Quanah answered. "It is our Comanche grass that makes them fat!"

"And tasty!" McKnight added.

"But not as tasty as our buffalo," Quanah said. "My people say that the white man's buffalo is too tough. It causes the Old Ones to chew too much!"

McKnight did not wish to be drawn into a losing argument. "Truly! I, too, prefer your buffalo. But I manage to choke down our beef."

Quanah smiled. "As do I." he confessed.

McKnight pointed to the watching Comanche. "I see you bring your friends!"

Quanah waved his hand in their direction. "They wish to see with their own eyes if the white man can keep a promise."

McKnight's locked eyes with Quanah's. "Yes, I understand. Tell your people that they are not dealing with someone in Washington far away! They are dealing with me, Gray Face! And I keep my word! I keep my promises!"

"Yes, I have told them that. But they wish to see for themselves!" Quanah replied.

"Fair enough!" McKnight responded. "Now, as we agreed, I will pay you one dollar for each head I drive across your land. I have about three thousand cattle here, so I owe you and your people three thousand dollars. Bose!" he called out. The trail boss hurriedly rode over to join the two. "Give him the envelope, Bose." Bose dug into a pocket and produced a soiled, wrinkled envelope, which he handed to Quanah, then rode back to join the drovers. "Here it is, like we talked," McKnight said. Quanah accepted the envelope without counting its contents. "With this money you can get many things for your people. Even new teeth for the Old Ones!"

"Yes, that is so," Quanah acknowledged. "I will tell them that." He paused. "One last thing," he said benignly. "As you know, my people are fond of gifts . . ."

"Seems you told me that before," McKnight interrupted, one jump ahead. He waved his hat at the trail boss. "All right, Bose, cut out a dozen head for Quanah. Make sure they're fat!" He turned to Quanah. "Take these cattle to your people as a gift from me."

Quanah gestured toward the herd. "This is a good thing for you, Gray Face, and a good thing for my people."

McKnight gripped the Comanche's hand. "Yes, it is a good thing. I will tell my friends that you and your people protect our herds!" Quanah wheeled his horse to leave.

"Hold on my friend," the rancher called out. "Here is something between us." He produced packets of tobacco and several pairs of earrings. "Enjoy the tobacco in your lodge tonight. And give these earrings to Weckeah, your first wife if I remember correctly." He paused. "Um . . . how many are there now?"

Quanah accepted the gifts with a smile. "Only six, Gray Face. You are learning our ways! That is good! Maybe some day you will become a good Comanche!" He whirled his horse. "Be well!"

As Quanah rode off, McKnight stood in his stirrups and called after him. "How can I become a good Comanche when I only have one wife?"

Quanah reined in. "My father had only one wife and he was a great Comanche!"

"A smart man, Quanah! A very smart man!" McKnight replied. "And he probably had a nice, peaceful lodge."

Quanah smiled and pointed toward the river. "Be warned, Gray Face. The sucking sands in the river are very bad."

"Thanks. Appreciate the warning," McKnight answered, and rode off to join the herd.

THIRTY-FIVE

Fort Sill
November 1904

Inside the Fort Sill post office, the Postmaster was shuffling through a stack of incoming mail. Suddenly a envelope caught his eye and sent him rushing out into the street.

"Anybody seen Quanah?" he asked a few bystanders.

"Yup. Seen him down by the Injun Court coupla minutes ago. Bein' a judge, he's prolly still there," said one. "What you want him for?"

The Postmaster waved an envelope bearing the presidential seal. "Got a letter here from the President of these Yew-nighted States of America! That's what I got! Old Teddy! T.R. hisself! Old Rough an' Ready!"

The bystanders were intrigued. "That right?"

"Damned straight! Special handlin', you might say!" The Postmaster walked briskly to the Court and entered. Inside he found Quanah in deep conversation with two Comanches. "Dint mean to butt in, Mr. Parker, but you got an important letter here!"

"Tell me the words," Quanah replied.

The Postmaster ripped open the envelope. "It's from President Theodore Roosevelt, hisself!" He took off his hat in respect. "Yessir. It says right here he requests the honor of your par-tiss-e-pay-shun in his Inawgural Pee-rade in Washington, on January 20, nineteen-hunnert an' five. It says here that there's gonna' be a ree-ception an' dinner afterwards that you're s'posed to go to!" The Postmaster shook his head in admiration. "Well, I'll be all go to hell! If this don't beat all! Gonna have beans an' bacon with old Rough 'n' Ready!"

"Tell Chief President in Washington I will come," Quanah said.

The Postmaster was ecstatic. "Sure thing! I'll tell him! Never writ to no President before. Lessee . . . do I say 'Dear President Roosevelt'? Or maybe 'Dear Teddy'? Wonder how he'd like 'Dear T.R.'?"

"Just tell him I come," Quanah repeated.

The Postmaster returned to earth. "Yup. Right away. You can sign the letter all official-like when I'm done." He started back to his office, waving the letter boisterously.

"Old Quanah's goin' to Washington to ride in Teddy's pee-rade! Ain't that somethin'! Our Quanah! Betcha that's gonna' turn some heads! Yessir!"

It was a clear, chilly day as Washington, agog with anticipation, scrambled with last-minute preparations for its Big Day. At the appointed hour, thirty-five thousand marchers stepped out, rife with pomp and circumstance, in the Inaugural Parade of 1905, which stretched for several miles. The military, in its gorgeous uniforms, dazzled the eye. Bands, both military and civilian, thumped and thundered. Flags of every description snapped briskly in the wind. President Roosevelt, with family and dignitaries, viewed the parade from a special platform above the crowds, which lined the avenue. As the military units passed in review, there was a roar from the crowd as forty members of Teddy's Rough Riders, veterans of the Battle of San Juan Hill, came into view. As they approached the reviewing stand, they broke into an exuberant gallop, skidding to a stop in front of their old commanding officer. A small boy, caught up in the excitement, was lassoed by a Rider, much to the merriment of the crowd. The Riders milled boisterously around the reviewing stand, waving and shouting to Roosevelt. One Rider whirled his horse in circles, and when his mount knelt, he swept off his campaign hat and bowed elegantly from the saddle. The President applauded vigorously. Animated by the appearance of his old comrades-in-arms, Roosevelt doffed his top hat and shook his fist in appreciation. As he took the salute of his old unit, a band enthusiastically blared "There'll Be A Hot Time In The Old Town Tonight," the Riders' anthem. Smiling broadly, the President danced a little jig to the music and waved his arms.

Following the blue-shirted Rough Riders, the Congressional Medal of Honor winners rode into view—Billy Dixon dressed in buckskins followed by Amos Chapman. As the medal winners passed in review, Teddy doffed his hat and placed it over his heart, bowing his head in honor.

The crowd responded with a roar. President Roosevelt turned to a dignitary. "By Godfrey, Senator," he said. "I'd give my right arm for that medal! Damned if I wouldn't!"

"Pretty strong statement, sir!" the Senator commented.

"It's the mark of a real man, sir!" Roosevelt replied. "By thunder, that's why there are so few of them!"

Next came six Indian chiefs riding abreast—their horses painted and decorated, tails tied up, ramrod straight in their saddles, and dressed in their best finery. Quanah was a striking figure, astride a white horse, brass earrings glinting in the sun and bridle bells jingling with each step of his horse. The crowd strained forward to see.

At the edge of the platform, two newspaper correspondents took note. Roland Phillips nudged his colleague Chris Ford. "There he is! Quanah Parker himself, in the flesh!" he exclaimed. "Last time I saw him was at Medicine Lodge Creek."

"Yeah. Who are the other five?" Ford asked.

"Wait a minute, check my notes. Let's see, second one in line is Little Plume, Blackfoot. Next two are Sioux, American Horse and Hollow Horn Bear. Next to last is Buckskin Charley. He's a Ute," Phillips explained."

"And the last one?"

"That's Geronimo. Apache. Hard case."

"I'm surprised that Quanah is here, what with the Medicine Lodge Treaty and all," Ford said.

"Can you believe the Government's land grab of Indian Territory?" his companion asked.

"It's a travesty! A disgrace! Shameful!"

"They called it the 'Oklahoma Land Rush,'" Phillips said. "Turning Indian Territory, guaranteed by treaty, mind you, into the state of Oklahoma. The state should be named 'Grand Larceny,' not 'Oklahoma!'"

"Yeah, white man's way not always the right way, that's for sure!" the *Boston Times* writer replied.

As the six Chiefs rode along the parade route, parents hoisted their children to their shoulders so that the little ones could see a "real, live Indian." There was much pointing and applause, as Geronimo, the sly showman, waved and bowed to the public.

A small boy excitedly leveled an imaginary rifle at the Chiefs. "Bang! Bang! Bang! Bang! Bang! Bang!" he shouted. "Gotcha!" He turned to his father.

"I got 'em, Father!" he exulted. "I got all six of them redskins!"

The father proudly patted his son on the head. "Atta boy, Will! Good boy! Only good Indian is a dead Indian!"

As the Inaugural Parade marched into history, Washington celebrated with a lavish reception for lawmakers, military notables, dressed in plumes and gold braid, society belles, Texas cowboys, political hangers-on, Indians, and Rough Riders from Arizona, New Mexico, and Texas, in their distinctive blue tunics. Overflowing punch bowls did a booming business. The buzz of conversation drowned the musical efforts of an overtaxed orchestra.

Burk Burdette, who had accompanied Quanah on his journey, guided him expertly around the hall, introducing Quanah to those who might be of help to the Comanche. As they made their rounds, they bumped into Billy Dixon and Amos Chapman, who were sampling the punch.

"Whoa, there, Quanah Parker!" Dixon said. "This is a little different than Adobe Walls!" Quanah smiled.

"We on same side, now," he answered.

Amos Chapman poured himself another cup of punch. "At least I had the brains to ske-daddle outta there afore it become downright unfriendly," he said.

Dixon laughed. "Not so long ago, we were tryin' to kill each other!"

"It was simpler then," Quanah replied. "Honored enemies. Not like this!"

"Amos an' me are pullin' out tomorrow mornin'," Dixon said. "Too many people here. Too many houses. No breathin' room."

"Me too," Quanah said. "After I see Chief President."

Burdette took Quanah by the arm. "C'mon, Quanah, maybe we can find him now."

President Theodore Roosevelt, the center of an admiring group, was talking with typical animation, waving his arms and showing his famous teeth in uproarious laughter. The old cowman was enjoying the occasion. Quanah and Burdette edged closer to him. When he turned and saw the Comanche, he pushed through the crowd surrounding him and strode to Quanah, hand outstretched in welcome.

"By Godfrey! Quanah Parker!" The President exclaimed. "I am pleased to see you, sir! I have heard good things about the work you have done for the Comanche people. I am honored by your presence, sir! And, Mr. Burdette! How's your herd back in Texas? Can we look forward to a plentiful supply of steaks?" Before Quanah or Burdette could respond, Roosevelt turned to the crowd. "Ladies and gentlemen, I want you to meet Chief Quanah Parker of the Comanches and Burk Burdette, a rancher friend of mine from Texas." There was a chorus of greetings from the crowd.

"We go home now," Quanah announced. "But ask Chief President to come hunt with me and this friend in my country."

"Mr. President, it's Indian land. Called 'The Big Pasture,'" Burdette added.

"Bully!" Roosevelt replied enthusiastically. "When?"

"At the Moon of the New Grass," Quanah answered.

"Moon of the New Grass?" The President was puzzled.

"That'd be April, sir," Burdette explained.

An administrative assistant waved a notebook at Roosevelt. "Your schedule, sir!" he said.

"Schedule be damned!" the President said emphatically. "We will make the necessary arrangements!" He turned to Burdette. "I would be obliged, sir, if you would notify my office of the dates."

"My pleasure, sir," Burdette replied.

Roosevelt smoothed his mustache. "I am honored by your invitation, Mr. Parker."

"We talk better when you come to my country," Quanah said. "Too many people here. Too much noise!"

"Couldn't agree with you more," Roosevelt said, beaming. He extended his hand.

"Until the Moon of the New Grass, then!"

Quanah returned the gesture and turned to leave with Burdette. As they wove their way across the hall, the President's gaze followed the Comanche. "By thunder," he said reflectively, "That man is the real thing. An American hero with the bark still on!"

Crossing the hall, Quanah noticed a punch bowl surrounded by unsteady patrons. "Is that foolish water they drink?" he asked.

"Sort of. Fixed up some. Tastes different. Same effect," Burdette replied wryly.

"I will ask Chief President why he gives foolish water to his people. It is not a good thing!" Quanah said solemnly.

"Good idea," Burdette said innocently. "He'll probably thank you."

As they approached the doorway to leave, a tipsy party-goer, glass overflowing, accidentally bumped into Burdette, spilling his drink over the Texan. Muttering an apology, the man vanished into the crowd, leaving Burdette to mop his shirt and coat. "Ah . . . hell's bells!" he exclaimed in disgust.

"See? Did I not say so?" Quanah said with a slight smile.

Burdette laughed. "You probably put him up to it!"

"No. Not have to," Quanah responded. He waved toward the crowd." See? Many more have too much foolish water." He surveyed the hordes of celebrants. "There are too many," he said reflectively and lapsed into the Comanche tongue, "I do not think we could whip them."

"Whip who?" Burdette asked.

"The soldiers," Quanah said in English. "Soldiers. Very many in parade. Too many horse soldiers! Too many big guns!"

"Biggest parade I've ever seen," Burdette said.

Quanah shook his head. "Too many! Indian people should see this! Change their hearts! Glad to be at peace!"

Burdette placed his hand on Quanah's shoulder. "I know that surrender always stuck in your throat like a sharp bone, Quanah. Now you can see that you did the right thing for your people, especially the children!"

Quanah's expression softened. "I know you speak the truth. The grandfathers knew this! Now, I know this. It makes my heart better."

Burdette took Quanah by the arm. "C'mon, honored friend," he said. "Let's go home."

THIRTY-SIX

Frederick, Oklahoma
April 1905

A train chuffed into the railroad yard at Frederick, Oklahoma, a sleepy, dusty cow town. It disgorged a small party of men, dressed in city clothing, and President Theodore Roosevelt. A large reception committee comprised of local ranchers, hunters, and the press met the visitors. A makeshift band struggled enthusiastically, but discordantly.

The President stepped to the platform at the rear of the caboose. He was his usual ebullient self, waving to the small crowd, who shouted welcoming remarks. "Ladies and gentlemen," he announced. "I am delighted to be back out west again, and to be welcomed to this fine town. As many of you know, I am here at the invitation of Chief Quanah Parker to join a hunt on the Indian land you call 'The Big Pasture.' And I expect to have a bully time!" He searched the crowd. "Chief Parker! Where are you?"

Quanah pushed his way through the throng and joined Roosevelt on the platform.

"I'm hoping to shoot a buffalo, Chief Parker! Can we do that?"

Quanah shook his head. "Buffalo all gone," he said. "White hunters shoot them all! We shoot wolves and coyotes. No buffalo. No."

President Roosevelt was unfazed. "Bully! When do we start?"

Quanah gestured dismissively. "We go now."

President Roosevelt the politician took over. "I want you good folks to know how much I value Chief Parker's friendship. And the fine job he is doing for his people. I appreciate that." There was a smattering of applause from his audience. "And now, ladies and gentlemen, I am going to step off this train and go hunting!"

The crowd erupted in laughter and applause. "Good huntin'. Mr. President!" someone yelled from the crowd. "Keep yer socks, dry, TR!" shouted another.

The President waved farewell to the crowd and climbed aboard a buggy driven by Burk Burdette. The hunting party and its growing entourage mounted up and rode out of town. Quanah was mounted on a black horse, decorated in Comanche fashion. The chuck wagon was driven by a grizzled cowhand, who doubled as the cook. A baggage wagon, loaded to capacity, was drawn by two mules. Clive McEnroe, the sole newspaper correspondent invited along for the hunt, climbed tentatively onto the wagon's seat. Dressed in city clothes, he had only recently graduated from Yale.

After an hour's ride the hunting party arrived at its campsite, a flat meadow nestled by a small stream. As the welcoming camp fires cast their flickering shadows on the chuck wagon and nearby tents, the hunters gathered their gear and hunkered down with mugs of hot coffee before drifting off to their bed rolls.

An hour after sunrise the next morning, a breakfast of beans, bacon, biscuits and scalding black coffee was served.

In his tent, Clive McEnroe was attempting to shave with a straight razor, cold water, and a poor mirror. The result was ragged and bloody.

Roosevelt, nursing a mug of coffee, lingered by the cooking fire. "Well, Burk, about time we saddle up, I should imagine. Sun's pretty far up."

"Pull out in twenty minutes, sir," Burk replied. "Horses and dogs are ready."

Clive McEnroe, bloodied from his first encounter with frontier toilette, walked by, blotting his bleeding face. The President looked up. "What the Sam Hill happened to you?"

The young correspondent was embarrassed. "Um, shaving, sir. No hot water."

The President laughed. "Hot water? Come on, lad, you're not back in New Haven!"

"I know that, sir. Maybe I'll grow a beard," McEnroe said sheepishly.

Roosevelt persisted. "When you were pestering me for permission to come on this hunt, remember, I warned you we'd be roughing it!"

"I remember, sir. I'll be all right. I'll catch on." Burdette watched the exchange with interest. "Can you ride, Mr. McEnroe?" he asked.

McEnroe blotted his face. "You mean a horse, Mr. Burdette?"

Burdette winked at the President. "Yup, of the four-legged variety. Only kind we got out here!"

McEnroe hesitated. "I may need a little practice."

"Afraid we ain't got time for that. Got some huntin' to do," the rancher answered.

"Burk's right, Clive. Probably better if you stay in camp," the President added.

Clive was crestfallen. "I've come all this way to cover the hunt, sir. At least let me try to ride!"

Burk glanced at Roosevelt. "All right, son, we'll get you a horse." Burdette hailed a wrangler, and an innocent looking pinto mare was saddled and the reins handed to Clive.

By now, a circle of spectators had assembled, anticipating the show. Clive struggled to mount, and after several attempts, succeeded. As he settled into the saddle, the mare, docile during the mounting, flipped her tail up and became a bucking, fishtailing nightmare. McEnroe was unceremoniously dumped on the ground. Three more attempts had the same result, much to the hilarity of the onlookers. As Clive, yet again, rose unsteadily to his feet, brushing dirt from his new "cowboy" clothes, Burdette had seen enough. He helped the young man to his feet. "All right, young feller, tell you what," he said. "Old Sally here, seems to be in a bad mood this morning. Now, I'm gonna be drivin' that buggy over there on the hunt. Could use some company. Whatta you say, Clive?"

"Bully idea, Burk," the President interjected. He slapped Clive on the back. "Good show, young man! I like your sand!"

"Thank you, sir," Clive said wanly. "The buggy sounds better than Sally."

"Probably feel better, too!" President Roosevelt added, laughing uproariously.

With the morning's entertainment concluded, the party set out on its hunt. Six greyhounds strained at their leashes, and their owner, renowned wolf hunter John Abernathy, struggled to keep them in check. After a short ride, the dogs became frantic, whining and yelping, signifying a game trail. Upon Abernathy's release, the greyhounds raced across the prairie. The hunting party followed at full gallop, led by an exuberant Roosevelt riding side by side with Quanah. Trailing behind was the buggy, flying across the prairie at top speed, bouncing and lurching, as Burdette urged his horses on, while Clive clung, wide-eyed and terrified, to the buggy's seat. This scene was repeated all morning, with several coyotes run down and killed. After a quick lunch, the party wound its way back to camp, arriving in late afternoon. Climbing down from his seat in the buggy, Clive wobbled unsteadily back to his tent to record the President's day. As the shadows lengthened, supper was dispensed from the tail of the chuck wagon, together with much laughter and camaraderie. After supper, in the growing darkness, the men lounged about the fire, sipping coffee and re-living the day's adventure. As the fire diminished, the usual banter among hunters subsided.

Sitting cross-legged on the ground, President Roosevelt spoke to Burdette. "Burk, why is this land called the 'Big Pasture'?"

Burdette refilled his mug. "Well, sir, it's the last of the Comanche-Kiowa Treaty land. Us cattlemen have been grazing our stock on it for some time now, for a fee."

"I see," the President said. He turned to Quanah. "Back East there's some who think this Big Pasture should be opened up for settlers, for farmers."

Quanah nodded. "Yes, I have heard that talk. But this is our land. All others taken away. Not right. We are few, but we are right! This is our homeland!"

Head cocked, Roosevelt listened intently. "I understand what you say," he said.

Quanah persisted. "When we fought the Bluecoats, we fought because they take away our country. Would you not do same if soldiers try to take away your country?"

The President shifted uneasily. "Your point is well taken."

"My people need Chief President's help. Tell Washington people leave our land alone," Quanah said.

"We should talk more about this," Roosevelt suggested.

"You make my heart glad," Quanah answered. "My people have lost our brothers, the buffalo. Gone. Buffalo sacred to my people." He waved his hands. "Buffalo and Comanche are one. Without them, Comanche are nothing!"

Roosevelt nodded without speaking. Quanah looked into his eyes. "Does Chief President have medicine to bring buffalo back?"

The President met Quanah's gaze. "Perhaps. Possibly," he replied.

"Comanche without buffalo are like white man without money," Quanah said.

"Yes, I see what you mean," Roosevelt said. "To see the buffalo on this land again would make both our hearts glad! Tell your people the Chief President will try to make this medicine!"

Quanah gripped the President's outstretched hand. "I will ask the grandfathers to help you," he said softly.

"Quanah, I will need all the help the grandfathers can give me," Roosevelt acknowledged.

"And then some," Burdette said.

"And then some," the President repeated.

The flickering shadows gradually subsided and the fire turned to coals, as the hunting party made its way to its bed rolls spread under a midnight blue sky sprinkled with stars.

The hunt was a success. President Roosevelt reveled in the experience, reminding him of his earlier days as a rancher in the Dakota Badlands. Traveling back to Washington, Roosevelt knew he was leaving with a greater purpose in mind, something that would help rebuild shattered U.S.-Indian relations.

As the Washington-bound train gathered speed, Clive McEnroe, looking more comfortable in his western garb, approached the President. "Sir, may I ask a question?" he asked.

The President looked up from a newspaper. "Fire away, my boy."

"Thank you, sir. Several nights ago, around the fire, I heard Chief Quanah Parker ask if you had the 'medicine' to bring back the buffalo."

Rosevelt nodded. "Yes, I remember."

"And you said, and I quote, 'Perhaps. Possibly.'" McEnroe said, consulting his notes.

"That's accurate," the President replied.

McEnroe looked puzzled. "How in the world can you bring back animals that are almost extinct, sir?"

President Roosevelt bent over confidentially and beckoned McEnroe closer. "Because, my boy," he whispered dramatically, "I have good medicine."

"Good medicine?" Clive repeated quizzically.

President Roosevelt maintained a straight face. "I'll let you in on a little secret," he confided. "Not only do I have 'good' medicine, I have excellent medicine. Some say even superb medicine!"

"I don't understand, sir," Clive said blankly.

The President beamed. "You will, my boy. You will."

THIRTY-SEVEN

Several months later, President Roosevelt was seated at his desk in the White House. A male secretary entered with his appointment book. "Mr. President your ten o'clock appointment, Mr. William Hornaday of the New York Zoological Society, is here."

"Send him in," Roosevelt said. Hornaday entered the office, and the President leapt from his chair beaming. "Hornaday! Wonderful to see you. Thank you for coming down from New York!" The old friends shook hands warmly. "Sit down, sit down."

"I am pleased to be here, old friend," Hornaday replied. "How are you and your rambunctious family faring?"

"Couldn't be better!" the President declared. "We're are all surviving Washington better than we expected!"

Hornaday smiled. "I am glad to hear that."

The President came right to the point, leaning across his desk. "William, I asked you here today to help me fulfill a promise."

Hornaday was intrigued. "How so?"

The President picked up a paper weight shaped like a buffalo from his desk and pointed it at Hornaday. "Quanah Parker, Chief of the Comanche, an old friend of mine, has asked me if I have the necessary medicine to restore the buffalo to his lands."

Hornaday corrected him. "You mean 'American Bison,' not 'buffalo.'"

"Buffalo, American Bison, you know what I mean," T.R. said impatiently.

"Yes, of course," Hornaday answered. "And do you have this medicine?"

Roosevelt leaned back in his chair and showed his teeth in his famous smile. "No, but you do!"

Hornaday extended his arms, palms up. "Theodore," he said. "I am a simple man, as you know. Completely devoid of medicine. Of any kind."

The President tightened the noose. "Ah, my friend, but you're not. Your medicine is that little herd of buffalo your Zoological Society maintains!"

"No medicine there, " Hornaday said innocently. "Just bulls and cows, and a calf or two."

"Exactly!" Roosevelt said triumphantly. "I couldn't have phrased it better!"

Hornaday feigned resignation. "You win, Theodore," he said. "Where do you want our American Bison shipped?"

"By thunder, William, you're a man after my own heart!" Roosevelt said fervently. "Ship them to Cache, Oklahoma. Closest railhead to Fort Sill."

"Then what?" Hornaday asked

"We've just set aside eight thousand acres in the Wichita Mountains as a preserve. Going to fence the whole shebang in. We'll release the animals there as breeding stock. Good range. Protected. They'll do just fine!"

"Indeed! I am impressed! You are to be congratulated, sir!" Hornaday marveled. "A most laudable plan!"

"It's just a start, old friend," the President said expansively. "Now, when can you ship the animals?"

"I'll make the necessary arrangements as soon as I return to New York," Hornaday answered. "You probably can expect them to arrive in mid-October. I believe the Indians refer to that time of the year as 'The Moon of the Falling Leaves.'"

Roosevelt was overjoyed. "Bully! Cows, bulls, and calves, I should expect?"

Hornaday laughed. "Just the way Mother Nature intended it. And bye the bye, Theodore, do you realize that there are only five hundred and fifty bison left out West, down from sixty million a few years ago? Five hundred and fifty bison left out of sixty million animals? It's an atrocity!"

Roosevelt was appalled. "A national disgrace! A national disgrace! Let's hope we can help turn the tide!"

After a few pleasantries the meeting ended, and the President summoned his secretary. "Take a letter to Mr. Frank Rush, manager of the Wichita Mountains Preserve. *Dear, sir, please be advised that you will receive a shipment of American bison from the New York Zoological Society. These animals will arrive by rail in the town of Cache, Oklahoma, in the Moon of the Falling Leaves. Please make all necessary arrangement to transport them from Cache to the Preserve. Sincerely . . ."*

The secretary was perplexed. "'Moon of the Falling Leaves,' Mr. President?"

"That's mid-October. Indian talk," Roosevelt explained casually.

The secretary was impressed. "Yes, sir, Moon of the Falling Leaves. I'll explain that to Mr. Rush."

It was mid-October, the Moon of the Falling Leaves, in Cache, Oklahoma, and the town's rail yards were bustling. Two rail cars, bearing some fifteen buffalo, stood on a rail spur. A noisy crowd of onlookers and curious townspeople ogled the cars and their cargo. Fifteen large, mule-drawn-wagons, each containing a barred holding pen, were arrayed around the cars. Each animal was gingerly prodded from its rail car into a wagon by sweating, cursing freight men. The crowd thoroughly enjoyed the show.

"Damn! If old T.R. wanted them animals so bad, least he coulda done is give us a hand!" a freighter said.

Another freight man cleaned a suspicious substance from his boots. "Earned my wages for today and into next week, I want to tell ya," he declared.

The wagon master spat copiously "Stop yer bitchin'! At least you're shut of them smelly things! Us drovers gotta live with them, up real close, until we unload their sorry-assed selves!"

"Better you than me," the freighter answered.

The wagon master climbed aboard the lead wagon. "Awright, you drovers, climb aboard and let's get this sorry sight outta here!"

In single file, fifteen wagons, creaking and groaning under their bellowing cargo, set off for the Wichita Mountains Preserve near Fort Sill, Oklahoma. As they left the crowd drifted back into the saloons for a review of the day's events.

Billy Dixon and Amos Chapman had heard the rumor of the return of the buffalo. Curious, they set off for the Preserve to see for themselves. As they neared their destination, they were surprised to see a number of Comanches camped in the area. Families with children, even grandchildren, dressed in their best finery, awaited the fulfilling of a Comanche prophecy: the return of their brothers, the buffalo.

Frank Rush, Manager of the Preserve, hailed the visitors. "Glad to see you fellers! Climb down and join the party!"

"Frank, when did all them Comanche get here?" Dixon asked.

Frank waved toward the encampment. "Some been here for a week or so!"

"That so?" Amos said. "How'd they know about it?"

"When I got the President's letter, I told Quanah about it. He done the rest," Rush answered.

"Guess so!" Dixon said, impressed by the crowd. "Quanah here?"

"Yeah, somewhere. You'll see him."

While they talked, there was a stir among the crowd, as the first wagon lumbered into view. As more wagons arrived, they were swarmed by eager Comanches, who strained to catch a glimpse of their long-awaited brothers. Despite the confusion, the wagons, one by one, approached the open gate of the Preserve and disgorged an agitated buffalo into its new home. Upon release, the animals grazed hungrily on the abundant grasses. The Comanche pressed their children against the wire fencing, excitedly pointing to the buffalo. A few old warriors wore their traditional buffalo head dresses, recalling past days. Fathers and grandfathers hoisted toddlers to their shoulders for a better view. It was a poignant scene, foretold in tribal legend, now realized, albeit under different circumstances. The emotion and fervor of the day were best exemplified by an elderly Comanche, seated cross-legged on a buffalo robe, arms extended skyward to the Great Spirit, as tears streamed down his weathered cheeks.

Billy Dixon, a man who contributed to the demise of the great buffalo herds, sought out Quanah, his ancient enemy. He rode slowly up to the Comanche chief, and made the historic, now outdated peace sign. "Well, Quanah, I never thought I'd see the day."

Quanah shifted in his saddle. "We Comanche have prayed for this day."

Dixon nodded. "So have I."

"You? Known to my people as 'Buffalo Killer'!" Quanah replied. "Why? So you can take more hides?"

"No! No more! That's over!" Dixon replied, chastened. "The buffalo belong here. Like the Comanche. They belong here. Maybe my people will realize that now."

There was a long pause. "White man took away our buffalo. Now he gives them back!" Quanah paused again. "White man took away our country. When will he give that back?"

"I don't know, Quanah," Dixon said awkwardly. "But what I do know is that more and more of my people are asking that same question."

Quanah looked into Dixon's eyes and motioned with one arm in an all-inclusive gesture. "Your people! My people! Maybe some day all same people! Our people, yours and mine! See how my people smile! They are happy! Their brothers, the buffalo, have come back! That is a good thing. And your people brought them back! That, honored enemy, is the best thing!"

The old adversaries looked over the happy crowd, as Comanche families introduced children and grandchildren to their heritage. Events had truly come full circle. With a full heart, Dixon reached for Quanah's hand. Surprised by the emotion shown by the old hide hunter, Quanah hesitated briefly and then gripped his hand.

Dixon nodded. "Honored enemy," he said softly.

Quanah smiled. "Yes that is so," he said. "Honored enemy yesterday, honored friend today."

EPILOGUE

Cynthia Ann Parker (Naduah) died from fever near Fort Worth, Texas, in 1870, following the death of her daughter, Topsanna. At Quanah's request, Cynthia was re-buried in the Fort Sill, Oklahoma, cemetery in December 1910.

Quanah Parker's extraordinary life included entertaining President Theodore Roosevelt and British Ambassador Lord Brice at his ranch house, and a part ownership in the Quanah, Acme and Pacific Railway Company. The town of Quanah, Texas, was named in his honor. On February, 1911, Quanah died of pneumonia and was laid to rest next to his long-lost mother at Fort Sill.

Billy Dixon and Amos Chapman were forced to return their Congressional Medals of Honor because, as civilian scouts for the U.S. Cavalry, they were not considered to be enlisted personnel. However, on June 12, 1989, the United States Government reconsidered, and restored the Congressional Medal to both Dixon and Chapman. Billy Dixon, a retired rancher in his later years, died in 1913 and was buried at Adobe Walls. Amos Chapman died in 1929 in Oklahoma.

Colonel Ranald Slidell Mackenzie was promoted to general and died of military disablilities brought on by his wounds in Staten Island, New York, in 1889.

Bat Masterson became a legendary frontier marshal, and concluded his career as a respected newspaper man and sports writer for the *New York Morning Telegraph*. He died in New York City in 1921.

Newspaper man, Henry Morton Stanley, on assignment from the *New York Herald*, searched for, and discovered, the missing British explorer, David

Livingston, in central Africa on November 10, 1871.

On November 10, 1907, the three million-acre Indian Territory, supposedly preserved for the sole use of the Indian people, was blatantly usurped by the U.S. Government, assisted by a number of illegal "land rushes" and the congressional Jerome Act. The end result of this fraud was the establishment of the State of Oklahoma.

In 1924, Congress passed the Sullivan Act, an act of gratuitous insolence that permitted Native Americans to become citizens of the United States.

The fifteen American Bison (buffalo) released on the eight thousand-acre Wichita Mountains Preserve has since multiplied into herds of thousands. The area is now designated as the Wichita Mountains National Wildlife Refuge and encompasses fifty-nine thousand acres.

An enduring legend maintains that on moonlit nights, a ghost herd of Indian ponies can be seen galloping along the rim of Palo Duro Canyon, their manes and tails streaming in the wind.

POSTSCRIPT

In 1887, the Dawes Act was passed, calling for Indian lands to be subdivided among the various tribes—160 acres per family, and 80 acres to a single subscriber. Included in the distribution were plows, farm tools, and crop seed, the necessary ingredients for basic farming. All land not subscribed would be put up for public sale. At the time, Senator Henry Teller of Colorado stated, "The real aim of the Dawes Act is to get the Indians' land and open it up for settlement." And when many tribesmen subscribed to the plan, they were allotted some acreage nearby, but the balance was in non-contiguous land in faraway locations, such as mountains and forests, all in an effort to discourage neophyte farmers, and with an eye towards fracturing tribal unity. In 1887, the U.S. government placed some 54 million acres of these lands in a trust fund (Indian Money Trust) to be managed by the Department of Interior for the benefit of the Indinas. For the next 100 years there was no accounting of any of these funds by the Interior. On the contrary, documents were "misplaced," records inexplicably disappeared, and the beneficiaries of the Trust, the hundreds of thousands of Indians, received virtually nothing. (In the meantime, Indian range land was being leased or sold. Oil wells were gushing royalties and timber stands were sold or leased to other interests. The proceeds of all these activities disappeared into government hands as did the contracts and agreements.)

Impoverished, bewildered, and infuriated, the Indian people brought a class-action lawsuit against the Department of Interior in 1996. Leading the fight was Elouisa Cobell, a lady of the Blackfeet tribe, who devoted her life to righting this wrong, marshaling her forces and raising substantial funds. From the beginning, her cause gradually won her recognition. She was awarded "warrior" status by the Blackfeet tribe.

As the trial progressed, a series of scandalous allegations came to light regarding the Interior's mismanagement of the Indian trust funds. An elderly Blackfeet Indian whose land included five producing oil wells received $30 a month in royalties from the Interior. Royalty checks for eight cents per month were sent to a number of Indians. Jim Thorpe, the legendary Sac and Fox athlete, requested money for his travel expenses to Sweden where he was to represent the United States in the 1912 Olympics. He was denied. Later the Bureau of Indian Affairs sent him $25. Thorpe won two gold medals despite the government's indifference. Commenting on the allegations as a whole, presiding judge Royce C. Lamberth wrote:

"The Department of Interior's administration of the individual Indian Money Trust has served as the gold standard for mismanagement by the federal government for more than a century. As the trustee-delegate of the United States, the secretary of Interior does not know the precise number of Indian Money Trust accounts that she is to administer and protect, how much money is or should be in the Trust, or even the proper balance for each individual account. In short, the Department of Interior has managed the Individual Indian Money Trust disgracefully."

The events of the trial certainly seemed to favor the plaintiffs. In 1999, Secretary of the Interior, Bruce Babbitt, was held in contempt of court when his department ignored a court order to deliver files to the courtroom. In the same year, Secretary of the Treasury, Robert Rubin, was also held in contempt of court for his failure to deliver documents to the court room. In 2001, new Secretary of Interior, Gail Norton, was ordered to stand trial on contempt charges, accusing her of mismanaging a billion dollars of Indian Trust Fund monies. Assistant Secretary of Interior, Neal McCaleb, was also cited for this offense. Furthering the incrimination of the Treasury was the Federal Reserve Bank's reporting the destruction of 162 boxes of related documents by the department. This action was covered up by the government lawyers.

In 1996, the Interior spent $21 million for defense attorneys for this case, followed by another $21 million in 2000, excluding salaries and normal expenses of the Department.

Cobell's accountants, after much research, reported that the government owed the Indian nations $176 billion for its mismanagement and hypocrisy over the past 100 years. When the Interior challenged the figure, Cobell fired back. "It's not your money, and never was," she said. Judge Lamberth concluded:

"The fund is not the government's money. It belongs to the beneficiaries. The Trust Fund is supposed to be administered in their best interest, and not in a manner that is most convenient to the government. Instead, throughout its management of the Indian Individual Trust funds, the Interior has chosen to behave almost as though the trust fund were a toy, one that it can abuse and mistreat if it wants to, and no one can tell it differently. The United States was founded upon the principle that its government derives its powers from the consent of the governed. But the Interior has stood this proposition on its head."

On December 8, 2009, Elouisa Cobell's quest ended, not with a bang, but not with a whimper either. An agreement was reached and the following terms were embraced. The United States government will provide its Indian citizens:

A $1.4 billion Trust and Accounting Administration Fund.

A $2 billion Trust Land Consolidation Trust.

A $60 million federal Indian Education Scholarship fund to improve access to higher education for Indian youth.

A commitment to appoint a commission to oversee and monitor specific improvements in the Department's accounting for management of individual Indian trust accounts and trust assets from now on.

After the historic signing of the agreement, Elouisa Cobell spoke to her people:

"Indians did not receive the full financial settlement they deserved, but we achieved the best settlement we could. This is a bittersweet victory, at best, but it will mean a great deal to the tens of thousands of impoverished Indians entitled to share in its financial fruits, as well as to the Indian youth whose dreams for a better life, including the possibility of one day attending college, can now be realized."

There followed a year of wrangling over the terms of the agreement and its payment schedules by Congress. Late in 2010, agreement was reached by the lawmakers, and on December 8, 2010, after President Obama signed the legislation, it was announced that the nation's Native American population would receive 3.4 billion dollars. Elouisa Cobell said, "It took my breath away."

Joan of Arc is alive and well and living in Montana.

LIST OF CHARACTERS

This book was written in an effort to illustrate the interconnection of seemingly unrelated events in the American southwest in the late 1800s. While adhering to the authenticity of historical events, the reader will understand that some creativity was needed by the author to bridge the years between these events. Hence the introduction of fictional characters. Those names bearing an asterisk (★) were real characters. Those unmarked are fictitious.

★**Baylor, John**. Discredited ex-agent of the Texas Comanche Reservation, he reviled anything Comanche. In the past, he had led an attack on a Comanche village and murdered a number of tribesmen and their families.

★**Beaumont, Eugene**. Hard-riding officer whose capture and containment of the pony herd at Palo Duro Canyon figured hugely in the operation's success.

★**Black Eagle**. A Kiowa representative at the Medicine Lodge Council.

★**Boehm, Peter**. A captain in the Fourth calvalry. Shared the position of chief of Scouts with Lt. Thompson.

Burdette, Burk. A Texas cattleman who befriended Quanah upon his surrender.

Carlos. A part-Mexican interpreter with the militia. Had ability to speak some rudimentary Comanche.

★**Carter, Robert**. Mackenzie's chief of staff.

Cass, Donny. A Private in the Fourth Cavalry.

★**Chapman, Amos**. Respected scout and frontiersman who lived off and on with the Cheyenne. Married Mary Longneck, daughter of the Cheyenne chief, Stone Calf.

Davis, Whit. A Connecticut Yankee and seasoned veteran of the Civil War, he served under Mackenzie in a number of battles.

*Dixon, Billy: A young man, mature well beyond his years. He left home in Missouri at the age of fourteen to seek adventure in the far West, and became a renowned buffalo hunter, taking an active role in the slaughter of the Texas herd. A quiet leader of men, he was renowned for his accuracy with a rifle.

Elias, Ben (Eli). A trooper in the Forth and a career cavalryman. Ben and others like him were the backbone of the southwestern campaigns.

*Ethan. Tonkawa scout for Mackenzie.

Falling Water. A young Comanche warrior intent on performing acts of heroism and bravery in front of his elders.

Five Wolves. A tribal elder known for his wisdom and fairness. Among the Comanche he was a "civilian" chief by acclamation of his fellow tribesmen.

Forbes, Peter. Young newspaper correspondent for the *St. Louis Post*.

Ford, Chris. Newspaper correspondent for the *Boston Times*.

*Frenchy. Dixon's hired cook.

Gallup, J. Commissioned officer in the Fourth Cavalry.

Gaudet, Lucas. A Private in the Fourth Cavalry.

*Harney, William. An Army General present at the Medicine Lodge Treaty Council.

*Hanrahan, Jim. Prominent business man in Dodge City. Helped establish the trading post at Adobe Walls and ran its only saloon.

*Hornaday, William. President of the New York Zoological Society.

*Ikard, Bose. Charlie McKnight's trusted trail boss. A pioneering black man in the history of the West.

*Isa-Tai. Comanche medicine man whose flawed yellow magic cost the attackers of Adobe Walls unexpected losses. Thereafter known as "Coyote Droppings."

*Job. Tonkawa scout for Mackenzie.

Kosack, Paul. Regimental surgeon for the Fourth Cavalry.

*Lawton, Henry. A genius in the intricacies of military supply.

*Lee, John. Young officer with the Fourth Cavalry.

*Leonard, Fred. Partnered with Myers in opening the trading post at the Walls.

*Long Hat. A Comanche representative at the Medicine Lodge Council.

Lopez. A part-Kiowa mule skinner, pressed into service as a translator during the encounter with the Kiowa Chief, Satanta.

*Loving, Jim. A local rancher, destined to make a name for his family in the Texas history books.

*Mackenzie, Ranald Slidell. A West Point graduate and Civil War hero who was charged with the pacification of the Comanche, Cheyenne, and Kiowa in the Southwest.

*Masterson, Bat. At age twenty, Bat started his famous western career as a buffalo skinner in the employ of Dixon. He was destined to leave his mark on Western lore as the Marshal of Dodge City in his later years.

*McCabe, Cranky. The second skinner with the Dixon hunting party.

McCarthy, Kenneth. Post commandant at Fort Cooper.

*McCusker, Phillip. Official interpreter for the Treaty Council.

McEnroe, Clive. Greenhorn newspaper correspondent.

McKnight, Charlie. A rancher and noted tracker.

McSorely, Patrick A. Reenlisted after the Civil War's conclusion. The Fourth Cavalry was the only home he knew . . . and loved. His kind of non-com made Commanding Officers better by association.

*Mooar, John and Wright. Storekeepers in Dodge. The brothers were responsible for creating the profitable demand for buffalo hides.

*Myers, Charlie. Co-owner of Myers' store at Adobe Walls. Sold supplies and bought hides. A prime mover in the expedition to Adobe Walls.

*Nokona, Pecos (Peanut). Younger brother of Quanah. Second son of Peta Nokona and Cynthia.

*Nokona, Peta (He Who Travels Alone and Returns). Comanche war chief, husband to Cynthia Parker, and father of Quanah and Pecos. A man whose courage and leadership abilities became legendary among the Comanche.

*Nokona, Quanah (Fragrance). Son of Cynthia Parker and Peta Nokona. Later in life, became known to the whites as Quanah Parker. Became one of the most famous men in the southwest. Led the Quahadi band of Comanche throughout the Red River War where he was pitted against Col. Ranald Mackenzie's Fourth Cavalry. Recognizing his unusual talents, local cowmen built him a famous ranch house. Later he became a judge in the Indian Court, a friend of cattle baron Charles Goodnight, part owner of the Quanah, Acme and Pacific Railway, and gave his name to a new town, Quanah, Texas.

Nolan, Wayne. A trooper with the Fourth Calvalry. Irish, fair skinned, with a prized head of hair.

*Ogg, Billy. Made his living among the buffalo herds. Was part of Billy Dixon's hunting outfit.

★Old Man Keeler. An old-time frontiersman. Lived with the Cheyenne for some time.

★Olds, Hannah and Bill. Managed the restaurant at Adobe Walls.

★Oscar. Bartender in Hanrahan's Saloon at Adobe Walls.

★Parker, Ben. Brother of Silas Parker.

★Parker, Cynthia. Mother of Quanah and Pecos, and wife to Peta Nokona. She was captured by the Comanche when she was nine years old from her family's cabin in west Texas. The Comanche renamed her *Naduah*, meaning "Someone Found."

★Parker, Elder. Grandfather and patriarch of the Parker family. He was shot and scalped before the horrified gaze of his wife, Sally.

★Parker, Isaac. Uncle to Cynthia Parker.

★Parker, John. Little brother to Cynthia. Was captured and adopted by the Comanche. Later became a Comanche warrior. Was eventually ransomed and returned to his white family.

★Parker, Lucy. Mother of Cynthia, John, Orlena, and Silas. After the attack upon the fort, Lucy was able to save her two babies.

★Parker, Orlena. Infant daughter of Lucy and Silas.

★Parker, Sally. Wife of Elder Parker and grandmother to Cynthia.

★Parker, Silas. Husband to Lucy, and father of their four children. Gave his life to the protection of his family.

★Parker Jr., Silas. Infant son of Lucy and Silas.

Phillips, Roland. Newspaper correspondent for the *Chicago Sun*.

Pinney, Lem. Veteran cavalry non-com.

★Rath, Charlie. Partner in Rath and Wright's general store.

Red Elk. An elderly Comanche hunter of mighty exploits. Revered by his tribesmen for his heroism and ability to make excellent bows and arrows.

Rogers, James. Post physician at Fort Cooper.

★Roosevelt, Theodore. Twenty-sixth president of the United States who had seized the imagination and affection of United States citizens. His appreciation and regard for Native Americans was well in advance of the times.

★Ross, Sam (Sul). Newly commissioned officer in a local militia, the Texas Rangers. A tough, fearless man whose name still commands respect in Texas.

Running Bird. Mother to White Rain. A widow for a number of years.

★Rush, Frank. Manager of the newly created Wichita Mountains Preserve.

*Satanta (White Bear). Legendary chief of the Kiowa.

*Shadler, Ike and Shorty. Freight haulers for the hide men.

*Silver Brooch (Toshaway). A Comanche representative at the Medicine Lodge Council.

Simpson, Jared. Wagon master and trail guide for hire.

Singing Woman. A Comanche widow who raised Cynthia Parker. Originally captured by Peta Nokona from a Mexican settlement.

Stage, John. Post sutler at Camp Cooper.

*Stanley, Henry Morton. Correspondent for the *New York Herald*.

*Stone Calf. Chief of the Cheyenne.

Stubbs, J.D. A Texas cattleman.

*Sturms, J.J. Post physician at Fort Sill. Considered a fair man by the Comanche, his presence at peace talks with Quanah was key to Quanah's ultimate surrender.

*Tafoya, Jose. The leader of a band of Comancheros. He was captured by Mackenzie's scouts and convinced to guide the Fourth Cavalry across the Staked Plains to Palo Duro Canyon, an area largely unknown to the military.

*Taylor, N.G. U.S. commissioner of Indian Affairs.

*Ten Bears. An eloquent and thoughtful elderly leader of the Comanche.

*Thompson, William. Shared position of chief of Scouts with Captain Boehm.

*Tonks. Tonkawa tribal members who possessed a fierce hatred of all things Comanche and became a source for scouts for the Fourth Cavalry.

*Topsannah (Prairie Flower). Young daughter of Cynthia and Quanah.

*Toviah. A Comanche scout for Mackenzie.

*Tyler, Billy. A young freighter seeking safety from rumored Indian attacks.

Waggons, Dan. A Texas cattleman.

*Watebi. A Comanche scout for Mackenzie.

*Weckeah. A pretty young lady infatuated with the youthful Quanah. Became his first wife.

White Rain. A teenaged girl of the Comanche village who looked down upon Cynthia, as a captured, white know-nothing.

Wirth, Wiley. Company clerk for the Fourth Cavalry.

*Wright, Bob. Partner in Rath and Wright's general store.

Yellow Bear. A respected elder among the Comanche and father of Weckeah.

BIBLIOGRAPHY

Barrett, S.M. *Geronimo's Story of His Life* (New York: Duffield and Co., 1905).

Brandon, William, et al. *The American Heritage Book of Indians* (Rockville, MD: American Heritage Publishing Co., 1961).

Brooks, Chester L., and Ray H. Mattison. *Theodore Roosevelt and the Dakota Badlands* (Washington D.C.: National Park Service, 1958).

Brown, Dee, and Martin E. Schmitt. *Fighting Indians of the West* (New York: Charles Scribner's Sons, 1948).

Brown, Mark H., and W. R. Felton. *Before Barbed Wire* (New York: Bramhall House, 1956).

The Buffalo Hunters (New York: Time Life Books, 1992).

Connell, Evan S. *Son of the Morning Star: Custer and the Little Bighorn* (San Francisco: North Point Press, 1984).

Curtis, Edward Sheriff. *Visions of a Vanishing Race* (Boston: Houghton Mifflin Co., 1976).

Dixon, Olive K. *Life of Billy Dixon* (Dallas: P.L. Turner Co., 1914).

Eastman, Charles A. *Indian Boyhood* (New York: McClure, Phillips & Co., 1902).

Erdoes, Richard, and Alfonso Ortiz. *American Indian Myths and Legends* (New York: Pantheon Books, 1984).

Fleming, Paula Richardson, and Judith Luskey. *The North American Indians in Early Photographs* (New York: Barnes and Nobles Books, 1992).

Gard, Wayne. *The Chisolm Trail* (Norman: University of Oklahoma Press, 1954).

Graham, W.A. *The Custer Myth* (Harrisburg, PA: The Telegraph Press, 1953).

Grinnell, George Bird. *Blackfoot Lodge Tales* (New York: Charles Scribner's Sons, 1892).

Grinnell, George Bird. *The Fighting Cheyennes* (New York: Charles Scribner's Sons, 1915).

Grinnell, George Bird. *Pawnee Hero Stories and Folk-Tales* (New York: Charles Scribner's Sons, 1892).

Hagan, William Thomas. *Quanah Parker, Comanche Chief* (Norman: University of Oklahoma Press, 1993).

Haley, James L. *The Buffalo War: The History of the Red River Uprising of 1874* (Austin, Texas: State House Press, 1998).

Higginson, Thomas Wentworth. *Army Life in a Black Regiment* (Boston: Houghton Mifflin & Co., 1900).

Hill, Ruth Beebe. *Hanta Yo: An American Saga* (Garden City, NY: Doubleday & Co., 1979).

Hoebel, E. Adamson, and Ernest Wallace. *The Comanche, Lords of the South Plains* (Norman: University of Oklahoma Press, 1952).

Hook, Jason. *American Indian Warrior Chiefs* (Dorset, England: Firebird Books, 1989).

Izzard, Bob. *Adobe Walls Wars* (Amarillo, TX: Tangleaire Press, 1993).

Kenner, Charles L. *The Comanchero Frontier: A History of New Mexican-Plains Indian Relations* (Norman: University of Oklahoma Press, 1969).

Künster, Mort. *Mort Künster's Old West: Indians* (Nashville: Rutledge Hill Press, 1998).

Lafarge, Olvier. *A Pictorial History of the American Indian* (New York: Crown Publishers, 1956).

Leckie, William H. *The Buffalo Soldiers: A Narrative of the Negro Cavalry in the West* (Norman: University of Oklahoma Press, 1967).

Locke, Raymond Friday. *The American West* (Los Angeles: Mankind Publishing, 1971).

Matthiessen, Peter, *Indian Country* (New York: Viking Press, 1984).

McHugh, Tom. *The Time of the Buffalo* (New York: Alfred A. Knopf, 1972).

The Mighty Chieftains (New York: Time Life Books, 1993).

Neeley, Bill. *The Last Comanche Chief: The Life and Times of Quanah Parker* (New York: John Wiley & Sons, Inc., 1995).

Neihardt, John G. *Black Elk Speaks* (New York: William Morrow & Co., 1932).

Newcomb, Jr., W.W. *The Indians of Texas: From Prehistoric to Modern Times* (Austin: University of Texas Press, 1961).

Peattie, Donald Culross. "The Ballad of Cynthia Ann." *American Heritage Magazine* Apr. 1956: pp. 38–41.

Remington, Frederic. *Crooked Trails* (New York: Harper & Brothers Publishing, 1898).

Remington, Frederic. *Frederic Remington's Own West: The Great Western Artist's Eyewitness Accounts of His Expeditions and Adventures on the Frontier* (New York: Dial Press, 1960).

Reynolds, Jr., Charles R. *American Indian Portraits from the Wanamaker Expedition of 1913* (Battleboro, VT: Stephen Green Press, 1971).

Rister, Carl Coke. *Comanche Bondage* (Lincoln: University of Nebraska Press, 1989).

Robinson III, Charles M. *The Buffalo Hunters* (Austin: State House Press, 1995).

Rollings, Willard H. *The Comanche* (New York: Chelsea House Publishers, 1989).

Roosevelt, Theodore. *Ranch Life and the Hunting Trail* (Lincoln: University of Nebraska Press, 1983).

Sandoz, Maria. *Cheyenne Autumn* (New York: Hasting's House Publishers, 1953).

Sandoz, Maria. *Crazy Horse: The Strange Man of the Oglalas* (New York: Alfred A. Knopf, 1942).

Schultz, J.W. *My Life as an Indian* (Greenwich, CT: Fawcett Publications, 1935).

Smith, Winston O. *The Sharps Rifle* (New York: William Morrow & Co., 1943).

Stirling, Matthew W. *National Geographic on Indians of the Americas: A Color-Illustrated Record* (Washington, D.C.: National Geographic Society, 1955).

Storm, Hyemeyohsts. *Seven Arrows* (New York: Harper and Row Publishers, 1972).

Taylor, Colin F. *The Plains Indians: A Cultural and Historical View of the North American Plains Tribes of the Pre-Reservation Period* (London: Salamander Books Ltd., 1994).

Tchakmakian, Pascal. The *Great Retreat: The Nez Perces War in Words and Pictures* (San Francisco: Chronicle Books, 1976).

Thomas, David Hurst, et al. *The Native Americans: An Illustrated History* (Atlanta: Turner Publishing, 1993).

Vestal, Stanley. *Jim Bridger – Mountain Man* (Lincoln: University of Nebraska, 1970).

Wallace, Ernest. *Ranald S. Mackenzie on the Texas Frontier* (College Station: Texas A&M University Press, 1993).

The Way of the Warrior (New York: Time Life Books, 1993).

Wilson, Claire. *Quanah Parker, Comanche Chief* (New York: Chelsea House Publishers, 1990).

Weston, Marybeth. *The Squaw with Blue Eyes* (Provincetown, MA: Shank Painter Co., 1986).

The World of the American Indian (Washington, D.C.: National Geographic Society, 1974).

Wunder, John R. *The Kiowa* (New York: Chelsea House Publishers, 1989).

Yenne, Bill. *The Encyclopedia of North American Indian Tribes: A Comprehensive Study of Tribes from the Abitibi to the Zuni* (New York: Crescent Books, 1986).

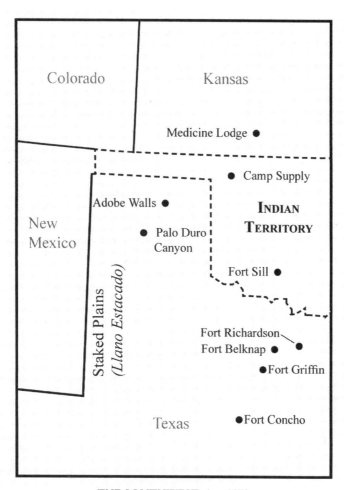

Colorado

Kansas

Medicine Lodge ●

● Camp Supply

INDIAN TERRITORY

Adobe Walls ●

New Mexico

● Palo Duro Canyon

Fort Sill ●

Staked Plains *(Llano Estacado)*

Fort Richardson
Fort Belknap ● ●

●Fort Griffin

Texas

●Fort Concho

THE SOUTHWEST circa 1872

CYNTHIA ANN PARKER (Naduah) Captured by the Comanche at the age of nine, she later married a Comanche chief and gave birth to three children, two sons and a daughter. The eldest, Quanah, became a legend in the southwest..

SATANTA (White Bear) Kiowa Chief. "The soldiers cut down my timber, and they kill my buffalo. When I see that, my heart feels like bursting. I love this land and the buffalo and will not part with it."

HENRY MORTON STANLEY. As a senior correspondent for the New York Herald, Stanley was moved by Ten Bear's eloquent speech at the Medicine Lodge Treaty council.

AMOS CHAPMAN, frontier scout for the Army, lost a leg in a fight with the Comanche and Kiowa, married a Cheyenne woman, and lived off and on with her people..

TEN BEARS, Comanche chief, shown wearing his spectacles. He noted that important Whites wore spectacles, so he acquired a pair of his own. His speech at the Medicine Lodge Treaty Council has rarely been surpassed.

BILLY DIXON; Buffalo hunter and
Army scout, known for his "one mile"
shot in the battle of Adobe Walls.

ISA-TAI, COMANCHE SHAMAN. The
Comanche medicine man, who claimed to have
risen into the clouds where he was instructed by
the Great Spirit to rally the restless warriors of
the Kiowa, Comanche and Cheyenne, and attack
the buffalo hunters at Adobe Walls.

QUANAH PARKER, Chief of the Quahadi Comanches, an honored enemy, and subsequently, an honored friend of the Whites.

COLONEL RANALD SLIDELL MACKENZIE (BAD
HAND). Commanding Officer of the United States
Fourth Cavalry.

PALO DURO CANYON. Some eight hundred feet deep
and several miles wide, provided a major obstacle for Colonel
Mackenzie's pursuit of the Comanche, who sought its protection
from the weather and sudden attack.

1905 INAUGURAL PARADE PARTICIPANTS. Quanah Parker, Comanche, (third from right) surrounded by Buckskin Charlie (Ute), American Horse (Sioux), Little Plume (Blackfeet), Hollow Horn Bear (Sioux). Geronimo (Apache) is third from left.

PRESIDENTIAL INAUGURAL PARADE 1905. Five of the six Indians who rode in Theodore Roosevelt's inaugural parade in Washington D.C.
(Quanah Parker is third from left).

RETURN OF THE BUFFALO. Shipped from New York's Zoological Society, by rail, in special cages, the fifteen buffalo arrived in Cache, Oklahoma unscathed.

WAGON TRAIN. The unusual wagon train, with its complaining cargo, provided a new challenge to its teamsters.

TRANSFER. Prodded into wooden crates at the railhead, the buffalo set out on the last leg of their incredible journey to the newly created Washita Wildlife Refuge.

HOME ON THE RANGE. Released from their wooden crates onto the grasslands of the Wildlife Refuge, the buffalo were welcomed by joyful Comanche and Kiowa families in fulfillment of tribal prophecy.

WOLF HUNT. At the tail of the chuck wagon on the Oklahoma wolf hunt in 1905, President Theodore Roosevelt pauses, cup in hand (fourth from left). Quanah Parker, also with cup, stands third from right. (1905)

ELOUISA COBELL, the Blackfeet Indian leader who won a hard fought lawsuit over the US Department of Interior.